NEVER STRIKE TWICE

ALEX SIGMORE

Storm
PUBLISHING

ALSO BY ALEX SIGMORE

The Forgotten Wife

Oak Creek Thriller

The Darkest Game

Emily Slate FBI Mystery Thriller

His Perfect Crime

The Collection Girls

Smoke and Ashes

Her Final Words

Can't Miss Her

The Lost Daughter

The Secret Seven

A Liar's Grave

The Girl In The Wall

His Final Act

The Vanishing Eyes

Edge of the Woods

Ties That Bind

The Missing Bones

Blood in the Sand

The Passage

Fire in the Sky

Oh What Fun

Ivy Bishop Mystery Thriller

Her Dark Secret

The Girl Without A Clue

The Buried Faces

Her Hidden Lies

PROLOGUE
25 YEARS AGO

"Dawes!"

Charlotte snapped her head up, taking a hot second to focus her eyes on the man beside her desk. She'd been so deep in her research that she'd lost track of the time—which used to be a regular occurrence but hadn't happened lately. Usually, she got bored quickly—her interest moving from one topic to another with little regard for extenuating circumstances. But in this case she'd been looking into the background of a well-known politician who had been rumored to be taking bribes in exchange for passing local ordinances. She was sure it was all business as usual in a big city like Chicago, but it was intriguing to see just how far some people would go for money. Not only that, but she thought there was a case there, if she could just uncover it.

Having only been a detective for the past six months, she had been determined to come into this job with a bang. And she'd seen this politician as her big chance. Her ticket to make a name for herself.

Her partner—Joseph Ortega, a veteran cop with more than twenty years under his belt—had been encouraging her to go out there and get her "big fish." But now here he was interrupting her in the middle of her work.

Charlotte glanced up at the man who was probably two hundred pounds of pure muscle fueled by a constant diet of hot dogs and steak. But he was as strong as an ox. Ortega might not be fast, but you didn't want to let him catch up to you. She'd seen him break someone's arm—by accident—just holding him in place to get the cuffs on him.

"Yes, sir," Charlotte replied, grinning at the man. Her partner was a pretty easygoing guy most of the time, but as soon as she saw the look on his face, she dropped the cavalier demeanor. "What's going on?"

"We've got a call in from Roberts. Multiple victims. And we need to get out to the site ASAP."

Charlotte gathered her stuff, pulling on her jacket as she closed her computer. She didn't have a ton of experience with Ortega yet, but she figured she knew him well enough she could tell when something was serious or not. They'd already had more than a few cases with multiple victims, but something about the way he said it was different. More serious.

"How many are we looking at?" she asked as she fell into step beside him.

"Five from the reports," he replied. "Homeless guy found them."

Charlotte's heart rate picked up. "Found them where?"

"Abandoned iron foundry, on the west side of town. We've got first responders out there and the area is being secured as we speak. Roberts requested us specifically."

"Got it," Charlotte said. One thing she'd learned in this job was that you didn't question whether you could handle the cases that were given to you—you just did the best you could. A five-victim case was a lot. One that would definitely attract the media and all other sorts of attention. But she didn't want to get ahead of herself. Better to wait until they arrived on scene before she could determine just how bad this would be.

Ortega—normally the talkative type—remained silent the entire drive out to the site. The sun had already set and a chill had come off the lake that blew through the city, dropping the temperature quickly. Charlotte kept forgetting to bring a spare pair of gloves with her to work, though it wasn't as if her hands got cold anymore. But given what had happened, she needed to be careful. With the nerve damage she couldn't always tell when they were getting *too* cold. Heat never seemed to be an issue for whatever reason. She would burn her hand on a hot mug just as easily as the next person.

But the cold—for some reason her hands just wouldn't register the sensation properly. As Ortega drove, she rubbed them together in preparation, given they would probably be out in the elements all night.

Charlotte spotted the lights from the emergency vehicles while they were still three blocks away. Chicago Fire, Emergency Services and three patrol cars surrounded the large structure as they approached. Ortega pulled up to the side of the building where a white van was being unpacked by men and women in full-body jumpsuits.

"CSI didn't waste any time," she remarked as she followed Ortega across the lot to the broken entrance to the foundry. Two firemen were coming out of the side of the building, both of them looking a little worse for wear as another patrol officer stood at the entrance.

"Joe," the officer said to Ortega, nodding.

Her partner turned to her. "Charlotte, this is Officer Poleski. I worked with his dad back in the day."

"Poleski," Charlotte said, nodding. Ortega hadn't given her very much information either before or on the way over, and Charlotte knew better than to ask. Whatever there was to see, she would see it soon. But something about all this was leaving a dark pit in the bottom of her stomach.

"Did you go in?" Ortega asked Poleski.

"For a second," Poleski replied. "Couldn't stay. I needed air."

"Shit," her partner replied, looking up into the clear night sky and taking a deep breath. Nothing about this was doing anything to alleviate any of Charlotte's anxiety. But she was the new detective. The low man on the totem pole. She didn't have the luxury of getting a heads-up.

Ortega turned to her. "It's not going to be pretty in there. But I want you to look past all that. I need your honest opinion of what you see, understand?"

"Yes, sir," Charlotte said, though she wasn't exactly sure what he meant. She expected to see five bodies inside, but what else? What was he asking her?

"Okay, thanks. Poleski," he said, clapping one of his giant hands on the man's shoulder as they passed.

The factory was dark, the result of not having working lights for twenty years; though there was some illumination at the far end of the room where CSI had already begun to set up spotlights. Charlotte tried her best to get a look at the scene as they approached, but the skeletons of the old equipment that had been decaying in the factory blocked most of her view. She was conscripted to follow Ortega, her heart nearly pounding out of her chest at what they would find ahead of them.

When they finally squeezed through two pieces of equipment into the area that had been lit, Charlotte took an instinctive step back.

It was a scene out of a horror movie. Five low tables had been set up in a semicircle around a central point. Each of the victims remained on each table, stripped of all their clothes. However, their wrists and necks had been cut with deep gashes, causing them to bleed out all over the place. There was so much blood it didn't even look real. It was as if someone had painted the place with buckets and buckets of crimson, smearing it over every surface in every way possible.

The victims themselves were relatively untouched other than the cuts, though even a cursory look told Charlotte whoever had done this hadn't been delicate about it. She could see the bone of the wrist on some of the victims' arms, the gashes so deep and ragged it looked like someone had taken a handsaw to them.

Above the cuts on their wrists, dark marks on the insides of their arms. From here they looked like deep bruises. Or maybe... burns?

Charlotte found herself taking in deep breaths, the tang of copper coming back to her with each inhalation. "H—how...?"

"That's what we need to find out," Ortega said, his hands in his pockets as he surveyed the scene with the cold detachment of someone who had seen it all. Charlotte envied that about the man —turning off his emotions so he wouldn't go through the turmoil of wondering what the last minutes of these people's lives must have been like. Had they been conscious? Had they been terrified? Who did they think about in their final moments? And who missed them now that they were gone?

Charlotte felt something on her cheek, and for a brief second she thought she might have gotten some of the blood from the crime scene on her face. But when she pulled her hand away, it was just clear and wet. No blood. She quickly wiped her eyes before her partner could see, but it was too late. Ortega regarded her with disappointment in his eyes. *Dammit.* She could handle this. She'd seen blood before, mostly when she'd taken an opponent out in the ring. This was the same thing. Just... more.

"Pull yourself together," Ortega said.

"I'm fine," she said, wiping her eyes a final time to make sure they were dry. "Let's get to work."

"Okay," he replied.

As far as Charlotte could tell, the blood was mostly contained to the circle that had been created by the tables. The tables themselves didn't have wheels, which meant they'd probably been pulled in here from somewhere else. Maybe another area of the foundry, maybe whoever did this brought them with them.

"First impressions?" Ortega asked as CSI continued to set up equipment before they entered the area.

"Looks ritualistic," Charlotte said. "Maybe some kind of cult."

Ortega didn't reply. He just continued to stare at the scene. She wasn't sure if he was testing her or if he was just thinking.

Charlotte checked her cheeks again, finding they were dry this time.

"I'm going in for a closer look," she said, taking a few more careful steps toward the bodies. Some of the blood had seeped onto the ground, running in rivulets away from the circle depending on the slope of the room, some of it toward drains that had been built into the foundry's floors, presumably for cleaning.

But as she took a closer look at the victims, she began to realize they were all young—probably in their early twenties or maybe even teens.

"Recognize any of them?" Ortega asked.

"I don't think so," Charlotte said automatically, but the truth was she didn't know. They looked so... strange. Their eyes remained open, staring out into nothingness. Was that how they died? Somehow paralyzed while their literal lifeblood seeped away? There didn't seem to be restraints on the tables, or anything that would have held them in place.

"Footprints," Charlotte said as soon as she got a better look at the circle itself. There were clear footprints in the blood that hadn't yet coagulated. But they were few and far between. Most of the blood had pooled in one area and had been smeared all over the floor in swirls—almost as if someone were *painting* with it.

"Was it a joint suicide?" she asked, looking around for anything the victims could have used to cut their own wrists and throats. But she didn't see any evidence of weapons.

"Doubtful," Ortega said. "The likelihood of getting five people to all take their own lives at exactly the same time? Not to mention we know someone else was here. Probably a few someones. People making sure it went according to plan." He pulled out a cigarette and stuck it in his mouth.

Charlotte promptly pulled the cigarette from his lips, causing him to glare at her. "Contamination." She handed it back to him.

"You're right. But sometimes a man needs one." He stuck it back in his mouth and lit it. "Don't ever pull a cigarette from me again."

"Yes, sir. Sorry," she said. She had a reputation for being impulsive—something that served her well in the past but she wasn't sure how well it would help her now. "So... where do we go from here?"

Ortega looked around, watching as CSI continued to prepare their equipment for the go-ahead to start processing the scene. "Out-of-the-way place. No cameras. No witnesses. A mess of a crime scene. Even if we do manage to pull some trace evidence from this, I'm not sure how much it will help us. Everything here is probably contaminated. See the colors of their faces? This didn't happen tonight. They've been here a few days. We need IDs. Then we'll go about contacting next of kin."

He was right. And while the weather had been cool, it hadn't been cold enough to preserve bodies exposed to the elements. To Charlotte, this looked like it would be impossible. Still, she had to try.

But as she worked, she couldn't quit thinking about what their last moments would have been like. The terror they must have felt. And again, she could feel herself welling up as she and Ortega worked with the CSI team to gather evidence. So much that she finally had to excuse herself and take a minute outside.

"It's rough, isn't it?" Poleski said coming up beside her after a few minutes. He held out a pack of cigs to her, but she shook her head. He nodded and pulled one out for himself. "You gotta wonder what was going through their heads, you know? At the last second."

"I can't quit thinking about it," Charlotte said, the tears beginning to fall again. Why was she having so much trouble? She was better than this. *Had* to be better.

"Hey, it's okay," Poleski said. "No one is really prepared for it. You worked beat?"

"Patrol," she said. "Mostly domestic stuff."

"And before that?"

She didn't feel like getting into her failed career and the injury that prevented her from doing the thing she'd loved for so long. "College athlete."

He crouched down beside her, blowing the smoke from his cigarette in the opposite direction, away from her face. "There's a trick to it my old man taught me," he said. "You take all the feelings you've got about what you're seeing in there, all your emotions, and you just box them up."

"Box them up?" she asked.

"Yeah, like you're putting away old clothes for the winter. You box 'em up. Stick 'em in the back for a while and you bring 'em out later. You know, when you're alone and you got some time."

"That really works?" she asked.

He shrugged. "I dunno. He said it worked for him. I've never really had much of a problem with stuff like that in there. I mean, I'm more than happy to let you deal with it. But I could handle it if I needed to. Anyway, food for thought." He stood back up and returned to his position beside the door, the light from the end of his cigarette a pinprick in the dark.

Charlotte thought about it for a second. Maybe walling herself off was the best way to get through this. She couldn't afford to lose any more face with Ortega—otherwise he would never respect her again. Maybe her politician wasn't her "big fish." Maybe this case was. And if she was going to crack it—if she was going to make a name for herself as a Chicago Police detective—then she needed to use whatever tools were available to her to get the job done.

Charlotte stood up, took a deep breath and looked to the night sky, imagining all her emotions were physical objects she could just store away until later. She mentally picked up each one, placed them gently into a large box and closed it back up. She then turned and strolled back into the foundry, giving Poleski a nod of thanks on the way.

But as she headed back inside, her fingers began to ache.

ONE

You can do this, you can do this, you can do this.

Mona LaSalle sat at the small table, hunched over her phone like a gargoyle as she tried to calm herself down. The past six months had been a whirlwind. The fallout from Robin's case and all the attention that followed had pushed her to the limit... including all the interviews she'd been subjected to as soon as the media found out the man who had been behind the killings in Oak Creek had been her biological father.

Then came the therapy, which had been a new challenge all on its own. At first the therapist had encouraged her to keep a "safe space"; a physical or emotional place for herself while they began to unpack everything she'd experienced during Robin's case. But apparently that had become more of a crutch than the therapist had hoped and had required pulling Mona back out of the depths again.

She knew that her recovery path would never be a straight line, and the therapist even said as much. But it was infuriating to seem to make some progress one week only for it to be erased the next. It felt like all she was doing was treading water. What was worse, she had hoped that opening herself up emotionally and allowing herself to be vulnerable would make her a better detective. But it had only made things harder. Cases she wouldn't have had a problem with six months ago she was finding herself agonizing over when she got back home at night. Not only that, but she was still having a hard time forgiving herself for what happened to Robin.

Dr. Cross said that would all come in time. That her journey would take effort but eventually it would all be worth it. Mona just had to trust that she was right. Because as far as she could tell, emotions were just a big ol' pain in the ass and barely worth the trouble.

But every time she thought along those lines, she'd think of John McCormick, her biological father, sitting in that mental institute talking to himself. And how much she didn't want to be like him. If anything, his presence was the only thing keeping her going to therapy, keeping her from falling back into her old, more comfortable habits.

Habits like never going out on dates. Because in her original estimation, she didn't want to waste anyone's time. She was a mess and she knew it, but Dr. Cross had encouraged her to start trying to meet new people. The one close friend she'd made—Charlotte— had gone back home to Chicago to begin living out her retirement in peace. Mona didn't want to bother her. She still had Adam, of course, but he was a good ten years younger than her and more like a brother than anything else. She needed friends her own age.

Unfortunately, the life of a police detective didn't leave much time for socializing. And most of her peers in the department were older than her by a good mile. Those that weren't still harbored some resentment towards her for advancing through the ranks so quickly, and she hadn't missed the whispers about her in the hall- ways, the other officers debating the wisdom of keeping the daughter of a serial killer on the payroll.

That's not the truth. That's the story you're telling yourself to justify your behavior. Dr. Cross's words echoed in Mona's own voice in her head. She was here; she was making the effort. She just had to see if it would be worth it or not.

The little bell over the restaurant door jingled and Mona

glanced up. A man in a pullover sweater with a pair of stylish glasses and his hair combed back nicely stepped into the restaurant, looking around. Well, he looked like his profile, that was a good sign at least. As soon as he spotted her, he grinned and began walking over.

Mona offered a weak wave too late as he'd already seen her, but it was all she could manage. She was practically vibrating with energy. The only "date" she'd ever had was with Chad Rooker in the ninth grade where they went to catch a movie and he tried to cop a feel. She'd been coldly detached then, asking him in a very measured and emotionless voice what he thought he was doing. He had tried to play it off, but she'd pushed, asking him where he'd hoped to put his hand until finally he'd gotten so weirded out by her behavior that he left her there at the theater. The following days at school hadn't been easy, but by then Mona had been an expert at not caring what people thought of her. Or at least, taking all those cares and shutting them away.

This was something different. She hadn't tried to cultivate anything other than a working relationship with anyone other than Robin in a long time. If she and Robin had met later in life, she probably never would have approached her. That's just how Mona had seen the world. She'd been the outsider—the person who would never fit. She was the one who didn't have shared experiences, who couldn't relate to other people.

Which was why she was so nervous now.

"Hi, Mona?" the man said, stopping short of the table. "I'm Caleb."

She brushed her dark hair back and stood, forcing herself to lock eyes with him. "Hi." She stuck out her hand and took his, shaking it quickly. Hers was clammy and covered in sweat, but she hoped she was fast enough that he didn't notice.

"You're very pretty," he said as he took a seat. "Your picture doesn't do you justice."

"Oh," she said, allowing the hair to fall in her face again as she nearly missed her seat. "Uh, thanks. You're... pretty too."

He chuckled. "Thanks."

Inside her head she felt like she was running around a burning building. *What kind of thing is that to say to a guy?* "Um... nice... sweater."

He looked down, almost like he was seeing the sweater for the first time. "Thanks. I bought it special for tonight."

"You did?"

"No, I'm just kidding," he replied. "But it is one of my nicer sweaters."

What are you doing? Talking about sweaters? Get it together, Mona!

"So you work for the Oak Creek Police?" he asked.

She nodded.

"I've been over to Oak Creek a few times," he replied. "It's a cute place. Were you born there?"

"No," she answered quickly. "I was born—on the east coast." *Shit.* Now she'd already lied to him. How was she supposed to explain that her mother had taken her as a small child and fled her abusive husband in an attempt to hide them from him, and then lied to Mona about her early childhood? She was still trying to unpack all the memories Dr. Pekannen had helped her suppress when she was still young, though that had been a daunting task on its own. "What about you? Were you born in Crystal Lake?"

She'd figured it was better to start her dating adventure *outside* Oak Creek, seeing as she already knew everyone in town. And considering everyone was either pissed at her for how she handled Robin's case, or afraid of her because of her association with her father, the odds of finding someone willing to date her there had been astronomically low. Probably on the Planck scale.

"No, I was born in Florida," he replied. "Moved up here for work a couple of years ago. So I guess we're both transplants."

"Do you like it?" she asked.

"I like the summers. Hate the winters. But the money is good, and I enjoy my job."

Crap. What was his job again? She remembered seeing it on

his profile, but she was drawing a complete blank. And he'd remembered her job! Why was this so difficult? She never had trouble remembering details. But it was like there was a black screen over the part of her brain that normally worked properly.

"What, uh, what do you like to do for fun?" she asked.

"Fishing, hiking, outdoors stuff when I can," he replied. "What about you?"

She thought back to her "hobbies," which Dr. Cross said were little more than extensions of her work. Her attempts to build a computer program that could predict crime, for example. Dr. Cross had said that she needed things that took her mind *off* her work, that it wasn't healthy to obsess over something all the time. Especially if that thing was a job as stressful as hers. She needed pressure valves. The only problem was she hadn't found what those valves were yet. "I guess... finding bodies?" She gave him a weak smile.

Unfortunately for her, her date didn't reciprocate. In fact, he looked a little put off.

"Sorry, that was a poor attempt at a joke," she replied.

"Oh," he replied, giving her a weak smile. "Got it."

This was going *swimmingly*. She couldn't *wait* for her next session with Dr. Cross so she could be sure to *thank her* for suggesting this course of action.

"Good evening, sir. May I offer you a drink?" the waiter said as he came up to the table. Mona looked at the barely touched wine glass on her side of the table, half filled with merlot.

"It's okay if you want to go," Mona said before he could answer. "I wouldn't blame you."

The man across from her frowned. "Why would I go?"

"Because I'm weird and awkward and probably not at all what you expected," she said. "I can also pretty much guarantee we're not having sex tonight."

That comment seemed to startle both of them, but where the waiter seemed uncomfortable, her date only smiled. "You're very direct."

"I can't help it."

Caleb turned to the waiter. "I'll take a glass of whatever she's having."

The waiter looked from him to Mona and back again before turning and heading off to the bar.

"I'm serious. You can just go. I'll leave you a positive rating or whatever on the app," she said.

"Okay, first of all, I'm not that easy to scare off," he said. "And second, do you know how hard it is to find someone who actually says what they mean? Do you know how many women out there want to play games? Some of them even get off on it."

The mention of *games* caused Mona to involuntarily shudder. She'd had enough of games for a while, making a point to avoid The Dragon's Hoard every time she walked across Oak Creek's town square.

"I definitely don't do that," she replied.

"Me either," he said as the waiter brought over his glass of wine.

"Would you like a few minutes to look over the menu?"

Mona caught the man's smile, which involuntarily made her smile herself. Maybe this wasn't so bad after all. That was another thing Dr. Cross told her she needed to watch: catastrophizing everything. One poorly timed joke didn't mean the end of the date.

"Yes, please," he replied for both of them. As soon as the waiter was gone, he leaned closer. "Have you ever had their scallops here?"

Mona shook her head. "Before a few months ago, I didn't get out of Oak Creek much. I'm... trying a lot of new things lately."

"Then I highly suggest them," he replied. "Unless you're allergic to shellfish."

"Not that I know of," she replied. "But if I am, I hope you have an EpiPen handy." *Chiropractor!* He was a chiropractor. Now she remembered. God, why had that been so hard to recall? It wasn't like it was a rare job.

He chuckled again. "I don't generally carry them, but I'd say if there's any risk—"

"No, I eat shrimp all the time," she said. "I was just joking... again. Sorry, my sense of humor can be a little... dark."

"I imagine in your line of work it would have to be," he said. "You don't exactly get to see the bright side of life much, do you?"

She offered him a pinched smile. "Not as often as I'd like."

Just as the waiter was returning and Mona had decided that she was definitely going for the scallops, the phone in her pocket vibrated.

"Sorry," she said, pulling it out. "I'm kind of always on call."

"Sure, of course," he said, turning to the waiter.

Mona turned away from the table before answering. "LaSalle."

"It's Bowman. We got a hit-and-run out on Route Thirty-Four. One victim. Sergeant wants us out there right now."

"I'm supposed to have the night off," she replied. "I'm... in the middle of something."

"Well, get out of it," Bowman replied. "I'll meet you out there. Six miles from the intersection with Highway Twenty." He hung up before she could protest.

Mona turned back to the table and her very handsome, smiling date. "I'm sorry to do this. But I have a work thing. It's sort of an emergency."

"Oh. Sure, I understand," he said without even an ounce of hesitation. Which caused *her* to pause momentarily.

"Really?"

"Yeah. I know what I'm getting into here, Mona. I know you're going to have stuff that can't wait."

"But... it's only our first date," she said as she stood, gathering her things.

He shook his head. "Let's call this a preview of what's to come. We'll reschedule." He stood and held out his hand again. "It was a real pleasure meeting you."

She took his hand, somewhat bewildered. "Yeah, you too."

"Good luck tonight. I'll message you."

"Oh-kay." Honestly, Mona couldn't believe this. She'd expected things to end badly or at best neutral, with both of them walking away agreeing never to see each other again. But the promise of things going well left her feeling lighter than when she'd arrived. And given that she was probably about to face death yet again tonight, that wasn't such a bad thing at all.

TWO

As she drove to the site, Mona couldn't help her good mood. Maybe Dr. Cross wasn't full of it after all. Meeting someone hadn't been the end of the world, and Mona actually felt better than she had before it began. She hadn't expected a net positive.

But still, she had a job to do and couldn't let her personal life interfere. It had been a difficult transition, from a new up-and-comer with little to no "experience" to one of the most reliable and famous detectives on the force. The whole ordeal with Robin and her father had given Mona a new perspective on her job, and it had given her co-workers a new perspective on her. No longer was she the strange loner who worked on her computer all day. She had been given a commendation for her role in stopping John and saving any future victims while her department underwent a significant transformation.

The loss of Sheriff Franklin had upended the entire town, requiring an interim sheriff to be hired by the mayor until another election could be held sometime later in the year. He brought in a man with almost as much experience, having come from a town somewhere in Wyoming. Where Sheriff Franklin had been something of a father figure to Mona, Sheriff Earle was less friendly, more action- and results-oriented. She had thought maybe he'd be running for the position when the election came up, but on his first day in the office he made it known in no uncertain terms he was here on a temporary basis and that he would not be sticking around permanently. Apparently, the man had a ranch with a large lake for fishing he was very much looking forward to returning to.

Still, in the few months he'd been in the job, Mona had developed a good working relationship with him. He trusted her with more than Franklin ever had, and way more than her former partner, Jack Ramsey, who was still under federal investigation for his role in what the FBI was calling a cover-up.

Regardless, Mona had been working with Detective Bowman for almost two solid months and they'd developed a good rapport. Bowman hadn't been like some of the others in the office—curious about Robin's case or her father's condition. Instead, he treated her like an equal, despite being almost ten years her senior. The subject had only ever come up once, and Bowman had told her in no uncertain terms he didn't care about that kind of stuff. He was here for the job and the job alone. As long as she was reliable, that's all that concerned him. He was a good cop, and they'd meshed as well as she could have hoped.

It took her longer than she'd like getting to the site, but as she did, the lights from the nearby patrol cars directing traffic guided her in. She pulled up next to Bowman's car and stepped out just as the ambulance was pulling up.

Bowman was in the road along with the other emergency responders, all of them standing around a specific area, presumably where the hit-and-run happened. They'd erected what looked like some kind of portable canvas to try and block the scene from the road to keep traffic moving, but people had slowed down anyway, creating a backup on both sides. Fortunately, Mona had had no trouble riding the shoulder all the way here.

"Hey, Will," Mona said as she made her way across the traffic and over to where the men stood.

"LaSalle, took you long enough."

"I was in Crystal Lake," she replied. "It was *supposed* to be my night off." She turned to the fire chief who stood close by with another of his men. "Tomly." She turned to the portly man standing nearby with his long hair pulled back in a low ponytail. "Whittle."

"LaSalle," the man replied, nodding. He was the medical examiner for the surrounding counties, including Oak Creek. She and Charlotte had nearly run Whittle and his team into the ground with the number of bodies in their last case. Fortunately, this one looked to be limited to just one victim.

Mona crouched down, pulling on a pair of gloves as she gave the woman a cursory examination. "Definitely a hit-and-run?"

Bowman pointed to a pair of black marks on the road leading away from the scene. "May have been intentional."

Mona glanced behind her, presumably from the direction the car had been coming. There were no skid marks on that side to indicate the car had slammed on its brakes. But the tracks on the other side indicated the driver may have floored it *after* the hit, to get away quicker.

"So someone is just out here hitting whoever they come across?"

Bowman shrugged.

"What about the victim?" Mona asked. The body was turned away from her, lying on its side. Some blood had seeped onto the pavement, presumably from where the body had skidded or had been dragged, depending on what happened.

"Mallory Wakefield," Bowman said. "ID was in her pocket." He handed over a see-through plastic baggie with a small wallet inside. It was already open to a driver's license. According to the document, the victim was only twenty-four years old.

Mona, still hunched, worked her way around to the front of Mallory's body. Her face was a mess of road rash, blood covering eighty percent of it and the front of her clothes were soaked in blood from the hit.

"Best I can tell, they hit her going between forty and fifty miles per hour," Whittle said. "From down there." Mona glanced in the direction he was pointing to a small crosswalk from a parking lot on the other side of the road. The crosswalk headed into the woods, on a trail that wove into the wilderness.

Mona indicated the lone car sitting in the parking lot across the street, partially blocked from the traffic heading back and forth. "That her car?"

"Still waiting on the DMV," Bowman said. "But probably. We haven't gotten into it yet."

"Time of death?" she asked Whittle.

"About forty-five minutes ago," he said.

"We got the call from a driver around then," Bowman said. He pointed to a man leaning up against his car in the parking area while a patrol officer spoke with him.

"Did he see it happen?" Mona asked.

"Nope, but he almost ran her over," Bowman replied. "Came up on her quick. Nearly wrecked his car getting out of the way."

She turned back to the skid marks on the road. "Then those marks could have been his and not the killer's."

Bowman exchanged a look with Whittle, then with Tomly. "I suppose so."

"Where's her phone?" Mona asked.

"Missing," Whittle replied. "Presumably somewhere in the brush. We were going to wait until daylight before—"

"I don't think you're going to find it out there," Mona said.

"Why not?" Bowman asked.

"Because I don't think any part of this was an accident. What was she doing out here, crossing the road at seven thirty at night, with no lights anywhere? She wasn't going hiking." She pointed in the direction of the trail.

"What are you saying?" Bowman asked.

"Someone lured her out here to hit her," she said. "Then took her phone as evidence. And drove away at a leisurely pace."

"You can't *know* that," Whittle replied.

"No, but you spend a few days looking for a phone you're not going to find and then tell me I'm wrong," she said. The group of men stared at her, drawing an uncomfortable silence. She was doing it again. The very habits she'd sought to avoid were becoming more noticeable.

She cleared her throat. "Where does she live?"

Bowman held up the wallet, looking at her license again. "Red Grove Lane."

She was right, and she *knew* it. But given her father's reputation... Mona needed a softer approach. "On the other side of town. Look at her clothes. Dark jeans and a nice top. She's dressed for a night out. Not a hike in the middle of the night by herself. Someone might have set her up for the hit. Planned it."

"You're saying it can't be an accident?" Tomly asked.

"I'm saying let's keep an open mind," she replied, turning to Whittle. "And I think the evidence will support my theory."

He sighed. "We'll get her into the morgue as soon as we can. I guess I know what I'm doing tonight."

"I want to block off as much of this road as we can, to preserve anything that's still out here," Mona said. "Maybe we'll get lucky and he broke a headlight when he ran into her."

"We didn't see any traces of the car left behind," Bowman replied.

Mona nodded as she continued to inspect the body. She had all the normal trauma one would expect from a hit-and-run like this, probably at least a few broken bones. Depending on how she was hit, she could have died instantly. Or she could have bled out here on the pavement. Either way, it was a poor way to go.

"What do we know about next of kin?"

"I was working on that when you pulled up," Bowman replied. "Still trying to track someone down. It's gonna take a minute."

The lights of the nearby cars passing by illuminated the scene before plunging it back into darkness every few seconds. It was a strange strobe effect and it was giving Mona a headache. But as a car with particularly bright headlights—probably halogens— passed, she caught something beneath the blood on the woman's arm.

Mona pulled out her phone and shone the light along the woman's skin along the arm, realizing there was something hiding beneath all the blood.

"Did you see this?" she asked Bowman.

"What?"

"This marking here."

Her partner made his way around to her side of the body, crouching down with a grunt as he strained to see what she had seen. "That's just a bruise."

"No, it's something else." She carefully wiped back the blood with her gloved fingers. Even through the material, she could feel the roughness of the skin where it had been seared. It was a distinct symbol, though she hadn't seen anything like it before. It resembled a shepherd's hook, with the letter Y piercing it perpendicularly.

"Is that a tattoo?" Tomly asked, having come around to take a look himself.

"It's a brand," Mona said. "Burned into the skin. See where it's been cauterized and blackened?" She turned back to Whittle. "And it's recent. Is there any way to tell if this was done pre- or postmortem?"

"As soon as I get her back to the morgue, I'll have a better idea," he replied.

"You think someone did this to her *after* they hit her?" Bowman asked.

Mona sat on her haunches, staring at the strange symbol that etched into the body. It was unlike any symbol she'd ever seen before. She pulled off one of her gloves and retrieved her phone, taking a close-up picture. "I don't know. But it had to have been within the past few hours. Right?"

Whittle nodded. "The blistering indicates that much."

While the others continued to examine the body, Mona did an image search on the symbol. Strangely, nothing came back. There were some that looked close, but nothing that was a direct match to whatever had been burned into Mallory's body.

Shoot. She had thought it might be a Greek or Sumerian letter, or at least something similar. But it could just as well be something someone made up. That was better for the investigation—a unique symbol would be easier to track down than something more ubiquitous.

Mona stood, looking around the scene. Her high from the pseudo-date had completely worn off, leaving her feeling much like she had before it had begun. Anxious and worried. She didn't like the implications of what this scene might mean. Despite the others' reservations, it *was* an intentional killing, that much she was sure. One that had happened just as she was waiting on Caleb to arrive at the restaurant. How could she even pretend to think she could find a potential companion when she had to face things like this on a near-daily basis?

Not only that, but she just couldn't seem to help letting everyone know she was right. Just like her father. It was almost enough to make her want to quit and start over with botany or something.

Her thoughts turned back to Charlotte, as they often did. The woman had made a career of these kinds of cases, working the worst of the worst. And look what it had cost her. Was that the future in store for Mona? Or could it possibly be worse? At least Charlotte had tried to balance a family life with work, but given all of Mona's... proclivities... she wasn't even certain she'd ever get that far. Caleb may think he knew what he was getting into, but the truth was he didn't know Mona. Not really.

And she wasn't sure anyone ever would.

THREE

It was close to one in the morning by the time Mona and Bowman left the site. They'd spent the better part of five hours processing the scene, gathering evidence and coordinating with the other departments. Not what she'd planned for her Friday night off. Afterward, Mona headed back home for some sleep before heading back into the office early. A case like this had a certain kind of urgency that other cases didn't necessarily have. They had a killer out there somewhere who apparently had no problem mowing down a young woman in the middle of a dark country road.

What really intrigued her and kept her from falling into a deep sleep were the circumstances of the death. How did he lure her out there, only to come around and hit her at the exact correct moment? And what was the deal with the symbol? She had done a more thorough search on the image before leaving for the office only to come up empty yet again.

"Morning," Mona said, trying to remain chipper as she made her way into the morgue.

Whittle looked up as he was writing something on a clipboard adjacent to the main examination room.

"Is it?" he asked, hunching back over and continuing his notes.

"Yeah. You were here all night?" she asked.

"I was," he replied. "Bowman implied it couldn't wait."

"He was right. We didn't find much out there last night, and I doubt the teams will find anything this morning. The only clue to who killed her would be on her body."

Whittle finished his notes before inserting the clipboard into a slot beside the wall. "Then I'm afraid I won't be much help."

"I'll take whatever I can get," she replied, following him into the examination room where Mallory Wakefield lay face up on a metal slab, covered with a white sheet.

"Do you want to wait on your partner?" he asked as he flipped on an overhead light twice as bright as the fluorescents.

"He's working on tracking down the family," she said. "Let's get this over with so you can go home and get some sleep."

"Fair enough," he said, pulling back the sheet. Mallory had been cleaned of all the blood, but the damage to her skin from where she skidded across the pavement remained, leaving dark marks all over her face and making it hard to distinguish her features.

"Cause of death was blunt-force trauma, which resulted in massive internal hemorrhaging. The hit broke six of her ribs, collapsed her lung and punctured both her liver and spleen, not to mention all the external damage from her exposed skin."

"Immediate?" Mona asked, hoping.

"More or less. And the shock of it probably meant she didn't feel much," he replied. "But still... there was probably a short time where she knew what was happening."

Mona winced but forced herself to continue. "Anything that would indicate *what* hit her?"

"Probably a sedan of some sort, but if you mean the impression of a hood ornament, I'm afraid we're not that lucky. But I estimate the speed of the vehicle was at least sixty miles per hour to do that kind of damage. Based on what was found at the scene, I imagine she was airborne for a short time before she skidded at least twenty or thirty feet across the pavement. I found hairline cracks in her femur as well as her hips and her collarbone, most likely from the secondary impact."

Mona stared at the woman—the girl, really—for a moment. She was only a few years younger than Mona herself, her life cut short so early. "Anything else?"

"Stomach contents indicated she ate about an hour before she died, and it was a solid meal. Steak and potatoes with a couple of vegetables mixed in."

"Okay... that's something at least." Her theory about Mallory having gone out earlier that evening was starting to coalesce. She had been dressed like *she* was on a date as well. Maybe she'd had a fancy dinner.

"Fingernails were clean and I didn't find any evidence that she even had a chance to fight back in any way. No other foreign DNA on her anywhere."

"Sexual activity?"

"Not in a few days at least. Other than that, not sure."

"What about time of death?"

Whittle went back over to the computer on the desk against the back wall. "Estimated at seven forty-five... given when the driver found her and the amount of traffic on that road. She wouldn't have been out there long before someone else drove up."

Mona pulled the sheet back to reveal the brand on the woman's arm. "Tell me about this thing."

Whittle came back over, snapping on a pair of gloves. "You were right that it's a brand. Burned into the skin *post* death. But probably not long after. Seconds even. As you can see here"—he gently lifted her arm and twisted it, causing the brand to crack where it had begun to scab—"some healing had begun to take place, but it was so minimal I have to estimate it was when she still had sufficient blood flow to the arm."

Again, it fit with Mona's suppositions. "So someone hits her —hard enough that she is lifted into the air. They then stop, get out, brand her with a symbol and then leave before the next car can come up behind them." She looked to Whittle for confirmation.

"I guess that's about the long and short of it," he replied.

"It doesn't make much sense, does it?"

"No. It doesn't."

"Thank you, Andy," she replied. "The report on the way?"

"Just finishing up. You should have it within the hour," he replied.

"Great. Get some sleep. Appreciate you staying on for this one."

The man smiled. "Let's just try to prevent a pileup like last time, huh? I don't want to call in help from Hebron again."

She gave him a sad sort of smile. "No promises."

"I got you coffee," Bowman said as Mona headed into the office. He'd taken over Ramsey's desk, which suited Mona just fine. She hadn't been sad to see Ramsey put on permanent leave while under investigation. The man had been a certified menace, to Mona and everyone else in the office. Since his dismissal, things had been quieter. But it had also been like working somewhere foreign. Without him or Sheriff Franklin around, Mona often pretended like she was in a different precinct altogether.

"Thanks," she said, taking a seat, noting the cup of coffee still warm on the edge of the desk. She removed the lid and took a tentative sip, finding he'd also managed to add a couple of sugars for her, just like she liked it. Bowman might come across as a hard-ass sometimes, but at his core he really was a sweet person. It was why Mona liked working with him. When they were around other people, he would often project this image of toughness, of someone not to be messed with or bothered. But when it was just the two of them, a different side of him came out: a more sensitive side.

"Did you talk to Whittle?" he asked.

She nodded, opening her computer and looking for the final report, but it wasn't in the case file yet. "Just left there." She gave him a quick rundown of everything Whittle had given her, including the information about the mark being burned into her arm. "Make any progress on the family?"

"Yes, and it's not good. Both parents are dead. The only other relative is a grandmother who lives near Gary in a nursing home. No brothers, sisters or cousins that I can find. I already called the nursing home; they told me the woman is in the late stages of dementia. So I doubt she'll be able to help."

Mona sat back, sighing. Secretly, she was relieved. Delivering the news about Robin's death to her mother and brother had been one of the hardest things she'd ever done, even *with* Charlotte there to support her. She hated delivering news like that, but it was an integral part of the job. There was no escaping it. It seemed she'd be spared that horror this time at least.

"What about her car?"

"It's in impound. They're still working on it, but initial examination didn't reveal any foreign prints and nothing in the car of note. No phone anywhere."

She had to suppress a grin. "Told you."

"That doesn't mean it isn't still out in the woods somewhere. I ordered the K-9 unit out there to take a look this morning. Hopefully, they'll come back with something."

"If you ask me, it's a waste of time." But she knew it was a box they had to tick. They couldn't very well go to Earle without telling him they'd exhausted all options.

"Boyfriend? Husband?" Though she knew the latter was unlikely because she hadn't been wearing a ring.

"Nothing yet. I was hoping you'd be willing to head over to her place to take a look."

"Wait," she replied. "Now?"

"Sure. I'll treat you to a breakfast burrito."

They pulled up to Mallory Wakefield's home a little after eight thirty. It was a quaint one-story cottage home with a small garage behind the house. A tiny plot of dirt on either side of the stairs up to the front door told her there were probably flowers growing here in the summer. And yet, the yard was almost bare from where the grass had either died off or had been overpowered with weeds.

Mona took a quick look around the sides of the house, not finding anything out of the ordinary. No sign of outward struggle or a break-in anywhere. The door to the garage was locked with a heavy padlock.

"Looks clean back there," she said as she returned to Bowman who stood on the front step, keys in hand.

"I knocked, but no one answered," he said, fumbling with the set until he found the right one for the deadbolt. A small charm hung from the keyring, a high-heeled shoe what had been molded in aluminum. Maybe Mallory had an affinity with Cinderella.

Mona followed Bowman into the home, noting there didn't seem to be an alarm system on the door. Inside it smelled of patchouli and oranges. A cursory glance revealed the house was practically immaculate.

"Wow," Mona replied. "I wish my place was this clean."

"There's a solution for that," Bowman said, heading deeper into the home. Mona shot him a look behind his back and then began looking around for anything that might give them more information about Mallory Wakefield. She was obviously someone who valued order and cleanliness, but other than that she couldn't find much personal information about the woman. There were no pictures of people anywhere on the walls, instead hand-painted canvases of a child's art decorated the hallways.

"Oh God. Does she have a child?" Mona asked, her stomach dropping.

"I didn't see anything in the records," Bowman replied. "Maybe they're from a friend's kid?"

"We better hope so." Mona hadn't considered Mallory might be a mother. She seemed too young, but she had known plenty of people her own age and younger who had become parents early. Some by choice and some by accident. It was just that being a parent always seemed like something "older" people did, not someone her age. And she wasn't sure if that was ever going to change.

"Check the kitchen, I'll head down to the bedrooms," she told her partner. He headed to the back while she turned down the short hallway, her heart thumping.

Please don't let there be a kid in here, she thought to herself over and over as she reached each door in the hallway. The first led to a small bathroom, while the second opened into a bedroom that had been turned into a sort of yoga retreat. The carpet had been stripped from the floor, leaving the hardwoods, and a yoga mat sat in the middle. A small pile of foam blocks sat off to the side, and the only other items in the room were a plant in the corner and a small bench with a docking station for a phone.

Mona let out a sigh of relief. Checking the last room down the hallway revealed Mallory's bedroom, which was as neat and tidy as the rest of the house. But there, in the middle of the comforter, was what looked like a pitch-black hole. Mona had to shake her head a second before realizing the hole was staring back at her with two green eyes.

"Oh," she said.

"Hey, Mon," Bowman called from the kitchen. "I think she has a cat."

"I just found it," she called back. She turned to the animal, approaching slowly. "Hey there," she cooed. "Hi, kitty."

The cat uncurled itself from its black ball and stretched out on the bed, extending its paws as far as they would go. Mona noticed no claws came out as the cat did so.

"Oh, you're an indoor kitty, huh?"

The cat mewed softly and approached her, burying its head in her outstretched hand.

"You're very friendly," Mona said. "What's your name?" A green collar around the animal's neck ended in a small gold medallion. "Perigee. Huh. That's an odd name." But as she reached for the animal, its eyes went wide and it bounded completely over her head, landing on the floor behind her and skidding down the hallway. "I guess it fits." She cupped one hand over her mouth to try and amplify her voice. "Cat incoming!"

Turning, Mona inspected the rest of the bedroom. A small dresser held a few pieces of jewelry, but still no personal pictures of Mallory or anyone else for that matter. Apparently, the woman hadn't liked looking at images of herself, which could indicate a possible self-esteem issue. Then again, Mona could be reading too much into it. She made her way over to the dresser, opening it up to find little inside other than clothes. Mallory's bedside table only had a few personal items inside, nothing out of the ordinary.

Frustrated, Mona sat on the bed, looking around for anything she might have missed. But there was nothing here. Maybe she had been the kind of woman who played her cards close. They needed to find some of her friends, figure out who had been in her sphere of influence, because her home was a complete bust. Finally, Mona stood and headed back down the hallway to find Perigee rubbing up against Bowman's leg as he searched through the remaining drawers in the house.

"Anything?" he asked.

"Just the cat."

He pointed to the kitchen table. "Laptop charging there."

"That's something at least," Mona said. "We'll get it to tech, see if they can't get inside."

Bowman shut the last of the drawers. "Garage?"

"Not unless you have bolt cutters. It's got a padlock this thick." She held her finger and thumb an inch apart.

"We'll come back," he replied, looking down at the cat. "What about it?"

"*It* is a *her*, and her name is Perigee," Mona said bending down and scooping up the cat in one quick move. "I'm not leaving her here to starve. Grab her stuff, I'll take her back to my place for the time being."

"Your place? Why not just drop her by the humane society?"

Because, Mona wanted to say, *black cats are typically adopted last, if at all.* If she dumped Perigee there, there was a good chance she'd sit there for years waiting for someone to come by and take her. Besides, she could use some company at home for a change. Ever since everything had happened with Robin, her house had felt emptier than ever.

"Maybe it's just her lucky day."

FOUR

"You're telling me we have *nothing* to go on," Sheriff Earle said from across his desk.

Mona and Bowman were seated opposite him, both of them more than a little frazzled. It had been a full day since they'd investigated Mallory Wakefield's house and still hadn't come up with anything substantive. The laptop had been clean—nothing to indicate she was being stalked or harassed. Her garage had turned out to be mostly empty, only a few boxes of old mementoes and expired tax returns. There had been a few small pictures in the boxes of Mallory when she was young, but little else. At this point, Mona had begun to question *why* there was an absence of any semblance of family in the house at all.

The paintings on the wall had apparently come from one of Mallory's friends—her kid anyway. They'd been a present given to her at church where she was a regular attendee. Mona and Bowman had spent the morning speaking with her friends and acquaintances in the church, only to come up empty. No one knew if Mallory was dating anyone, had dated anyone or was having trouble with anyone. Apparently, the woman kept things *very* close to the chest. Everyone they spoke to only knew her tangentially, no one seemed to be close with her, even the friend who gave her his kid's paintings.

In fact, it was *weird*. Mona knew all about cutting yourself off from others, but Mallory had taken it to the extreme, not letting anyone get close in any capacity. Her grandmother turned out not to be much help—as her partner had predicted. She couldn't even remember having a granddaughter, much less her name.

"It's all right there in the file," Mona said. "The woman was an island. No personal connections, no family. In some ways, she was the perfect victim. Whoever targeted her knew she was isolated. Easy to kill without making a lot of fuss."

"If that's the case, then why the elaborate setup?" Earle asked, looking over the documents. "Why not just jump her in her home? Or on the way to work?"

"We can't speak to that point. No one seems to know if she was seeing anyone, if she was having trouble with anyone—anything. She was like... like a ghost in her own life."

The words surprised her even though they were from her own mouth. In a way, she was describing what her life used to look like. She was completely isolated from almost everyone, save a few people here at the office. It wasn't until Charlotte came in that things had begun to change.

"A hundred and thirty dollars in cash left in her purse," Earle remarked. "So robbery is out. And her car was still in the lot, so it wasn't about the vehicle."

"I don't know who would want to steal a 2015 Corolla anyway," Bowman added.

"And no phone. The K-9 units didn't pick up anything else on the scene. Whoever hit her, they took it. Probably because they knew it could lead back to them."

"Then pull the phone records," Earle replied.

"We're waiting on them," Bowman said.

"But they won't include texts. Or any information that could be contained in her apps."

Earle sighed before tossing the file on his desk and standing.

He headed to the room's only window and looked out on the dreary day outside. "Tell me about the mark."

"Whittle confirmed it was branded onto her," Mona said. "Shortly after death. But we can't find anything that's a match for what the symbol represents."

"That doesn't make me feel very good, Detective."

"Us either. I've made some inquires but with it being the weekend—"

He turned back around. "Right, good luck hearing anything for a few days at least. Look, I don't like the idea of a crazy-ass driver plowing people down around my town. There has to be a way to get a bead on this guy."

"The good news," Mona suggested, "if you can call it that, is this seems to be targeted, not random. So I don't think we have to worry about a series of road accidents just on chance. Mallory knew her killer. Or the killer knew her. I'm sure of it."

Earle eyed her for a moment before turning to Bowman. "You agree?"

"Detective LaSalle might be young, but she has good instincts," Bowman said. "She called it the night of the accident. I think we're looking for someone with a vendetta."

Earle seemed to mentally chew the information for a minute. "Keep working on the symbol. That's going to be your best bet for success. Pull cold cases, talk to whoever you need to talk to. *Someone* has seen that image before. Find them."

"Yes, sir," they said in unison.

"Okay, that's it. Dismissed." They stood and headed for the door. "Oh, and LaSalle. I understand you have a new houseguest."

Mona turned back to her boss. "I couldn't leave her there. She'd starve in a few days."

The man grimaced. "Just make sure you fill out all the appropriate paperwork. And if we find a next of kin that actually has some mental capabilities, you be ready to give that creature up, understand me?"

She nodded. "Yes, sir."

"Alright. Go on."

They headed back out to their desks to start the search all over again. "How was the first night?" Bowman asked as they sat back down.

"A little skittish, but she seemed pretty comfortable," Mona replied. "She's an easygoing cat. Which reminds me, I need to stop and get some toys or something on the way home."

"Ever had a pet before?"

Thoughts of her father flooded her mind. Of her asking when they'd get a dog or a cat and always being told no. It had taken time with Dr. Cross, but Mona was slowly beginning to uncover all her memories of her father, including the bad ones. Mona had attempted to talk to her mother about him but, given her failing health, hadn't gotten very far. That, and every time she brought up the subject, her mother would get into one of her fits. Still, she spent as much time with the woman as she could. She looked forward to letting her know she'd taken in a cat.

When she'd been a kid, Mona had desperately wanted a pet. Her poor mother had been too timid to speak her mind, and for good reason. But John—John always said a house was no place for an outdoor animal. That they were wild and deserved to be outside. But Mona always thought differently. "She's my first. Why?"

"Just curious," he said. "We used to have a couple of hound dogs. Got as fat as they could be thanks to my wife giving them table scraps all the time."

"I think it will be good for me," Mona said. "Plus, cats are self-sufficient. I don't need to be home all day."

"Good, because it doesn't look like either of us is getting home anytime soon."

Mona glared at the clock on the wall. It was a quarter to eight and she had been at this for a solid ten hours already with little to show for it. Bowman had given up somewhere around six and headed home so he could get a fresh start in the morning, but Mona had stubbornly stayed put. She was sure she could find *something* on this symbol, but the closest she'd come was running across a few made-up languages someone had posted on DeviantArt.

That's what this had to be, a made-up image. She wasn't even sure it *was* a symbol, but it had all the characteristics of one. And *someone* had gone to enough trouble to create a custom brand for it, something portable that they could carry around with them. It sounded insane when she tried to quantify it, but at the same time, those were the facts they were dealing with.

She thought back to when she had believed she could predict crime with enough points of data. But who could predict something like this? Even if she'd had all the information in the world, there was something very strange and almost... otherworldly about this case, and this symbol was the crux of it all. But if she'd never seen it before, how was she supposed to figure out what it meant? Even if she did, would it lead her to the killer? Or just in another series of circles?

Desperate for *anything*, Mona began pulling any case file in the state of Illinois that had to do with symbols or burns on victims' skin after Bowman went home. Needless to say, there were a lot, without even counting the federal files. These were all nothing more than local and state police cases, the ones that had been added to the shared database anyway. No doubt there were more out there somewhere.

But after about the sixtieth case file that had little in common with her own case, Mona was beginning to lose hope. It was possible whoever killed Mallory would actually get away with it, having planned something so precise and meticulous that they literally *couldn't* be caught.

No. She didn't believe that. There was always evidence to be found somewhere. Her father had tried to control everything and look where it had gotten him. He thought he'd been smarter than everyone else, that he'd been five or ten steps ahead, leading them along like a puppy on a short leash.

But he'd been wrong about one thing: people. He hadn't understood that not everyone had the same ambitions or desires in their cores that he did. He hadn't realized that not everyone wanted to be like him. He'd been so wrapped up in his own delusions of grandeur that he'd forgotten there were *other people* out there.

Thankfully, he hadn't tried to reach out to Mona since that last night in the hospital. And she had no plans on reaching out to him. In fact, she hoped he went crazy in there—talking to himself and seeing ghosts that weren't really there. It was a fitting end for someone who thought he was the smartest person on Earth.

Mona flipped to the next file on the screen, her eyes beginning to go fuzzy. Maybe it was time to call it a night and head back home. At least she had someone waiting for her when she got there. It had been nice, bringing Perigee to her place and introducing her to everything. The cat was extremely curious, but also seemingly very cautious. Unlike some cats who apparently lived to knock things over, Perigee had been deft enough not to even move the slightest cup... yet. There was no telling what condition her place would be in when she got back home.

But given how immaculate Mallory's place had been, Mona wasn't worried. Just as she was about to close the file and head out, something caught her eye. A picture of a mark on a victim with a burn on the arm in approximately the same place as Mallory's.

She looked through the rest of the pictures. Apparently, there had been five different victims, all found at once and all found with burns on just below their wrists. But from what she could tell, the burns didn't resemble the mark they'd found on Mallory at all. First off, they weren't brands, they were more like general burns, circular, like they had come from a flame having been applied to the skin.

It wasn't a slam dunk, but it was the closest she'd found so far. The only problem was the case was twenty-five years old, which meant it was unlikely that it was connected to her case. It had also occurred in Chicago. Mona was beginning to think maybe she was seeing a connection that wasn't really there when she happened to catch the name of one of the detectives assigned to the case.

She smiled. Sometimes a coincidence wasn't a coincidence after all.

FIVE

Where is that damn piece?

Charlotte Dawes stood hunched over the table like a predator looking for the weak spot on its latest prey. Beneath her, on the table in her kitchen, were hundreds and hundreds of little cardboard pieces of all shapes and colors.

She needed one very specific piece.

Her hands gripped the edge of the table harder, almost like she could break through the old wood if she squeezed hard enough. She'd been looking for the little man with the blue hat for nearly twenty minutes. At this rate, she'd be done with this puzzle somewhere around Christmas.

The phone beside her buzzed, but Charlotte didn't break her concentration. If she just stared a few seconds longer, she'd finally pick out the last missing piece of the mill, the one with the man's head as he helped raise the barn in the quaint New England scene on the box cover.

But her phone continued to buzz.

"Faaaack you," she hissed before giving up and grabbing her phone. "Dawes."

"Mom?"

"Haley," Charlotte said, taking a seat in the banquette, the fight against the puzzle immediately stricken from her mind. "Is every-thing okay?"

"Why do you ask that every time I call?" her daughter asked, seemingly annoyed.

"Sorry. I guess... I'm just not used to hearing your voice yet," she replied.

"Why do you still answer your phone like you're on call?"

Charlotte produced a rueful smile. "Old habits, I guess. How is your weekend?"

"Good, Paul and I went out last night to a movie."

"Oh yeah? What did you see?" Charlotte asked, turning away from the puzzle.

"Do you really care?" her daughter asked.

"If you're asking if I'm planning on seeing it? No. But I *am* interested."

Haley huffed on the other end of the line. It had been quite the battle for both of them ever since Charlotte had formally retired from the force. She'd reached out to Haley a couple of times, each of them apologizing for her behavior over the years and asking for forgiveness, though she never really expected to hear from her daughter again. She was okay with that. As long as Haley was healthy and happy—which she believed she was—then there was nothing else to be done. She had already been a drag on her daughter's life long enough. But the girl—the woman—at least deserved an *I'm sorry.*

So it was quite the surprise when Haley actually returned one of her calls. They had begun as short, five-minute calls to catch up and had been getting progressively longer, though they hadn't gone much deeper with each other than a few questions about their respective personal lives. That would probably come in time, if Charlotte didn't screw it up before then. She'd been trying to be careful, to continue to give Haley space, but it was hard. The girl lived five hours away in a completely different city with a man Charlotte had never met, but apparently had been introduced to Charlotte's ex and his wife. She figured if Ronson approved of him,

"Jack" must not be all bad. But still, she hadn't even seen a picture of the two of them together yet.

"It was called *One Over the Moon*," Haley replied. "It's an indie film."

"What's it about?" Charlotte asked.

"A woman who kills her mother because she asks too many annoying questions."

Charlotte smiled. Even though they hadn't been talking long, she still had no trouble discerning when her daughter was being sarcastic. "I'll have to look that one up."

"What are you doing?"

"Oh. Uh... a puzzle."

"A *puzzle*?"

"Yeah, you know. Trying to stay busy."

"What happened to gardening?"

"It's almost fall. Not much to do at the moment." A total lie. The truth was Charlotte had just about killed everything she'd tried to grow to the point where she'd finally decided to just get fake plants and call it a day.

"And the volunteering?"

She hesitated a beat too long. "It's going... well. They're looking for a place for me. There are a lot of volunteers." She neglected to mention that the volunteer coordinator practically threw her out because Charlotte tried to take control of the operation after being repeatedly asked not to.

"*Mom.*"

"Listen, you don't worry about me," Charlotte said. "You've got enough going on. Isn't Jack interviewing for that new job in London next week?"

Her daughter sighed. "Yeah. We think it'll go well. But you know what it means if he gets it."

"I do. And I fully support it."

"You're just saying that because you don't want me to yell at you," Haley replied.

It was true, Charlotte *didn't* want that. She was afraid the second they started yelling again, she'd lose contact with her daughter for good this time. She wasn't going to be that person anymore—the person who criticized her daughter's choices. Her time with Mona had given her a new perspective on young women that age. Plus, Haley had made it this long without Charlotte's interference. She probably thought of Helen—Ronson's wife—as more of a mom than Charlotte.

"We'll still be able to talk on the phone," Charlotte said. "Or chat. Whatever it is you do."

Haley snorted a laugh. "Yeah. There's no shortage of ways to keep in touch. I just mean... I won't see you in person for a while. We'll only be able to come back maybe once or twice a year."

"That's okay," Charlotte said. "It's only a seven-hour flight. I'll come to you."

"You sure?" Haley asked. "I don't want to... you know, be a burden."

"What else do I have to do?" Charlotte asked, her heart sinking. So many times she'd left her daughter as a kid, off on some case, trying to catch the next criminal, and her family life had suffered because of it. First Ronson left, and eventually Haley followed until Charlotte had no one. That was when she really dove headfirst into work, not coming up for air until a few months ago when she finally accepted her retirement. She'd planned on fighting tooth and nail to get Jeremy to keep her on a provisional basis—but it had turned out not to be necessary. Everything changes eventually, and all things end. And Charlotte had finally accepted that.

"Okay, I'll let you know how it goes next week," Haley said, optimism in her voice. Had she been worried about Charlotte's reaction if Jack *did* get the job? Did she think Charlotte would be upset? It made her a little proud that her daughter still gave so much weight to her opinion, especially considering how long they'd been estranged. But Charlotte didn't want to be an obstacle to her daughter, something to overcome or avoid. She wanted to support her in every way possible.

"That sounds great. Tell him 'good luck' from me."

"Okay," her daughter said, almost like she couldn't believe what she was hearing. They chatted for a few more minutes before the conversation began to drag as it always did after they updated each other on their respective weeks.

"Well, I guess I'll talk to you later," Haley said.

"It was nice talking to you," Charlotte replied. "Thanks for calling."

"Yeah, sure. I'll text or something."

"That sounds good," Charlotte replied. "I love you."

"Thanks. Talk to you later." Haley hung up.

Charlotte had to admit that still hurt. Her daughter hadn't said the L word since they'd reconnected. Not that she could blame her after everything Charlotte had put her through. Still... it didn't feel great.

But she didn't want to linger on the feeling. Instead, she turned back to the puzzle but had lost her taste for it. She grabbed the box and swept all the pieces back into it, destroying what little work she'd managed to do. She wasn't a puzzle person. Nor a sudoku person. Nor a gardening person.

Nor, apparently, a volunteer person.

These last few months she'd been restless. After speaking with her old partner—Dale Givens—about it, he'd suggested she needed to find something that *intrigued* her. Something that gave her purpose.

But the honest truth was the only thing that ever gave her purpose was serving as a police officer. She secretly wondered if maybe they could use someone on the call desk. She would even take third shift, if for no other reason than to get out of this house.

Her phone buzzed just as she was putting the puzzle away. At first she thought it was Haley, but when she looked she saw it was a text from Dale, "inviting" her to dinner tomorrow night. She groaned. It wasn't that she didn't like being around Dale and his wife and their kids. But every one of these dinners so far had been a poor attempt to introduce Charlotte to new friends, and she always ended up being the fifth, or seventh, or ninth wheel. Oddly enough, all of Dale's friends came in pairs. And no matter how well the dinner went, Charlotte was always the odd one out.

She appreciated the effort—she really did. But if she had to sit at Dale's dining table and watch other couples chat and laugh about the latest gossip, she might hang herself with Dale's hideous curtains.

She sent a quick text back letting him know she'd be busy but she'd take a rain check that she didn't actually plan on cashing. Though in the middle of the text, her phone began to buzz again, a familiar name flashing up on the screen.

It took Charlotte a second to realize just who was calling her. They'd been keeping in touch, but honestly she hadn't heard much from Mona in the past month or two. She figured the woman would reach out for a short time but eventually forget about Charlotte and get on with her life.

She took a deep breath and recalled what her daughter had just chided her about. "This is Charlotte Dawes."

"Hi there," a familiar voice said on the other end. And while the greeting was welcome, there was something underpinning her words.

"Mona," Charlotte asked. "Hi. Is everything all right?"

"Not exactly," Mona replied, causing Charlotte to furrow her brow and stand, on immediate alert.

"What is it?"

"Well... it's a little complicated," she said. "Are you doing anything right now?"

Charlotte looked at the puzzle she'd haphazardly thrown back in its box, noting a stray piece had fallen on the floor. When she bent over to pick it up, she realized it had been the piece she'd just spent half an hour looking for.

"Not a thing. How can I help?"

SIX

The following morning as she drove towards Oak Creek, Charlotte couldn't help but feel a familiar sensation throughout her body. It hadn't been more than a few months ago that she made this exact same drive in an attempt to salvage what remained of her career and ended up facing one of the toughest and most sadistic killers she'd ever encountered. She had barely survived that ordeal, but it had given her a new clarity; helped her to understand she couldn't hold on to everything forever. She'd returned to Chicago with a new determination to accept the next phase of her life.

Which made it strange, heading back again. It was almost like hitting rewind in a way, except this time she was coming as a civilian and nothing else. Mona asked if she could help consult on a new case, and while Charlotte didn't officially do police work any longer, she wasn't about to pass up the opportunity. If for no other reason than to get out of the house.

It had to be better than sitting around doing puzzles all day.

As she pulled into the familiar square, she couldn't help but think about the small mob that had once gathered there, demanding justice for Robin, Dr. Pekannen and the others. They had nearly caused a scene that night and the memory of just how volatile this community could be had stuck with Charlotte.

But she supposed she couldn't blame them. Their own people were being hunted down and killed. And this was a tight-knit community. They watched out for each other here. Small towns were like that, though she had to admit Oak Creek had been *particularly* invested. Some of that was due to McCormick's influence, but he'd only stoked the fires of what already existed. This town... it was special.

She pulled up to the small station beside the town's courthouse and stepped out of her car, noting it was still a bit cooler out here than in the city. Across the square stood the building that once housed Robin's art studio on the ground level and Dr. Pekannen's practice above. It was currently empty, with a *For Rent* sign posted on both windows.

"Oh good, you made it."

Charlotte turned to see Detective Mona LaSalle bounding down the stairs. They hadn't seen each other since Charlotte had returned to Chicago, and she had to admit Mona looked like she'd matured in the few months they'd been apart. There was a new confidence about her, and she walked with more purpose in her step.

Purpose, which slammed into Charlotte in the form of an unexpected hug. "It's great to see you."

Charlotte wrapped her arms around the younger woman's back. "You too. Keeping out of trouble?"

Mona pulled away. "Not exactly. We have a new interim sheriff and Ramsey is still under investigation. And up until this weekend, things had been pretty quiet. I thought we might be getting back to normal. At least, people have mostly stopped staring at me when they think I'm not looking."

"That's to be expected," Charlotte replied. "After news of your father got out."

A pinched smile crossed Mona's face. "Let's not talk about it. Come on. I've got someone I want you to meet." She took Charlotte by the arm and guided her up the stairs to the police station before opening the door for her and ushering her inside.

This was the part Charlotte had been dreading the most. She hadn't gotten along with most of the local cops in Oak Creek the last time she was here; they saw her as an interloper, someone who thought she was better than them just because she was a cop from Chicago. Which hadn't been the case at all, but you couldn't exactly tell someone that and have them believe you when you were specifically brought in because of your "experience."

"Jenkins, you remember Detective Dawes," Mona said as they approached the security door where the sergeant sat on the other side.

"It's just civilian Dawes now," Charlotte amended. "I'm officially retired."

The man inside the booth looked at the two of them for a second before buzzing them through without a word. Just as Charlotte had expected. The cold shoulder. "I hope everyone else is just as happy to see me," she said.

"Don't worry about him, Jenkins is..." Mona paused, resetting herself. "Jenkins is Jenkins. And he's not representative of the general opinion around here." Mona smiled as they headed down the familiar corridors. This was harder than Charlotte had expected, and she had expected it not to be a walk in the park. All her confrontations with Ramsey, with the FBI and even the few discussions with Mona's mentor, Sheriff Franklin... they had all happened in these halls. And even though they were exactly the same as they'd been when she last left them, something about the place seemed different. Emptier, somehow.

And yet Mona herself was so much more full of life than she'd been when Charlotte first met her. Gone was the shy detective who was afraid to speak up, who didn't let her personality shine through, and who kept every emotion guarded and locked away. Mona had blossomed into a vibrant and energetic person. It warmed Charlotte's heart.

"Wait a second," Charlotte said, stopping them in the hallway.

"Everything okay?" Mona asked.

Charlotte regarded her for a moment. "You really have changed, you know that?"

"Oh, I guess?" Mona replied, though something darkened her demeanor behind it all. "I'm in therapy now. We're working on it. At least that's what Dr. Cross says. I got the impression from Sheriff Earle if I didn't stick to it, my job might be in jeopardy."

"Because of your dad?"

She nodded. "But I don't call him that. He's just John to me."

Charlotte wanted to be delicate here. She knew John McCormick was being remanded in the Illinois State Mental Facility about an hour north of the city, but since her retirement, it had been difficult to get any additional information. Last she heard he was being held there indefinitely, pending an evaluation for standing trial.

"Have you... heard from him?"

Mona looked away, some of that guarded personality Charlotte had become so familiar with reappearing momentarily. "He's reached out on a few occasions. But I don't plan on responding."

"I think that's the smartest thing you could do," Charlotte replied. "How are you handling all of it?"

"Like Dr. Cross tells me. Day by day. Here, come on." Mona led the way down the hallway back to her same desk which happened to be right across from the sheriff's office. The desk where Charlotte had been temporarily set up had been removed completely, the office undergoing something of a rearrangement.

In the desk across from Mona's sat a man with a medium build, hunched over his computer while a cup of coffee and half-eaten egg sandwich sat on the edge of his desk.

"Will?" Mona asked.

The man turned and looked up. Upon seeing Charlotte, his eyes flashed with recognition. "Ah, you must be Dawes." He probably had about six inches on her, was clean shaven and didn't carry the weight of the job that she saw in so many cops of his age. Still, he'd begun to gray at his temples, an early sign of stress for someone who couldn't be older than thirty-five.

Charlotte stopped short. "That's right."

The man stood, extending his hand. "Will Bowman. Mona talks about you. A lot."

Charlotte shook the man's hand. "We had quite the case together."

"Will transferred up from Indianapolis," Mona said. "Earle thought it would be a good idea to get some new blood in the ranks after—well, you know."

Charlotte nodded. "The department went through a lot." She turned to Bowman. "How are you liking Oak Creek?"

"It's slow," he replied. "Which is good for my back. And it's good for my kids. Worst we've had to deal with are a few punks selling substances. At least, until Friday."

Charlotte turned back to Mona. "Okay. You brought me all the way up here. What's going on?"

Mona returned a sheepish smile. "I'm not trying to be cryptic, but I wanted to get your honest reaction when I asked you about the case without clouding your judgement."

"What case?" Charlotte replied. Mona had given her scant information over the phone, just asking if she could come help on an old case that Charlotte had worked once upon a time. But Charlotte had worked hundreds of cases over the years. There was no telling which one she was referring to.

"Maybe it's better if I show you," Mona said, tapping her forefinger to her chin.

"She's convinced you can help," Bowman replied. "Though I'm still skeptical." He struck her as a very practical kind of detective. One who would follow the evidence and little else. Unfortunately for him, that wasn't how Mona operated. At least not in Charlotte's experience. The woman had a knack for seeing patterns where other people couldn't. And she knew if Mona had stumbled upon something important enough to ask for Charlotte's help, it was real.

"Okay. Show me," Charlotte said.

"You've got to be kidding me." The man who was in the process of removing his white lab coat had practically stopped in his tracks as soon as he saw Charlotte and Mona coming down the hallway.

"Whittle, good to see you again," Charlotte said as they approached.

"Surprise," Mona said, wiggling her eyebrows at Whittle. "I wanted to show her Mallory."

"I thought you retired," Whittle said.

"I did. Only here as a personal favor."

"I can't allow civilians back there," Whittle said. "We have procedures—"

"Andy," Mona said. "C'mon."

The man sighed. "Fine. Follow me." He led them into the morgue as Mona gave Charlotte a quick wink. She couldn't help but be impressed with how Mona wielded her new confidence—it made her a force to be reckoned with.

Whittle took them over to the nearby freezers, opening one of the drawers to reveal a white sheet covering the body. The cool air from the freezer seeped under Charlotte's coat, sending a chill up her back.

"Mallory Wakefield, twenty-four years old. Victim of a hit-and-run," Whittle replied, pulling the sheet back.

It was nothing Charlotte hadn't seen a dozen times before. A young victim, killed before she could even really start the prime of her life. Clearly, they already had the cause of death, as well as an ID on the victim herself. It looked open-and-shut to Charlotte.

"Okay. So what do you need me for?" she asked, looking to Mona.

Mona kept her gaze on Charlotte for a second, before rounding the body and gently pulling back the sheet even further to reveal the woman's arms. Just above the wrist on her right arm was a dark burn in a shape that Charlotte had never seen before. But it wasn't the shape itself that caused her stomach to bottom out. It was the placement.

"Recognize it?" Mona asked.

"Is that—was it due to the accident?" Charlotte replied, her mouth suddenly dry.

"It wasn't an accident," Mona replied. "And no. We believe this was done after."

Charlotte took a deep breath, the air thick with the smell of chemical bleach as the memories came flooding back.

No. It couldn't be. Not after all this time. The mark wasn't the same... which meant it probably wasn't related. But still, she couldn't help but think back to that case all those years ago. To her own personal failure. It had been her first large-scale case. And she'd dropped the ball.

Not only that, but it had become the one case that had haunted her entire career. The one she'd never been able to get away from, and that had come back with every unsolved murder she'd faced after that day. What she had believed would put her on the fast track to making a name for herself had become a ball and chain she'd never rid herself of. Whatever this was, it couldn't be part of that. And even if it were, she wanted nothing to do with it.

"Sorry," Charlotte finally said. "But I don't think I'm going to do you any good."

SEVEN

"Wait a second," Mona said, trotting down the hallway after Charlotte.

After taking one look at that mark on the poor woman's arm, Charlotte had practically turned and walked back out of the room, leaving Mona and Whittle baffled. Mona had run after her, with Whittle asking if she wanted him to keep her out or not.

Mona didn't understand. She'd never seen Charlotte react like that, even when they found Robin's body, or Sheriff Franklin's. The woman wasn't the kind of person to get rattled. But it was as if Charlotte had seen an honest-to-God ghost.

"Charlotte," Mona called, finally reaching the other woman just before she got to the doors.

"I should really get back to Chicago," Charlotte said in a rush, not meeting Mona's eyeline. "I just spoke to my daughter and I may need to go to Philadelphia for a few days. I need to pack."

"Hang on," Mona said, taking the other woman by the arm. The action seemed to snap Charlotte out of whatever she'd fallen into as she almost went stiff, staring at Mona. Mona released her grip immediately. She hadn't grabbed on hard at all—but it was almost like she'd slapped Charlotte. "I'm sorry."

Charlotte seemed to come back to herself. "No, I..." She shook her head, and a bevy of emotions scrambled their way across her face all at once, like she couldn't decide how to react and instead reacted every possible way all at once.

"Are you okay?"

"I'm fine," Charlotte replied.

"You seem... rattled."

Charlotte shook her head, too quickly. "No. It's just... What happened? To your victim?"

Okay, so they were going for the professional approach. "Like Whittle said, it was a hit-and-run. But it was in a remote part of town where there is little foot traffic. It happened after sunset and the victim's phone was missing. We believe she was lured out there, then hit. We then believe the killer *branded* her with that symbol on her arm. I was going back through any case file I could find that might have something in common with it and I found—"

"My case was completely different," Charlotte interrupted.

Her abruptness caused Mona to pause. "I know. But you can't deny the placement of the marking. It matches exactly."

"Mine weren't markings either. They were just burns."

Mona nodded again, already aware of this information. "Yours was the only thing I could find that was even close."

Charlotte swallowed, looking at the door before taking her hand away.

"I'm not asking you to work the case. I just wanted to get your honest opinion on whether you thought they could be connected or not. If you say no, I'll close up book and move on."

"*You* think they are," Charlotte replied.

She couldn't deny it. As soon as Mona had read the case file, she had recognized something familiar about the case but she couldn't put her finger on it. Charlotte was right, there wasn't a lot connecting the cases. But seeing as Mona had found *zero* other cases with any relation, she was willing to take what she could get. Something told her she was on to something here.

"That case is over twenty years old," Charlotte finally said. "The odds of it being connected—"

"But you never found the person or people responsible," Mona said. "It's still an open cold case."

Mona couldn't tell what was going on behind Charlotte's gaze, but the woman was temporarily somewhere else. Maybe reliving the events of the case as they happened. Whatever she was thinking, it was as if a shadow had fallen over her friend.

"It might be possible," Charlotte finally said.

"Can we talk about it?" Mona asked. "Then I'll let you go, I swear."

Charlotte looked through the glass doors that faced a tree-lined street on the other side. "You're buying."

"Fair enough."

"It wasn't my first case, but it was my first *big* case," Charlotte said after she took a sip on her plain black coffee. They'd come to a little café that was just off Oak Creek's main square that served everything from ground Colombian to the sweetest sugar-filled "coffee" money could buy. Charlotte, predictably, got a plain Americano while Mona had splurged for something with a little more flair. She had wanted to tease Charlotte about it, but the look on the woman's face told her that now was not the time. Mona had always had something of a problem with reading social cues, but thanks to her recent efforts, it had been getting better over the past few months.

Thankfully, she was able to recognize just how much pain Charlotte was in. Even though she didn't know why, she also didn't want to put Charlotte through any unnecessary distress.

"I didn't realize this would be so tough for you," Mona said, staring at her own cup of butterscotch-colored liquid. "I just thought it was another case you worked."

"I've never had trouble with tough," Charlotte replied. "But when you're thrown into the spotlight and expected to deliver results, and then *can't*, no matter how hard you try... it starts to wear on you." She took a deep breath. "I never wanted to think about this case again. I thought, especially after I'd retired, that it was dead and buried. I didn't expect it to come back to haunt me."

"Did you ever have a reasonable suspect?" Mona asked.

Charlotte shook her head. "It took us weeks to even identify the victims." Those were five names she'd never forget. Gabrielle Ruiz, Rob Keppler, Blaine Weiss, Melissa Hocker and Lori Evans. "Me and my partner at the time—Ortega—we worked that case for months. Under the watch of all the cameras, the media, my boss... and we never made a dent in it. We talked to the families, looked for witnesses, appealed to the public. No one came forward. Things dragged on and we got dragged along with them. For the longest time I was afraid that was how they'd all be. Thankfully, it turned out to be the exception, not the rule."

"Why did they assign it to you?" Mona asked. "Weren't you still new?"

"Who knows why the bureaucracy does anything," she replied. "Short on staff, no one else wanted it, someone wanted to prove something, it was a political move to put someone else in power. Doesn't matter. What remains is, Ortega and I got it. The problem was, we couldn't do anything with it. We had the bodies, but the place was littered with contaminated evidence. Literally hundreds of people's fingerprints came back. None of them matching anything we had in the system except for a few people who had worked at the factory years before it closed. But we eliminated them as suspects quickly."

Mona nodded. "I read your initial report and the follow-ups. Must have been hard, not being able to make any progress."

"It was maddening," Charlotte replied. "No matter which way we looked, there was nothing. Nothing came back on all the blood spilled at the scene. As best we could tell, all the victims were chosen at random. None had any connection to each other. In fact, if I didn't know better, I would say they were all chosen *because* they were different and unrelated. None were even the same ethnicity."

"Must have been scary," Mona said.

"The city was terrified for a while, convinced someone was out there kidnapping people and then slicing them open. But it never happened again. At least, not in that exact same way. As far as we could tell, it was a one-time event. Eventually, my boss at the time wanted to rule it a mass suicide."

"But you knew better."

"I knew that getting five people to slice their wrists and throats all at once was like a bullet hitting another bullet in midair. It's possible, but the chances are so astronomically low that it might as well be impossible. Plus, we never found any weapons on the scene, so we couldn't make a determination one way or another." She took a sip of her coffee. "Our coroner at the time—old guy by the name of Ritehawk, I'm sure he's dead now—couldn't even confirm for us that someone else had cut their throats. He said it had been done in such a way it was possible that they could have done it themselves. We just didn't have the evidence." She took a deep breath, setting her cup on the table.

As she spoke it was like a dark cloud was forming over her head, drowning her in bad memories. Mona felt guilty for bringing all this back up; it was obviously hard for Charlotte. "When was the last time you checked on it?"

"I went back to it once. After I'd been on the job about five years. I figured maybe I'd missed something back then and I was too green to notice. But after spending another week getting nowhere, I realized that wasn't the case. I just decided to let it go. Try to forget it and move on with my career. Two weeks later, I broke the Moreno case. And everything changed."

"That's the one that put you on the map," Mona said. "I remember hearing about that on the news."

"After that, I didn't want to look back," Charlotte said. "Suddenly, things seemed brighter."

"And you don't know if there have been any developments on it since?"

Charlotte shook her head. "I haven't looked in years. The department is always looking for tips."

"What about copycats?"

"At the time that wasn't as prevalent," Charlotte replied. "We didn't release all the information to the press at once for that very reason. But no, we never saw anyone attempt something similar."

Mona sat back, thinking. Charlotte's case involved five people at once, hers was only one. And hers had been in a kind of ritualistic killing, while Mona's had been a hit-and-run. Not at all similar.

And yet there was the mark on the wrist.

"So then you don't recognize that symbol," Mona finally said.

Charlotte paused for a moment, went to grab her coffee and then thought better of it. "There was always something that really bothered me about that case. It was the fact that each victim had been burned in that exact same spot, just like yours. All on the same arm. And like yours, it appeared to have been done postmortem."

Hope flourished in Mona's chest. "Really? Was that confirmed?"

"We never released that information either." Charlotte leaned forward. "But I always thought that had something to do with... whatever happened that night."

Mona furrowed her brow. "What do you mean?"

"These weren't regular burns. They were third-degree burns. As in, someone had to have held a flame there for a long time to get that kind of charring. Why would someone do that *after* the person was already dead?"

"I'm assuming you're not thinking it was a fetish of some sort."

"I never had any evidence to prove this, but I always thought it was to cover something up," Charlotte replied. "Something that might have given us a clue to who the killer or killers were."

"That makes a lot of sense," Mona said. "But if that's really the case, then I don't think ours are related at all. I mean, whoever branded Mallory left a very specific symbol on her. Like they're almost *pointing* to something."

Charlotte nodded. "That's true. Yours seems very specific. It's... unnerving. Brings back bad memories."

"I'm sorry," Mona replied. "And I'm sorry for dragging you all the way out here for nothing."

"No," Charlotte said. "Not bad memories of my case. Of the one you and I worked together."

"Oh," Mona said. "Yeah... I guess leaving a clue like that..."

"We know it can't be him," Charlotte said. "He's under twenty-four-hour supervision."

Mona smiled, but it was forced. "I know. I think maybe I was just seeing a connection where there wasn't one. I should have just told you all this over the phone."

"I'm glad you didn't. It was nice coming out here—seeing you, meeting your new partner. You're making quite the life for yourself. How is your mother doing?"

Mona suppressed a wince. "The same. She's in and out of it a lot. But I still see her once a week or so."

"And Adam?" Charlotte asked.

"He's doing better. Getting back in a routine. We still talk often. I'm trying to help him with college essays. I owe Robin that much, at least."

Mona couldn't help but be a little deflated at learning more about Charlotte's case. As terrible as the details were, it made sense. If she had staged a mass murder, she would have taken every opportunity to obscure or destroy as much evidence as possible. This matter with her symbol on Mallory's arm... that was something she couldn't understand. Charlotte was right, it was very similar to what John had done: a lure of sorts. As if the killer was trying to pull them along, make them follow a pre-planned course of action.

But Mona wasn't about to get drawn into something like that again. "Well, we gave it our best shot."

She felt the pressure of Charlotte's gaze, much like she had when she first met the woman. Back then she had been Detective Charlotte Dawes, a legend in the community. But as Mona had grown to know her, that pedestal had slowly lowered itself until they were on level ground. Now she saw Charlotte for who she really was, a flawed person doing the best she could with what she had. Just like Mona.

But that didn't mean she still couldn't be intimidating as hell. Her face was drawn in the way that told Mona she was deeply considering something. She just didn't know what.

"Everything okay?" Mona asked.

"I was just thinking... I have a friend who deals with cryptology. He loves this kind of stuff. Why don't we go pay him a visit? At least I can be slightly useful. You can show him the symbol—maybe he'll be able to make something of it."

"I've already looked in every online catalog and database I can find," Mona replied. "There's no reference to it anywhere."

Charlotte grinned. "Kids. Think everything can be found on the internet. Believe it or not, there are people out there who know more than randos online do."

"You can just give me his information, I'll email him," Mona said. She'd already inconvenienced Charlotte enough; she didn't want to make it any worse. "I'm sure you don't want to be bogged down with this. You said you had that thing... with your daughter?"

"It's no trouble. He's in Chicago and I'm headed back anyway. We might as well go together," Charlotte suggested. "Sometimes he doesn't trust people he doesn't know. It'll be better if I'm there."

"You sure?" Mona asked.

"Absolutely." She stood, depositing her empty coffee cup in the nearby trash can. "How about we head over there now?"

"Right now?" Mona asked, looking around.

"Do you have something better to do?"

Mona got the distinct impression this wasn't all for her convenience. But she wasn't about to argue. Thirty minutes ago, Charlotte had been on the verge of walking out of here and she wasn't about to look a gift horse in the mouth.

"Ready when you are."

EIGHT

The drive back to Chicago was quiet. Charlotte didn't feel like playing the radio or even rolling down the windows to let in some fresh air. Instead, her mind was preoccupied with the case that almost ended her career before it began. Not that she would have been fired for not being able to solve a case such as that—the odds against them had been high from the beginning. But it had almost turned her off police work entirely. She hadn't been sure she could handle something so... depraved on a regular basis. It had taken a lot of soul searching to stick with it. That first night after seeing those people—those *kids*—splayed out on those slabs like that had nearly convinced her to go into another line of work.

But she'd stuck with it. It had taken every ounce of strength to keep going, but she'd managed it somehow. It had taught her how to manage her emotions in cases like that. In fact, back then she hadn't been that dissimilar from Mona, though she'd never been able to turn them off completely like Mona had.

It was probably why she had connected to Mona so deeply when they first met. Because even though the woman seemed foreign in her uncanny ability to shut herself off, Charlotte had seen something of herself deep in there. And she hadn't wanted Mona to turn out like she had.

Thankfully, the young detective had made leaps and bounds in the past few months, to the point Charlotte was practically astounded at how much she was blooming. The only problem was Mona had also uncovered one of the few cases Charlotte had hoped never to think about again. Because even though she'd found a way to survive the investigation without completely ripping her own heart out, it remained one of the biggest, if not *the* biggest, cases of her career that she never solved. Back then she had considered it the case that would put her on the map, fast-track her to a promotion and bring justice to the city of Chicago.

None of that had happened.

Instead, she and Ortega had struggled with it for months before her boss brought in another team, effectively removing them from the case. And yet, the media portrayed it as *their* failure, not the department's. Maybe someone at the *Tribune* had a grudge, but they'd called Charlotte out personally to say how ineffective the police were being in tracking down Chicago's biggest killer at the time. It had taken Charlotte a long time to finally allow that to roll off her back.

Predictably, no matter who eventually ended up with the case, they always ran into the same roadblocks. Charlotte had tried... She'd gone back to it a few times, but eventually she had to accept there was nothing else there before she stopped looking at all. She had hoped she could forget about it completely, but that wasn't possible.

Not really.

Charlotte glanced in the rearview mirror at Mona following in the car behind her. She hadn't wanted to entertain the possibility of even examining the case again at first, but the more she recounted the case for Mona, the more she realized it wasn't about her case. It was about getting a win for Mona. The cases probably weren't related, but that didn't mean she couldn't help in another way. And maybe in some way, helping now could make up for her failure a quarter century ago.

Was she being impulsive? Maybe. Was she using this opportunity as an excuse to come back to work in a way? She was pretty sure Jeremy—and everyone else, including Dale—would see it that way. But this was honestly the most stimulating thing that had happened to her since she'd officially turned in her badge. Mona had become like a lifeline to her old life.

She had tried. She really had. But investigating was in her blood. It didn't matter what else she tried to do, everything else just felt... empty. Maybe if she could get closure on this one case, it would change how she felt. But she knew somewhere deep in her heart that nothing would ever quench that fire. And she didn't want it to.

As the first spires of Chicago appeared over the horizon, Charlotte decided to put her future out of her mind for now. She needed to focus on helping Mona as much as she could with her own particular mystery. And there was no one who knew cryptology than Roger Kaye. He had been a mainstay for the department back in the day, though Charlotte had lost track of him in the past ten years or so. But if she knew Roger like she had back then, he was still kicking around, probably with his nose in some history book somewhere. They'd worked together on multiple cases, and she always found him affable and easygoing, despite everyone else thinking he was nothing more than a nerd.

She pulled off I-90 just past O'Hare and headed down the side roads, making sure Mona was still behind her. She had to admit, when Mona wasn't hamstrung by her own lack of self-confidence, she was a force to be reckoned with. When Charlotte had first met the woman, she had seen that fire in her almost itching to get out. Her only concern was John was still out there. He might be in custody in a mental facility, but that didn't mean he was completely invisible. It would have been better for Mona if he had died. Then she could have moved on with her life. But knowing he might still be able to influence Mona in some way left an uneasy feeling in Charlotte's stomach.

She pulled into a small parking structure, grabbing the ticket as the gate before her allowed her past. Mona pulled in right beside her, stepping out. "Your friend works in a parking garage?"

"No," Charlotte said, locking her car. "He works at the main branch of the library in the middle of downtown. But it'll take a good two hours to get there if we drive. Easier to take the El." She led Mona to the nearby station where they took a seat as they waited on the train to arrive.

She wasn't sure why, but she could almost feel Mona's tension, though she didn't know what the woman had to be nervous about. "Never ridden the train before?"

"Plenty of times," Mona replied. "I'm just worried I'm putting you out. I already brought you all the way out to Oak Creek for no reason. Now I'm taking up the rest of your day."

"It's no trouble," Charlotte replied. "One of the benefits of being retired is I don't have anything else to do today."

"How is that going by the way?" Mona asked as the train approached.

"Great. Love it."

Mona followed Charlotte onto the train and they took a seat. Thankfully, it wasn't too busy as they headed into the city. But the trains running opposite would be absolutely packed at this time of day.

"Doesn't really sound like you love it," Mona finally said as the doors closed.

Charlotte turned to her. "What do you mean?"

"Nothing, it's just... your whole face kind of darkened when you said it, that's all."

Charlotte didn't want to acknowledge the comment, partially because Mona was right. She didn't like it when people could read her so easily, but she should have known better than to think she could pull one over on Mona.

"It's been... a process."

"Still trying to find something to occupy your time?"

"Found plenty to occupy my time. Finding something that sticks is the key."

Mona nodded to her hands. "Those feeling okay?"

"Haven't felt so much as a twinge in months."

Mona smiled. "I guess you're doing something right, then."

It only took about twenty minutes for the train to finally reach the Harold Washington Library stop, thanks to Charlotte's knowledge of the train schedules. They both stepped off with a glut of other people who'd gotten on at the stops between, then descended the stairs to street level.

The Harold Washington Library itself was a massive brick-and-glass building, relatively modern by the city's standards, having been opened in the early nineties. Though somehow it still fit in with the rest of the city.

Charlotte led Mona in through the north entrance, which led to a massive two-story lobby made of marble and stone. In the center was a circular depression that looked down on the lower level while a large information desk sat just to the right.

A young woman in large glasses sat behind the desk, the light from the computer monitor reflecting in her spectacles as Charlotte approached. "I'm looking for Roger Kaye."

The woman looked up, confusion on her face. "Historical figure? Those are on level three."

"No, Roger Kaye, he's head of Archives and Collections."

"I'm sorry, Mrs. Dorsey is our head of Archives and Collections. Maybe you're thinking of a different branch?" She began typing on her computer.

"No, I'm pretty sure I'd remember if it was a different branch. The building is hard to miss."

"Oh, here we go," the girl said. "It looks like Mr. Kaye retired about five years ago."

"Retired?" That didn't make sense. Roger was one those people who always had his nose in a book and *loved* it. Short of going blind, Charlotte couldn't see any reason why he'd give up such a choice position. "Do you know where I can find him?"

"Sorry, I don't. But hang on, let me check with our Human

Resources." She picked up the phone and dialed, speaking quietly into it.

Behind her, Mona was looking up at the ceiling. "This place is *huge*."

"You should see the top floor. They have a winter garden up there," Charlotte replied. "All glass ceiling."

"I am definitely coming back here on my day off." Mona continued to gawk at the size of the room.

"I can't believe you've never been here before," Charlotte said.

"I don't make it into the city often. Before there hadn't been a reason. But more recently I've been matching with people online, and most of them are from the city."

"Matching as in... dating?" Charlotte asked.

"Uhh... well—" Mona began.

"I'm sorry," the girl at the desk said as she hung up the phone. "I was just informed we can't give out personal information about former employees."

"But you do know where he lives." Charlotte reached into her jacket pocket for a badge that was no longer there. Normally, getting them to give up his address would be a piece of cake. But without the authority of the police department behind her anymore, those doors were now closed.

A badge appeared on the desk in front of her. "I'm with Oak Creek Police. We need to find him," Mona said, having come up beside Charlotte.

"Oh," the girl replied. "One second." She picked up the receiver again as a few of the other patrons milling about the lobby glanced in their direction. Charlotte happened to catch Mona's eye and the younger woman gave her a quick smile.

"We don't have a home address on file," the woman at the desk finally said. "Only a forwarding one. I believe it's for a shop."

"A shop?" Charlotte asked. "Fine. Give us what you have."

The girl wrote down the address on a small notecard and handed it over.

"Thank you for your help," Mona said as they headed back toward the doors.

"Appreciate the save," Charlotte said once they were back on the street. She still wasn't used to not having her shield on her. After thirty years, it had become like an appendage.

Mona shrugged. "I figured if it was just an address, what could it hurt?"

Charlotte pulled out her phone and plugged the address into her maps. "Oh."

"Oh?"

"It's a bookstore," she said, unable to keep the surprise out of her tone. Roger had quit the library to open his own bookstore. There was something innately charming about that.

"Looks like it's only a few blocks away," Mona said.

"I don't mind the walk if you don't." Chicago could be cold and blustery as the narrow corridors created by all the tall buildings focused the wind down the streets. In the winter it could get unbearably cold, especially after the sun was down. Thankfully, even though the sun was beginning to set, it was still relatively warm out.

It took less than fifteen minutes to walk down State Street before they found the storefront they were looking for. Unfortunately, the sign on the door told them he was already closed for the day. Charlotte cupped her hands over her eyes to see if anyone might still be milling around inside, but the shop was dark.

"Damn."

"It's okay," Mona replied. "Really. I can come back another day on my own. Now that I know where he is."

"I suppose that makes sense," Charlotte admitted. But she was deflated that the "investigation" had ended so suddenly. It felt good to be back out on the street, chasing a lead, even if it was something as mundane as tracking down an address. She supposed she could come by first thing in the morning and give Roger a heads-up. But she had really hoped they could have spoken to him this evening.

"Are you okay?" Mona asked.

Charlotte gave her a wistful smile. "Just thinking that if this was one of my cases, I'd head out for a bite before getting a couple of hours sleep and then coming right back here first thing in the morning. But I guess there's no longer any need for that, is there?"

"Why don't we go grab a bite anyway?" Mona suggested. "It will give us a chance to catch up."

It was as if someone had lifted a heavy rock off her chest. "Are you sure? Don't you need to get back?"

"Bowman can handle it things. He's a good cop," Mona replied. "Besides. I want to hear about your daughter."

Charlotte hadn't spoken to anyone other than Dale about Haley. And she was sure her old partner was tired of hearing the scraps Charlotte had gathered through their conversations. It would be nice to have someone new to talk to. Maybe Mona could even help Charlotte figure out how to relate better to Haley. "I'd be happy to tell you what little I know."

"How hard is it to get a good pizza around here?" Mona asked.

Charlotte couldn't help but smile. "I know the perfect place."

NINE

One thing Mona had learned about herself as she'd began navigating new relationships was how *aware* she was of everything and everyone at all times. That was not a trait that other people seemed to share. Like when she had been waiting for Caleb at the restaurant, she had been mentally tracking not only her server, but half of the others in the room, while also subtly watching who came in and left the restaurant. She'd been able to tell exactly when her order was input into the computer and usually knew when it was on its way to the table before anyone else ever did.

Bowman—on the few times they'd been out to eat—called it uncanny, but it was just a matter of simple observation and of understanding general human behavior. It was easy to tell when the waitstaff was overworked versus not, or what they'd ordered too much of based on what was on special. Even though she tried to turn it off, she couldn't just *stop observing*. And maybe some of that was a trauma response. She'd spoken to Dr. Cross about it who admitted they'd need to do a deeper dive into Mona's past to really find out, but it had some similar hallmarks of underlying issues.

But at the same time, Mona didn't want to stop. She liked knowing what was going on around her at all times. So she found it slightly unnerving when two hours had passed at the pizza place and she'd barely noticed how much time had passed. Usually, she was hyperaware of the clock in addition to everything else, but there was something about Charlotte's company that just helped all that melt away.

In some ways, Charlotte was like the mentor Mona had always expected Sheriff Franklin to be. While he had always been supportive and helped Mona more than she could ever repay, he hadn't been a woman in this line of work. Especially not a woman with thirty years under her belt. In many ways, Charlotte was the woman Mona aspired to be one day, at least as far as her career went. She obviously didn't want her personal life to mirror Charlotte's, though she also didn't think that it was entirely Charlotte's fault. As the woman talked about how she'd worked to reconnect with her daughter, Mona considered that maybe it was part of the job itself, and how it was harder on women, who were traditionally expected to take on more of the domestic burden. Bowman had been great and all, but he couldn't see things from her perspective. It was impossible. And it was nice to have someone to relate to again.

After dinner it had been late, and even though it was only about a ninety-minute drive back to Oak Creek, Charlotte had insisted Mona stay at her place. She had a second bedroom that was never used, and she suggested they could head back over to Roger's bookshop early the following morning. Thankfully, Mona had already gotten Perigee into the start of a routine and wasn't worried about leaving the cat overnight. She still had dry food if she needed and could be self-sufficient until Mona returned the following day.

It also didn't escape Mona's attention that Charlotte kept using "we" when discussing the case. She supposed it was hard for her, working for the department for so long then suddenly being asked to let it all go. It made sense that she would fall back into old habits.

And honestly, Mona was glad to have the help. She really enjoyed working with Bowman, there was no question about that. But the man didn't have much of an imagination and always seemed to take things at face value. Charlotte, on the other hand, tended to think broader and outside the box. If she was offering up her services for free, Mona wasn't about to turn her down.

Not only that, but she could tell there was something else driving Charlotte. A deep-seated need that she'd first caught a glimpse of during their last case together. Charlotte had always desired justice—it's what had driven her career. And even though their cases might not be related, Mona was pretty sure she'd accidentally dug up some old demons for her friend. Demons that were not just going to go away quietly.

That hadn't been her intention and she felt somewhat responsible for it. But Charlotte was a grown woman, and Mona wasn't going to stand between her and whatever she felt like she needed to do. Too many people had done that to her in the past and she wasn't going to repeat the behavior.

In truth, Mona would have preferred to be back at her own place, with her own things. But part of this job was adaptability. She'd been lucky that she hadn't had to travel much yet, but that didn't mean it was off the table. Earle had let it slip that the governor was considering an overhaul of local law enforcement, which would mean they'd be sharing resources with some of the other nearby towns pretty soon. With that came a lot more collaboration.

And stress.

"Mona?" Charlotte asked, knocking on the door to her room. "Ready to get going?"

Thankfully, Mona had gotten up early but had forgone a shower, since she didn't have a change of clothes handy. Instead, she'd just done the best she could with what little had been in Charlotte's guest bathroom. She'd take a proper shower when she got home.

"Be right there." She'd hoped Charlotte's guest room—and her place in general—would have offered a few more personal touches, but the woman herself admitted she'd never paid much attention to any of that. She'd been too focused on the job to worry about decor. But the lack of personal photographs only reminded Mona of Mallory's place, of someone who had isolated themselves, maybe even without meaning to. But in many ways, the women were similar.

Still, a bed was a bed and Mona wasn't complaining. And given they'd shared a bottle of wine last night, maybe it had been smart not to try and drive all the way back home on her own.

She emerged into the hallway and headed down to the kitchen where Charlotte was waiting, two thermoses on the counter. "That one's for you," she said. "I didn't have any caramel, but it's almost the way you like it."

"Thanks," Mona replied. "I didn't realize—"

"What? That I paid attention?"

Mona had to work to keep the heat out of her cheeks. They were two sides of the same coin. Of course she noticed.

"C'mon," Charlotte said. "I want to get over there before he opens up. Let's knock this out so you can get back home."

When had this turned from Mona inconveniencing Charlotte to the other way around? She was certainly gung ho about something this morning. "In a hurry?"

"Just anxious to find out about your symbol," Charlotte said before shooting her a wink. Her mood had improved dramatically since yesterday in the morgue.

Mona followed Charlotte back out as they walked to the nearest El station. Twenty minutes later they were back in downtown Chicago, sharing the streets with people in suits, construction workers tearing up part of the street and food vendors getting an early start with the breakfast crowd.

Finally, they came back to Roger Kaye's store: The Quill and the Queen. Mona didn't know what to make of the place, but from the outside it looked like it had been there for a significant amount of time. Perhaps Mr. Kaye purchased the property from someone else after he retired.

Charlotte leaned up against one of the windows, sipping on her coffee as she placed one foot on the wall behind them. It was like she had de-aged ten years overnight. In an instant Mona saw the cool and collected cop she'd read so much about when she was coming up through the ranks.

Finally, a man wearing a tweed jacket came strolling down the street and Mona clocked him immediately as Roger Kaye. He had the distinguished look of someone who had made study their life's work, and though his face was lined with age, they weren't deep lines. His hair was a salt-and-pepper mixture, and he wore a pair of stylish glasses that fit his face well. As soon as he saw them, he stopped short, about twenty feet from the front door of the store.

"Can I help you?" he asked.

Charlotte turned, having been watching the traffic from the other direction and pushed off from the wall. "Roger?"

"Charlotte?" he asked, somewhat bewildered. "How... how are you?" He approached cautiously and held out a tentative hand.

Charlotte took it, shaking it, though Mona noticed she didn't give him as much grip as she was capable. "I'm good," she said. "Retired. But good. I hear you're living the easy life now too." She turned to Mona. "Oh, I'm sorry. Roger Kaye, this is Detective Mona LaSalle. She's with the Oak Creek PD."

"How do you do?" Roger asked, giving Mona's hand a quick shake. But he turned his attention back to Charlotte quickly. "*You're* retired?"

"A couple of months now," Charlotte replied, grinning. "Out of the two of us, though, I would have thought you'd keep that job forever."

He returned a terse smile. "Well. It wasn't exactly by choice."

"Oh," Charlotte replied. "Sorry to hear that."

Roger reset his smile. "Water under the bridge now. I assume you'd both like to come in rather than stand here on the street like a couple of pigeons." He headed over to the door, unlocking it from their side before bending down and unlocking the metal cage that sat right behind the door itself. He rolled it up before holding the door open for them as he walked inside, flipping on the lights.

"It's not much, but it's cozy."

The store had a very lived-in feel to it, like an old library. Books covered almost every surface and shelf, and there were a pair of chairs in the back of the main room with a small table between them, a vibrant green plant growing in a tiny pot on the table.

Roger disappeared through a door behind the counter while Mona and Charlotte took the place in. It carried the smell of old books and tea, and Mona instantly felt at home. If Roger had left the spotless and gleaming library for this place, she considered that a step up.

"There we go," Roger said, coming back through the door. "Just had to double-check the security feeds overnight. Seems we had a couple of hooligans hanging around last evening. Needed to make sure they didn't try anything funny." He gave them both a wink.

Mona smiled. Roger was friendly and personable. She could see why Charlotte trusted him. But her line about needing to be here to make an introduction for Mona had clearly been BS. Roger seemed like the kind of guy who never met a stranger.

"Well, we didn't want to rough up the place too bad," Charlotte said, taking a long look around the main room. "Lot of nice stuff in here."

"Thanks. I actually purchased the store from a man who'd run it his entire life and was looking to get out completely. Bought all the inventory, kept the rent going, just like nothing had happened. We have a very loyal client base. Of course, I've been adding new products here and there. But most of the regulars tell me they can't even tell anything has changed. Which was how I wanted it."

"It's very nice," Charlotte replied, taking another sip of her coffee.

"I doubt you decided to look me up because you wanted to talk about my shop," Roger replied. "What can I help you with?"

Charlotte turned to Mona, who pulled out her phone.

"I'm working a case... We had a victim who was killed in a hit-

and-run. But we found a strange symbol on her body. It's not one I could find anywhere, but Charlotte suggested you might be able to help." She scrolled to the image she'd taken from Mallory's body and handed the phone to Roger.

"You always were one of the best sources of symbology the department ever had," Charlotte said. "They lost a real asset when you left the library."

"They could still call," he said, smiling. "Though I'm not sure my credentials would mean as much now." He turned to Mona's phone, removing his glasses, and squinted at the image, bringing the phone close to his face. "Ah. It's a rune."

"A rune?" Mona asked. "What kind?"

He handed the phone back to her before making his way around the counter to one of his bookshelves. He ran his hand along the books until he found an old canvas-bound book. There was nothing written along the spine—or if there had been, it had long since rubbed away. Roger pulled the book from the shelf and began flipping through furiously until he found the page he was looking for. He turned it to show Mona.

The symbol on the page was a dead match for the one on Mallory's body.

"What is that?" Mona asked.

"A dead language," he replied. "Or at least the remnants of one. It's believed to have originated with the Welsh pagans, but there's no concrete evidence for that. Not much exists on the language, so most of the symbols remain unknown to us."

"Do you know what this one means?" Charlotte asked.

"It's generally understood to mean *life* or *life-giver*. Or some variation thereof. As I said, it's a dead language with limited sources of information. It could very well mean *carrots* and we wouldn't be a hundred percent sure."

"Can I see that?" Mona asked. Roger handed over the book. Inside were more runes, though none of them were close to matching the one Mona had found. The book also postulated potential explanations of the runes, as well as described where and when each instance of them had been found—most in Wales in the late nineteenth century. It was filled with photographs of stone versions of the runes, most taken in England. She handed the book back to Roger. "Thank you."

"The question is, what is someone doing burning a two-thousand-year-old rune on your victim?"

"That's what we'd like to know," Charlotte replied. "Whoever did it, obviously knows about this language. Enough that they went to the trouble to make a presumably iron brand for it."

"Has it showed up anywhere else?" Roger asked Mona.

"Not yet. But this just happened Friday. We're still looking for suspects."

"Roger, do you remember that case... the one with the kids in the circle?" Charlotte asked.

The man's face darkened. "I'd prefer not to."

"Me either. But remember how they each had burns on their arms? This most recent victim? The burn was in the exact same place."

"Wait," Mona said. "You've known each other *that* long?"

Charlotte nodded. "That was when we first met. I was looking for anyone who might be able to help me, which brought me to the library." She turned to Mona. "This was back before the internet was as widespread as it is now. In those days we still had to look things up."

"And walk both ways uphill to work," Roger said, grinning. "I had only been at the library for a year or so at that point. But I knew the face of desperation when I saw it."

Charlotte shot him a look. "I wasn't desperate."

"Agree to disagree. You were looking for *anything* that might help with your case. We spent hours poring through the microfiche."

"Much like you, I was trying to find if there had been any related cases in the past few years... pretty much anywhere," Charlotte admitted to Mona. "But you already know how that turned out."

"Did you ever figure that one out?" Roger asked. He wasn't just being polite; Mona could tell he really cared.

"I wish I could say we did," Charlotte replied. "This case from Detective LaSalle has dug up some old ghosts. But that case is long in the past. Right now, *this* is our primary concern."

Mona caught Roger tilt his head ever so slightly. He'd caught it as well. Charlotte referring to it as "their" case. Mona couldn't help but notice the way Roger kept sneaking glances at Charlotte when she wasn't looking. Like he was trying to see beneath all that armor that she always wore. Ever since they'd arrived, he'd been overtly friendly, though that could have just been his demeanor.

Still, Mona felt like there was more going on there than any of them realized.

But before she could ponder it further, her phone rang in her pocket. "This is LaSalle."

"It's Bowman. Where *are* you?"

"In Chicago," she said. "Following a lead. We might have a break on that symbol burned into Mallory Wakefield."

"You need to get back up here as soon as you can," he replied.

"Why? What's going on?"

"They just found another body."

TEN

The whole way back to Oak Creek, Mona's mind should have been on the fact that her colleagues had found another body—and according to Bowman, it probably wasn't related to the first one. She'd asked if it was another hit-and-run, but he'd been scant on the specifics, just insisting she get back as soon as possible as Earle was pulling all resources for this. She could imagine what kind of pressure the sheriff was under, especially since they had just wrapped up a multiple murder and things were only now beginning to settle down in Oak Creek.

But a second death within a few days was not a good sign. Mona would reserve judgement until she got a look at the evidence before deciding for herself whether it was related to Mallory Wakefield or not.

What occupied her mind on the drive was not the few specifics Bowman had given her, but instead that Charlotte and Roger had been *flirting*. Maybe not overtly, but they obviously harbored some feelings for each other. And it had only taken a quick glance for Mona to tell Roger wasn't married. She'd wanted to mention it, but as soon as she'd gotten the call from Bowman, Charlotte had snapped back into work mode. She was invested in the case now, so when she asked Mona if she could come back to take a look for herself, Mona wasn't surprised. Again, she wasn't going to look a gift horse in the mouth. If Charlotte Dawes wanted to consult on the case, Mona was more than happy to let her.

Mona pulled into Oak Creek's town square a little after ten, finding somehow Charlotte had beaten her there. She already stood outside her car waiting as Mona pulled up.

"How did you do that?" Mona asked, getting out of her car. "We left at the same time."

"Experience," Charlotte said, giving the woman a wink. "I know some reliable back roads."

Mona nodded. "Let me go speak with Earle and see what's going on, give me a minute?"

Charlotte nodded as Mona headed into the station. It was a flurry of activity inside, with the switchboards lighting up as word of another murder moved like a breath of wind through the town. By noon everyone within a hundred-mile radius would know and the vultures would begin to swarm. One additional death was an anomaly. Two was a pattern. And after what they'd been through with Mona's father, the media would be chomping at the bit to get all the details they could. They'd need to get assistance from some of the surrounding counties to help with traffic and media control.

"LaSalle!"

Mona turned as Sheriff Earle made his way over to her, sweat visible on his brow. "What are you doing here? I need you out on the scene."

"I don't know where the scene is, sir. I just got the call from Bowman an hour and a half ago. I was in Chicago doing some background—"

"I don't care, don't bother me with it," Earle said, cutting her off. "Sixteen-fifty-four Evergreen Road. Get out there right now. And don't talk to the media. I'll be making a statement after I confer with the mayor."

"Yes, sir," Mona replied. She wanted to ask him some details about the death, but he brushed past her, apparently done with the conversation. She hadn't known him long, but this was the most flustered she'd seen her new boss since he'd arrived. Coming in from Wyoming, he probably wasn't used to this many murders in such a short time. But then again, neither had Sheriff Franklin been before his untimely death.

But to Mona, this already felt like old hat. Maybe that's what Charlotte had meant by experience. Given what they went through on the last case, this one felt almost pedestrian in comparison.

"Sixteen-fifty-four Evergreen Road," Mona said, taking the stairs down to the parking area where Charlotte waited on her. "Media is incoming. We need to hurry."

"You want to drive or you want me?" Charlotte asked.

"I'll drive," she replied. "I know where it is."

The older woman nodded and got in Mona's passenger seat as Mona turned over the engine, backed out in one deft move and peeled away from the curb.

"Did they give you any more details?" Charlotte asked.

"Nothing. Apparently, I'll see it when I get there. But every single line was lit up. The town was just beginning to get used to not dealing with death on a daily basis. I can't imagine it's going over well."

"This kind of pattern is concerning," Charlotte replied. "And it's going to cause stress on the town. Stress you might not be able to mitigate." Mona glanced in her direction. She was probably thinking about how one local business owner had almost instigated a mob against them last time.

"I've spoken to Ken, he realizes he was out of line with us. I even think he's been going to anger-therapy meetings."

"It may not matter," Charlotte replied. "When push comes to shove, people will always revert to their base instincts. I'm just letting you know you need to be ready for it."

They drove the rest of the way in silence, though Mona kept trying to figure out how to bring up the Roger angle, or if this was even the time. She had a bad habit of bringing up sensitive topics when it was most inappropriate and had been working on trying to identify better timing based on context clues, but it was difficult. Everyone was different, which made every situation different. There was no single rule she could apply across the board, which only made it more confusing.

Which meant she decided to table that conversation for later.

As they approached the home, a small crowd of neighbors stood and gawked outside, almost all of them on their cell phones while patrol officers made sure everyone stayed back from the scene. Bowman's car was in the driveway, beside an ambulance, and a large fire truck sat along the side of the road. Three other vehicles Mona didn't recognize were also parked close by, and a news van from the local station had pulled up, though they hadn't set anything up yet.

"They don't waste any time," Charlotte muttered.

"Are you surprised?" Mona asked.

"No. People are more on edge, quicker to react. You can bet the pushback will be harder this time."

Mona nodded as she signaled to Officer Cahill who allowed them to pass through. Mona parked right behind Bowman's car and both women stepped out.

The front door of the home was open, allowing them to see the activity inside while the nearby neighbors craned their necks to try and get a look themselves. The home had been upgraded from an old split-level into something a little more modern. Large windows dominated the front of the house on both floors, and the entire home had been painted white, with detail paneling and sharp angles to complete the look. On either side of the front door were two lamps with small, flickering flames inside—gas fed. The whole home had undergone a massive renovation.

"Any information about the victim?" Charlotte asked as they walked up the front steps.

"Nothing. Bowman is like that sometimes. He's a man of few words until you get him alone. Then I can't get him to shut up." She shot Charlotte a knowing smile.

They headed into the house where they were almost stopped

again by another officer. "She's with me," Mona said, indicating Charlotte.

"No unauthorized personnel," Officer Wood replied.

"I'm authorizing her," Mona replied. "Beck... come on."

The officer sighed and allowed them to pass.

"Thanks," Charlotte told Officer Wood, though it wasn't in the friendliest tone.

"*Finally*," Bowman said, coming up to them. "Took you long enough." He noticed Charlotte over Mona's shoulder. "What's she doing here?"

"Professional courtesy. She helped with my last big case. The least I can do is repay the favor."

"I thought you were retired," Bowman said to Charlotte.

"Only semi," she replied, grinning.

"Right." Bowman turned to Mona. "He's upstairs. Boy hung himself."

"Okay," Mona said, furrowing her brow. "Suicide. So unlikely to be related to the Wakefield case. Why'd you tell me this was a homicide?"

"You'll understand when you see him," Bowman replied.

Why couldn't people just be direct? What was the point of all this cloak-and-dagger crap? "Okay." She headed up the stairs with Charlotte close behind, making sure not to touch anything until she got her gloves on. A suicide by hanging was about the furthest thing from being related to an intentional hit-and-run that Mona could imagine. So why the—

As soon as she entered the room she saw it. The symbol on the boy's wrist, burned into it just like it had been on Mallory Wakefield.

"Ah," Charlotte said from behind her.

There were only two other people in the room, one of which was from Whittle's team, taking photographs of everything. The other was Officer Roche, probably tasked with keeping an eye on everything to make sure no one touched the body. He looked a little green around the gills.

Because not only had the boy been hung from the fan on the high, pitched ceiling, he was swaying ever so slightly. He was also completely nude and other than the mark on his wrist, didn't have a bruise on him anywhere.

"Where's the chair?" Charlotte asked.

Both the tech and Roche turned at the same time to look at her. "What?"

"The chair. If he hung himself, he didn't get up there on his own. He had to have been standing on something."

A quick glance around revealed that the only chairs in the bedroom were a cushioned chair in the corner and a small stool that sat under the desk.

"Do you mind?" Charlotte asked the photographer who stepped back, allowing her to get to the stool. "I need a glove."

"Here," Mona said, already seeing what she was doing.

Charlotte snapped the glove on, then pulled the stool out and set it on the bed. The boy's feet were about six inches too high to reach even the stool.

"That kills that theory," Charlotte said. "Who said it was a suicide?"

"His mother." They turned to see Bowman in the doorway. "She found him first thing this morning."

Mona winced. She couldn't imagine finding someone you loved like this.

"I didn't want to argue with her," Bowman added. "She's downstairs. We've been trying to keep her calm, but..." He gestured to the victim. "It's been rough going."

"ID on the victim?" Charlotte asked.

"Connor Peterson," Bowman replied. "Works for a data center somewhere in town. Graduated from Arizona State before coming back here."

"How old?" Mona asked.

"Um..." Bowman pulled out his notebook and consulted his information. "Twenty-four."

The same age as Mallory Wakefield. Mona wasn't chalking that up to coincidence. "Family?"

"The mother, obviously. But also a father and two sisters. The parents live over on the other side of town. One of the sisters is in Texas. The other's still in college in Indiana."

"What was the mother doing over here on a Tuesday morning?" Charlotte asked.

"Apparently, she comes to clean every week for Connor. And drop off groceries. I already checked the property records. The house is in the parents' name."

That explained a lot. A twenty-four-year-old working in a data center couldn't afford a place like this on his own. Not without a little help.

Mona took a few tentative steps towards the body, looking carefully at the marking on his wrist. It was similar to the one they found on Mallory. Recently burned into the skin, probably just postmortem. However, it wasn't the same symbol.

"Charlotte? Can you send this to Roger?" Mona asked. "I think I'm going to need more of his help than I expected."

"Already on it," Charlotte said, snapping a picture of the wound with her phone.

"Wait a second," Bowman said. "She's not on this case. She can't—"

"She's an official consultant, and if you want to argue the point, take it up with Earle," Mona replied.

"Earle approved this?"

"He will when I show him what we've found. Her contact managed to identify the symbol we found on Mallory Wakefield's body." Mona couldn't exactly blame Bowman for being upset. Cops in general didn't like it when someone came in and "trespassed" on their turf. Though Mona never understood it—why not use all the available resources at your disposal—that was the culture. But it wasn't like Charlotte was going to take over the case and claim it for herself. She was here on an advisory basis only.

"Thank you," Charlotte whispered as she passed Mona,

heading to the en suite bathroom as the photographer resumed taking photos of the scene.

"How about we see if we can speak to the mother again," Mona suggested, hoping that by including Bowman she'd be able to temper his reaction.

"Yeah... okay," he finally said. "She's in the kitchen."

"Great. Lead the way."

ELEVEN

Charlotte leaned up against the marble countertop as she dialed. As strange as it seemed, she actually felt *good* about this. Not that a young man had died, but that she was here, helping, at least a little. It was the first time since she'd retired where she actually felt *useful*. She hated to admit she missed that feeling more than anything. Nothing that she'd done—save talking to Haley once a week—had filled that void for her. She didn't want to consider the implications of what it would mean for her future.

Instead, she cleared her mind as she waited for Roger to pick up. They'd exchanged numbers before she'd left this morning, him joking so she wouldn't need to stalk him anymore. He was an entertaining guy.

"Well, this is unexpected. Miss me that much already?" he asked without even saying hello.

"That's it, exactly," Charlotte replied, smiling. "I just wanted to make sure you hadn't given me a fake number."

"You wound me, Ms. Dawes," he teased. "What can I do for you this fine morning?"

"Do you still have that book on hand? The one you showed us with the runes?"

"I threw it away as soon as you left, figured it was useless," he replied without missing a beat.

"We've got a second victim with another marking. I'll text it to you. Completely different from the first."

"Oh," he said, his voice suddenly turning serious. "Of course. I'll take a look immediately."

"Apologies in advance if it's a little graphic," Charlotte warned. "It's another brand."

"I can handle it," he said. "If I find anything, I'll let you know."

"Great, thank you, Roger."

"It's my pleasure," he replied, a smile returning to his voice. Charlotte hung up and sent the image to his phone before taking a quick look around the bathroom. She opened the drawers, not really sure if she was looking for anything in particular or if she was just being nosy.

They were full of the normal things, clippers, creams, deodorant; nothing out of the ordinary. When she opened the second drawer, she found a couple of medications inside. She snapped off a few pictures and returned everything back the way she found it.

Coming back into the bedroom, more people from Whittle's team had arrived with a large black bag they were rolling out on the floor as two firefighters set up a ladder to begin cutting the man down. Charlotte nodded at the techs she recognized, though she wasn't sure they remembered her or not.

"Has anyone located the cell phone?" she asked. But she was only met with shaking heads.

She made her way downstairs and around the corner to where she found Mona and her partner sitting across the breakfast table with a woman in her mid to late forties. She had brown hair that was cut short and wore an oversized sweater and leggings. Her face was streaked with tears and her mascara had run down her cheeks.

"...I just don't understand," the woman said. She wasn't looking at either of the detectives; instead, she was staring at the crumpled-up tissue in her hand. "It doesn't make any sense."

"Can you tell us what Connor's normal day was like?" Mona asked gently.

"He was always an early riser," his mother replied. "He liked to get out and go for runs early. Then he'd come back for a shower and head to work. I usually don't get here until around ten or so to start cleaning, but it's a small house and it only takes an hour or two." Her fingers fumbled a small pendant around her neck with a design Charlotte had never seen before.

"And you do that every week?" Bowman asked.

She nodded. "Every week since Connor came back from college."

"And when was that?"

"About a year and a half ago," she replied. "His father and I got him this house as a graduation present. He was so excited. We were so proud of him for everything he'd done."

"Your son worked for Data Technologies Inc.?" Bowman asked.

Mrs. Peterson nodded. "He was one of their lead developers. He told me—said he was working on a new kind of app that would make some of the bigger companies' apps obsolete. It was going to be a game-changer for the industry."

Charlotte caught Mona exchanging a quick look with Bowman. A potential industry-changing app could have given Connor a few extra enemies.

"Was there anyone he was having trouble with, outside of work?" Mona asked.

Mrs. Peterson looked up. "I don't think so, why?"

Mona sighed and Charlotte could tell she was about to deliver the bad news. "Because unfortunately, your son didn't kill himself. We believe there was foul play involved."

"*What?*" his mother said. "No, that can't be right. Everyone loved Connor."

Charlotte had to repress the urge to tell her obviously someone didn't.

"The fact is, Mrs. Peterson, there is no way your son could

have gotten into the position he was in without someone's assistance. Now, whether it was an accident or not, someone else was here and they were involved," Bowman said.

"I don't understand what you're saying," she replied. "You just said there was foul play."

"There *may* have been foul play," Mona added. "We don't know yet."

Charlotte cleared her throat, causing Mona to turn. She motioned for the younger detective to join her in the living room. "Excuse me a moment," Mona said, and Mrs. Peterson nodded.

Mona followed Charlotte into the living room, both of them keeping their voices low. "I don't know how to tell that mother that Connor might have been involved in some kind of sexual game that got out of hand. You saw him up there."

"Then don't," Charlotte said, pulling out her phone. She showed Mona the picture of the medications from the bathroom. "You and I both know this wasn't some autoerotic experiment gone wrong. This was deliberate."

Mona's eyes went wide when she saw the medications. "Can you text this to me?"

Charlotte nodded.

"Thanks. This helps."

"Ask about his girlfriend," Charlotte added. "There was a picture of them up there on the dresser. And ask about his cell. They haven't found it yet."

Mona squared her shoulders and took a deep breath, like she was going back into battle. "Wish me luck."

Mona headed back into the kitchen while Charlotte thankfully stayed behind. She probably understood as well as Mona did that Mrs. Peterson was already under enough stress as it was and didn't need *three* cops bearing down on her.

Her phone buzzed with the text image from Charlotte, which Mona opened immediately. Ritalin, Adavan and Xanax. Three powerful drugs that painted a very different picture to the one Mrs. Peterson had been portraying.

Mona took a seat beside Bowman again, showing him the picture quickly. He nodded, allowing her to take the lead. "Mrs. Peterson, was Connor on any medications?"

She took her pendant in her hand again, gripping it until her knuckles went white. She'd been absently fumbling with it since Mona had first sat down with her. "Not that I know of, why?"

"Because we found these in his drawer upstairs." She turned her phone around to show the woman, whose eyes went wide.

"He—he was supposed to be off Ritalin. He hasn't been on that since he was a child."

"How long was he on it that you knew of?" Mona asked.

Mrs. Peterson's mouth formed a line. "Connor was always an... active child. To the point where he could get destructive if he wanted to. We had to start the medication around age five—we just didn't know what else to do. We thought he would grow out of the hitting phase, but it just got worse and worse."

"Hitting phase?" Bowman asked.

"He would hit me, his father. Sometimes his sisters. Lashing out when he didn't get what he wanted," she explained. "But we got it under control as soon as he was on the medication."

"And the others?" Mona asked. "Adavan is generally used for anxiety and Xanax is for depression."

"He wasn't anxious *or* depressed," his mother insisted. "I don't know why those were up there."

Mona watched the woman carefully. She had gone from grieving mother to being on the defensive. Part of that could be because she considered this line of questioning an insult. *Or* it could be because she knew more than she was telling them.

"When you arrived, did you happen to see Connor's cell phone anywhere?"

She screwed up her features. "No... I didn't even look. He usually keeps it on him." Mona had a feeling just like Mallory's, Connor's phone would turn up missing.

"What can you tell us about his girlfriend?" Mona asked.

Mrs. Peterson's face dropped. "Oh my God. I completely forgot about Kayleigh." Fresh tears ran down her cheeks. "What is that poor girl going to do? How am I supposed to tell her?"

"We can tell her," Bowman replied. "You don't need to worry about that. How long had they been dating?"

"Ever since before he left for college," Mrs. Peterson replied. "They grew up together. We're... Kayleigh's father is the head of our church. We've known them... forever. They started dating in high school. His father and I were so happy—they seemed like the perfect pair. Were planning on getting married soon... I had hoped Connor had already bought a ring..." She trailed off, pressing her hand to her mouth as a fresh wave of grief overwhelmed her.

The woman was struggling, but she'd given Mona something to work with. And while she preferred to sit here all day and get the answer to every question swirling around her brain, she recognized Mrs. Peterson was on the edge of cracking in two. She needed a break.

"Mrs. Peterson, my partner is going to drive you back home so you can be with your family, okay?" Mona said. "We can talk more later. With both you and your husband."

The woman nodded silently.

Mona stood and met with Bowman at the end of the room. "See if you can get anything else from the rest of the family. I'm going to investigate this girlfriend angle."

"You and the other cop?" he asked.

"Hey, she's here. We might as well use her. She's the one who found those meds."

"Only because we haven't had time to do a thorough search," he shot back.

"That's exactly my point. Three heads are better than two. She can help us split the work. And trust me, Dawes knows what she's doing. I wouldn't be here if it weren't for her."

Bowman extended one of his fingers, pressing it into the shoulder of her jacket. "Just make sure you're not doing this out of some sense of guilt. If she can really help, fine. But if you're trying to repay something that can't be—"

"No, it's not that," Mona insisted. "I swear."

Bowman regarded her for a moment. "Okay. Let me see if I can get the girlfriend's details for you."

"Thanks, you're the best."

"Just make sure you get Earle's approval," he said, heading back for the kitchen. "We don't need any more snafus. Not on something this sensitive."

She nodded. He was right, they needed to make sure this was by the book. But if Charlotte was willing—maybe her presence here would help stave off some of the pressure to bring in more help.

"Any luck?" Charlotte asked as Mona joined her in the living room again. She was staring at a painting hung on the wall above the fireplace.

"Not much. Girlfriend looks like she might be able to give us something, she's been a family friend a long time. I get the sense this woman is hiding something, but I don't think now is the time to pressure her. She'll just shut down."

Charlotte nodded, though she seemed preoccupied with the painting. "Give her a few days to get used to everything. Right now everything is raw, a full shock."

"Meanwhile, Bowman is going to talk to the rest of the family. I thought... you and I could go speak with this Kayleigh."

That got the other woman's attention. "You want me to help?"

Mona took a deep breath. "I know you're not just doing this out of the goodness of your heart. And I'm sorry if I dragged up some old demons. But I like working with you—I always have. You're smart, you don't screw around and you're a good cop. I want to talk to Earle about bringing you on... officially. If you're willing, that is."

"Mona, I'm retired," Charlotte replied.

"I think we both know how that's working out. I'm not asking you to wear a badge again. But I wouldn't mind the assistance on this one. Advisory role only."

"You think your boss will be okay with that? It didn't go over so well the last time and that was an official assignment."

"Earle isn't like Sheriff Franklin was. And I think he's worried about the optics of people dying in this town. We're going to need help, one way or another. I'd rather be working with someone I know than someone from three counties over who has never worked a murder investigation in their life."

Something seemed to soften in Charlotte. "You're too damn perceptive for your own good. Retirement has been... well, complicated. Not that I don't like a good challenge, but something has seemed off since I hung up the shield. Don't get me wrong, I'm glad not to be on the force anymore—officially. But I'd be lying if I said I didn't miss it."

"Then help me. Maybe you'll figure out what you're missing along the way."

The woman gave her a rueful smile. "And it wouldn't hurt if we happened to solve a couple of murders?"

"No, it wouldn't," Mona replied. "I won't say I *need* you because you'll just turn around and tell me I don't. But I would *like* to have you here. We're a good team."

Charlotte took a deep breath, clearly at battle with herself over what to do.

"If you weren't invested, would you have come all the way up here *twice*?" Mona asked.

"Okay, LaSalle," she finally said. "You've got a deal."

Mona couldn't help but beam. "Great. Now let's go make it official."

TWELVE

Charlotte didn't know what made her say yes. Maybe it was because she missed the job. Or maybe it was because she'd already invested a significant amount of mental energy into the case and knew the specifics. Another perspective was never a bad thing in their line of work.

Or maybe, deep down, she knew that she would have done just about anything to get back on the job again. If Mona hadn't asked for her help, she would be on her way back to Chicago right now to pester Dale to reopen the murder case from twenty-five years ago so she could go back over the details of everything.

Because while there didn't seem to be a concrete connection between Mona's case and Charlotte's from back then, there certainly were some similarities—similarities that needed consideration at the very least. And maybe a full revisit, taking in what was happening in Oak Creek.

Something about seeing that boy hanging had made her realize she didn't want to finish her career without at least trying to find some closure for those families. She and Ortega had sat with them for hours and days trying to understand what had happened to their loved ones. She recalled seeing the very same pain on their faces as she'd seen on Mrs. Peterson's. It was unimaginable that they still had no answers all these years later. Charlotte was better than that. Maybe there was some way to re-examine the evidence or at least fast-track the DNA evidence from the scene.

Depending on how this case went, she would make it her first priority as soon as she got back.

But as they drove to the house of Kayleigh Goole, she found herself replaying the thankfully short meeting with Sheriff Earle, approving her assistance on the case. Earle was clearly in over his head here, being pulled in a hundred different directions at once, and Mona had used that distraction to her benefit, making what should have been a rigorous process much less cumbersome. Charlotte now found herself Oak Creek's newest police consultant. And even though she still didn't have a badge or weapon, at least now she had some authority to work.

"Here we are," Mona said, her chipper demeanor a ghost of the last time they worked a murder case together. Back then, Charlotte had been worried that Mona's ability to truncate her emotions was a sign of something sinister. That maybe Mona had been capable of terrible things.

But that had turned out not to be the case. Quite the opposite, in fact. Mona felt things deeply, and it was only by turning off her emotions was she able to get through this job without going insane. She'd made a lot of progress since then, finding a balance somewhere in the middle.

But even so, old habits died hard.

"Mona," Charlotte said as they approached the apartment complex. "Drop the smile."

"Oh," Mona replied, pausing a quick second. "Right. Thanks. Sorry, I'm just excited that Earle approved you so quickly. It really means a lot that you're here."

"Just don't let her see that," Charlotte reminded her.

Mona's partner had gotten the girlfriend's information from Mrs. Peterson, who had then relayed it to Mona while they were still at the station. They'd then grabbed a quick lunch and made their way over to Forest Glen Apartments, where apparently Kayleigh Goole worked from home.

"Would you like to do the honors?" Mona asked as they approached the door.

Charlotte stepped back. "Just an advisor."

Mona turned and knocked on the door, stepping back so Kayleigh could see them clearly through the peephole.

"Who is it?" a young voice called from the other side.

"Ms. Goole?" Mona asked. "Oak Creek Police. May we speak with you a moment?"

They heard the chain on the other side of the door, followed by the deadbolt. It opened to reveal a young girl, probably in her late teens to early twenties with bright blond hair pulled back and to the side. "What's this about?" she asked.

Her face was cherub-like, almost as if she hadn't really grown up. She wore a tank top and cut-off shorts, clearly not suffering from the chill that had permeated the town. In fact, Mona could feel the warmth coming from the apartment.

"It's about Connor," Mona replied.

"Oh," the girl said, stepping to the side. "Is everything okay?"

Mona entered the apartment, followed by Charlotte as Kayleigh closed the door behind them. She indicated the couch. "May we sit?"

"You're scaring me," Kayleigh replied. "What's going on?"

Mona took a deep breath, but Charlotte beat her to it. "Ms. Goole, I'm sorry to tell you that Connor is dead."

The girl just stared at them for a minute, a blank look on her face.

"Ms. Goole? Did you hear me?" Charlotte asked.

"Um... can I... get a glass of water?"

"Why don't you allow me?" Mona said and headed for the small kitchen attached to the living room. Charlotte took Kayleigh by the arm and guided her gently to the couch where she remained perched on the edge.

Mona returned a moment later with a glass of water in hand. "Here you go."

Kayleigh took the glass but didn't drink it. Instead, she just held on to it.

Charlotte knew from experience that sometimes it was better not to say anything and let the family or friends of a victim come back to them. Hearing that their loved one was dead was always a shock, and you could never quite predict how someone would respond.

"H... how?" Kayleigh finally said after a solid five minutes of silence had passed.

Mona had taken a seat on the chair opposite her couch while Charlotte remained standing.

"Asphyxiation," Mona said gently. "When was the last time you spoke with Connor?"

"Yesterday," Kayleigh admitted. "Last night, I mean."

"Do you remember what time?"

"Around eleven... I think. We were just texting memes back and forth. Not really talking."

"Did... anything seem wrong last night?" Mona asked. "Was he acting strange at all?"

She shook her head.

"Did he say anything out of the ordinary when you *did* talk last?" Charlotte added.

Kayleigh looked over to Charlotte like she'd forgotten she was there. "No. Not that I remember."

Mona took a deep breath. "Ms. Goole, do you know anyone who might want to harm Connor? Anyone who had a problem with him?"

She shook her head back and forth very slowly, her eyes staring off into the distance. "No. I don't think so." Charlotte didn't like that look.

"Do you know if he was on any medications?"

"Um... yeah. Xanax, I think. And a few others."

"Adavan and Ritalin?" Mona suggested.

Kayleigh nodded. "I think so."

"Was he having problems with anxiety and depression?" Charlotte asked.

"Not since he'd been on the meds," Kayleigh replied. "But before that... yeah."

"Regarding?"

Her eyebrows lifted. "What?"

"What was the cause of his anxiety and depression?"

"Oh," she replied. "Just normal stuff. Work, I guess. His parents." Not exactly what they were looking for, but plausible enough. Though Charlotte wanted to dig deeper.

"His mother told us you two knew each other a long time. Ever since you were kids."

She nodded. "We grew up together. Our parents... they're friends."

"Have you left your apartment this morning?" Charlotte asked. Mona shot her a questioning look, but Charlotte kept her attention on Kayleigh.

"I went out for coffee like I always do," the girl replied, some of the life coming back into her. She blinked a few times and looked up at Charlotte. "Why?"

"We just have to cover all our bases," Charlotte replied. "How long were you gone and what time did you get back?"

"Wait a second," Kayleigh said, standing. "Are you saying I had something to do with this?"

"Do you own a key to Connor's house?" Mona asked, picking up on what Charlotte was doing.

"Of course I do, but I wasn't anywhere near there this morning," Kayleigh replied.

"Is there someone who can vouch for your whereabouts?"

"Well, no. I live alone. But I swear I just went out for coffee. I had to be at my desk by nine for my shift."

"What do you do for work, Ms. Goole?" Charlotte asked.

"I work for a local construction company. I field all their calls and get them to the right contractor. It's basically just scheduling and logistics."

"How long have you been working from home?"

"I don't know, maybe a few years now?"

"You like it?" Charlotte made sure the questions kept coming quick, hoping to throw Kayleigh off-balance a bit.

"I guess? It's a job." More of her emotions were beginning to show. "What does that have to do with anything?"

"Like I said, we're just trying to cover all our bases." Charlotte pulled out her phone and showed it to Kayleigh. "Have you ever seen this image before?"

The girl's eyes went wide. "Is that... Was that burned into his skin? I thought you said he was strangled."

"I said he was asphyxiated," Mona corrected. "He was found hanging from his ceiling fan."

Kayleigh put a hand over her mouth and sunk back into the couch. "Oh my God."

"Now, is there anyone that might have wanted to harm Connor?" Mona asked while the girl still processed what they'd told her. "Anyone who could have hurt him?"

A flash of recognition passed across the girl's face so brief it was practically invisible. But Charlotte had seen it. Kayleigh knew something—something she hadn't mentioned yet.

"I don't think so," she finally said.

"Don't lie to us, Ms. Goole," Mona replied. "Maybe we should finish our discussion at the station." She stood to take Kayleigh by the arm.

The girl jerked away. "You can't be serious," she replied. "I didn't have anything to do with this. I *loved* Connor."

"Then tell us the truth," Charlotte replied. "Who wanted to hurt him?"

The girl let out a frustrated and stressed breath, looking around as if she were trying to find the way out. Like she could almost convince herself this wasn't happening and all she needed to do was go on a walk and it would all just go away.

"I don't know why he would even want to..." She trailed off.

"Who?" Charlotte asked.

She pinched her features together, struggling with some internal battle Charlotte could only imagine. Whatever secret she was keeping, it was tearing her up inside. And right now, she was trying to decide if keeping it was worth going to jail over.

"Terry," she finally said. "My ex."

"Do you have a last name for Terry?" Mona asked.

"Barker," she finally said.

"And why would your ex have a problem with Connor?" Mona asked. "Did he not take the breakup well?"

"Not... exactly," Kayleigh replied. "I'm sort of... still seeing him."

Charlotte paused a moment to take it in. An ex who wasn't really an ex. "Still seeing him as in..."

"As in we're sleeping together," Kayleigh finally said. Tears formed in her eyes and she wiped them away quickly. "But it isn't what you think! I really do love Connor. I mean... I did, I still do. The thing with Terry... it's complicated."

"Uncomplicate it for us," Mona prodded.

The girl sat back on the sofa again, pressing herself into it. "I've known Connor forever. He was my first boyfriend. We've always been a part of each other's lives. A few years ago I just got... bored, I guess. I just wanted to try something else, you know? It didn't mean I didn't still love Connor, but he could be smothering sometimes, especially as we got older. So when he went off to college..."

"You took the opportunity to try someone new," Charlotte said, jotting down Terry's name in her phone.

"It wasn't anything special. Just sex at first. And then we hung out some more."

"Did Connor know?" Mona asked.

"Not at first. But when he came back for vacation one Christmas, he saw us out. I told him it meant nothing and I'd break up with Terry. At first he was mad, but eventually he forgave me."

"And did you? Break up with Terry?" Mona asked.

"Um... yes. And no." Kayleigh waited a beat. "We officially broke up but kept seeing each other on the side."

"For how long?" Charlotte asked.

"Two years."

Charlotte pressed a hand to her temple; she could feel a headache coming on. "Why not just break things off with Connor if you wanted to be with Terry so bad?"

"I didn't! At least, not all the time," Kayleigh replied. "You wouldn't understand."

Mona took a seat again, leaning forward. "Try us."

"Connor was... sweet. Attentive. Loyal. You know? Like the perfect boyfriend. But Terry... He was wild. Dangerous. Everything that Connor wasn't."

"You wanted the best of both worlds."

"Just for a little while. I knew Connor was close to proposing, I told Terry that we'd have to break things off for good soon."

"How did he react to that?" Charlotte asked.

"He didn't," she replied. "He didn't really seem to care."

Charlotte exchanged a glance with Mona. That kind of response could be indicative that he wasn't worried about losing Kayleigh because he knew in his mind it wouldn't happen. He had already planned to put a stop to it. It wasn't iron-clad, but Terry was definitely a person of interest. "Where can we find Terry?" Charlotte asked.

"He lives at Four-fifty-four Brookmoor Road," she replied. "Rents out the house with a couple of his friends."

"When was the last time you saw Terry?" Mona asked.

"Yesterday," Kayleigh admitted. "He came over for a few hours."

"Did he say what his plans were last night?"

She shook her head. "I don't ask. Terry... He doesn't like to be questioned. He does what he wants."

Charlotte stood, putting her phone away as Mona withdrew one of her business cards, handing it to Kayleigh. "Stay close. We may have more questions for you."

"You don't think Terry really did it, do you?" Kayleigh asked.

"We'll be in touch," Charlotte said. "Thank you for your time." She and Mona headed back out to the car. "Did you notice her demeanor?"

Mona nodded. "You'd think someone who just lost their childhood crush would have been more... crushed."

"I'm not one to tell someone how to grieve, but am I crazy or did she look relieved when we told her Connor was dead?"

"Want me to call in a patrol unit to keep an eye on her here? Make sure she doesn't run?" Mona asked.

Charlotte nodded. "I think that's prudent. In the meantime, we have a boyfriend to track down."

THIRTEEN

Mona found her anxiousness ramping up as they drove to the address Kayleigh had provided. She felt like they were making some progress already, and that in itself was exciting. But she was also intrigued by this case. While it was nothing like Robin's case, she couldn't ignore it had some of the same hallmarks. Multiple victims, each identified by the killer in a strange and unexpected pattern. And she couldn't help but wonder if whoever had killed Mallory and Connor was some kind of twisted copycat of her father.

Because this would have been right up his alley.

All of which made her thankful Charlotte was close. It meant she didn't have to face this alone. Not that Bowman or any of the others would have let her, but they still didn't really understand Mona. They accepted her, and she was happy for that. But they didn't go much deeper than surface level. Was that because of who she was at her core? Of what she represented? Or was it something more? She couldn't really say.

All she knew was Charlotte treated her like any other person, not some specimen to be studied from a distance. Not only that, but she knew how to get to the heart of what they needed. Like the way she'd worked Kayleigh back there into giving up what she knew. Mona could have done it too, but it would have taken longer and she might not have been as effective. And Kayleigh had dropped an atom bomb on this investigation. They needed to find and question Terry as soon as possible, before he got the heads-up the cops were looking for him. From Kayleigh's description of the boy, he didn't seem like the type who would just wait around for them. If they weren't quick, he would be in the wind soon.

"You want to take the lead on this one?" Charlotte asked as they pulled up to the house address Kayleigh had given them. Unlike Connor's place, this home was in desperate need of repair. The roof looked to be sagging in multiple places and there wasn't any grass on the lawn. Instead, two cars were all parked haphazardly on the property, like a disoriented valet had taken charge.

"What are you going to do?" Mona asked.

"Take a look around. I'll join you in a minute."

Mona had learned not to question Charlotte's motives. Whatever she was sniffing, it was probably worth it.

She headed to the front door while Charlotte made her way around the back. As Mona approached, she could hear what sounded like gunfire from inside, but she immediately recognized it as the soundtrack from a video game, more than likely a first-person shooter variety. She knocked hard, but there was no response from within. She slammed her fist on the door again, over and over, enough that it rattled in its hinges. Finally, the soundtrack paused.

A dark shadow covered the peephole. "Who is it?"

Mona held her badge up so whoever was on the other side could see it. "Police. I'm looking for Terry Barker."

A sudden shuffling from inside let Mona know whoever was on the other side wasn't going to be opening the door. She sprinted around the side of the house to the back where Charlotte had already tackled one man and had him on the ground as another sprinted off behind the house. Neither of them looked like they could be more than twenty.

Mona broke into a run behind the one who had taken off,

catching up to him quickly. She tackled the man to the ground, holding him down with one hand as he struggled under her grasp.

"Are you Terry Barker?" Mona demanded.

"Fuck you, pig," the boy spat. Mona wrenched his arms behind him and cuffed them together before pulling him to his feet. He tried to fall to his knees again until she elbowed him right in the middle of the back, causing him to cry out.

"You don't want me to drag you back to the house," she warned.

As she returned, Charlotte already had the other kid sitting on the steps. His cheeks were wet.

"Christ, Donnie, are you *crying*?" the kid in Mona's grasp said.

"Definitely not Terry," Charlotte said. She turned to the boy in her custody. "Who is that?" She pointed to the man in Mona's custody.

"Logan," he said, his voice shaky.

"Man, shut the *fuck* up," Logan replied as Mona sat him down beside the other boy.

"Take your own advice," Charlotte said. "I'm assuming you both know Terry Barker."

"You don't know anything, you dumb bitch," Logan replied, seething with anger.

Charlotte turned to Mona. "Anger issues. Typical." Mona had to hide her smile.

"Hey, I don't—"

Charlotte bent down and got in the boy's face. "You say one more word and I'll charge you with assaulting an officer. And trust me, Judge Coulter has no love lost for arrogant little shits like you, so you'll be spending a minimum of six months in prison. Got it?"

Logan shut up.

Mona nodded, getting the attention of Donnie. "Why did you run?"

He motioned to Logan. "He said to. He said you'd arrest us no matter what."

"And why would we arrest you?" Charlotte asked.

Donnie exchanged a glance with Logan, who practically shot daggers out of his eyes at the boy, subtly shaking his head.

"No reason."

"Uh-huh." Charlotte turned to Mona. "Might want to call it in. We'll need a warrant for the home."

"They're just relaxants, okay?" Logan yelled. "That's all. Everything legal."

"Wow, you really *do* think I'm dumb, don't you?" Charlotte asked, an amused smile on her face. She turned back to Mona. "Thoughts?"

"Probably Fentanyl. Maybe a few other things."

"My thoughts as well. We might have just stumbled on a nice little drug den here." She turned to Logan. "Just think, if you'd answered the door like a normal person, we wouldn't be in this situation. We weren't even looking for you."

Logan tried to spit at Charlotte, but it was poorly timed and didn't have very much oomph behind it, landing in the grass.

"What now?" Mona asked, pulling out her phone. "Barker might show back up."

Charlotte turned back to Donnie. "If he's not here, where would he be?"

"He's supposed to be at work right now," the boy replied. "Advantage Tree and Lawn. It's a local company."

"I know it," Mona replied. "Owner is Bill Jamison. I've spoken to him a few times before."

"What about family? Friends other than you two chuckleheads?"

They both shook their heads.

"Okay, let's get in contact with Jamison and get a couple of units over here to handle this. Maybe we'll get lucky and he's clueless at work. At the very least they should have some more information on him."

"What do you want with that loser anyway?" Logan asked. "It's not like he ever pulls his weight around here."

"You mean he doesn't help distribute your product like the rest of your lackeys," Charlotte replied. "Sounds like Terry might actually be the smartest person who lives here. Where was he last night?"

"Hell if I know," Logan shot back. "And I don't really care."

"Which means he wasn't here," Mona replied. "Do either of you know Connor Peterson?" Both of them shook their heads. "What about Mallory Wakefield?"

"Yeah, isn't she that artsy chick who makes her own baskets or something?" Donnie asked.

It was true, they had found some homemade items that Mallory probably sold on Etsy or a similar site in her home. "How did you know her?"

"We used to go to school together," Donnie replied. "Before I dropped out."

They spent another ten minutes questioning the boys and coming up with nothing but half answers as they waited for backup to arrive. Mona got the feeling neither of them knew anything about Mallory or Connor. If Terry was their unsub, he wasn't talking to his friends about his actions.

Bowman showed up with a couple of units in tow and took the two *men* off Mona and Charlotte's hands. He promised a thorough investigation as Mona informed him of the progress they'd made so far. Bowman had just finished processing the Peterson scene but said that Whittle's people hadn't come up with much that was usable. The only thing they had confirmed was there was no way Connor Peterson could have gotten himself into that position. Someone had placed him there.

Mona thanked him as she and Charlotte got back in the car and headed for Advantage Tree and Lawn. She sensed the pressure of this case building, and so far, Terry looked good for their primary suspect. He had motive in the second murder and may have had knowledge of the first victim, but that was still to be determined.

"I don't know about you," Charlotte said as they drove, "but I really worry for the next generation sometimes. You see what some of these kids are reduced to and you begin to wonder if any of us will ever find a way to make things better."

"How do you mean?" Mona asked.

"Those kids back there. They probably had bright futures. And yet they're out there slinging illegal drugs for a quick buck, living life minute to minute." She sighed. "When I was still a young cop, I always imagined that people would start to figure things out. That life would get better and each generation would have it easier than the last. It just feels like everything is going in reverse sometimes."

Mona had heard older people talk about this sort of thing before—that the older generations were holding everything back and once younger people came along, things would improve. But in her experience, everything moved in cycles. It was never just a straight line. Things would get worse, then they would get better, then worse again. And on and on forever. And most of that would happen with or without Mona. All she could do was the best she could with what she was given.

"Are you thinking of your daughter?" Mona asked.

Charlotte sighed. "Reconnecting with her... it's been hard. Good, I'm happy to talk to her. But she's still so guarded... so closed-off. And I know I've missed so much of her life that now I only get to see what little she's willing to show me. I'll never get to see behind the curtain. But Hayley... She's a good kid. Smart. Capable. Still, I can't help but worry about the world I'm leaving her. She's going to have it far harder than I did at her age."

"I'm sure she'll manage," Mona replied. "We all will. We have to. Otherwise we end up like Tweedledee and Tweedledum back there."

Charlotte snorted a laugh. "That's true. Hey, can you see if you can get Advantage on the phone? If we can pinpoint where Terry is before we get there, this will go a lot smoother."

"Yeah," Mona replied. "Let me see what I can do." She dialed the number on the website, but only an automated messaging system picked up, letting her know that they would call her back as soon as possible.

"Figures," Charlotte replied. "I'm sure they're busy this time of year."

"Do you really think Terry might be our suspect?" Mona asked.

"I don't know. But right now he's the closest thing we've got," Charlotte replied. "If I'm being completely honest, I really hope he is. Because right now we don't have another lead."

Mona knew what she meant. If he turned up clean, then they were dealing with someone much more difficult to catch—and who probably wasn't done. She couldn't see the whole picture yet because they didn't have all the pieces. But if one thing was for sure, it was that if Terry wasn't their culprit, this was far from over.

FOURTEEN

God, it felt good to be out investigating again. Charlotte was practically giddy with excitement as they pulled up to Advantage Tree and Lawn's office. Tackling that kid and wrestling him to the ground had pumped a full liter of adrenaline through her heart, and for the first time in *months*, she felt alive again. Looking back on how she'd been spending her days, she couldn't see how she'd even gotten through them. They had been so mundane and boring and *typical*.

But this... this was her life. This was what she was meant to do and it felt good to be back.

And yet, she knew that once this was all over, she'd return to that life and fall right back into the same mindset. The prospect loomed over her like a dark cloud on the horizon, threatening to swallow her whole.

No. She couldn't think about that right now. She needed to stay rooted in the present, continue to work the case. Live in the moment, because it could very well be her last. It was funny, the last time she'd worked with Mona, Charlotte had been all too aware that it would be her final case as a police detective. And yet, here she was, continuing the work, just in a different capacity.

What if there was some way that she didn't have to go back after this was all over?

That was... assuming they caught their culprit.

Advantage Tree and Lawn was a small unit that sat adjacent to a strip mall. Behind the building was a large parking area that had been gated off and which probably held equipment when it wasn't being used. But today it was mostly empty save for one pickup truck and a couple of partially disassembled riding lawn mowers.

"Think anyone is in there?" Mona asked as they approached the building. There were no other cars in the parking lot and the windows looked dark, though that could just be the anti-reflective coating.

"Only one way to find out," Charlotte replied, trying the door. It opened with ease and a cool blast of air hit them as they entered the bright space. Inside sat a small desk off to the right with the company's logo behind it. A young man, probably still in his teens, sat behind the desk. He was too young to be Terry and, from Kayleigh's description of him, too small as well.

He was in the middle of a call with the receiver to the landline on one shoulder and a cell phone in his other hand.

"Yes, I believe we can, just give me one moment," he said into the landline before putting the cell phone to his other ear. "She wants the full works. Today if possible. Uh-huh. Okay, thanks." He hung up the cell phone and turned back to the landline. "Yes, we can do that. I have the address." He paused. "Probably around five this afternoon. It's the soonest the crew can get out there. Yes, okay, thank you. You too."

He hung up, took a breath and reset himself for Charlotte and Mona. "Hi, if you're here for lawn services, unfortunately we're all booked up for the next two weeks."

The boy wore a nametag that said, *Preston*. "We're looking for Terry Barker," Charlotte said. "Did he show up for work today?"

"Oh, I'm not sure..." Preston said, looking at his computer. "He's scheduled on crew six, but I don't remember seeing him. Hang on, let me call my dad and find out."

"You're Bill's son, aren't you?" Mona said, her warmth palpable. It was so startling Charlotte almost took a step back. She wasn't used to that from Mona.

"Yeah," Preston said in the middle of dialing.

"I'm Mona... LaSalle," she said. "I used to live in your neighborhood. You were still little then, I doubt you remember me."

"Oh..." Preston said, "...right. How are you?"

"I'm good," Mona replied. "Thanks for asking." If she noticed the subtle shift in Preston's attitude, she didn't react, but Charlotte saw it clearly enough. As soon as she had said her name, the boy's demeanor had changed. He'd become more guarded. Mona's reputation in this town had swung from one extreme to the other.

They fell into an uncomfortable silence as Preston dialed. "Hey, yeah, it's me," he said. "There are some police officers here looking for Terry. Is he on site with you?" Preston listened for a second and nodded. "Okay, thanks, Dad."

He turned to them, setting the phone aside. "He never showed up for his shift."

"Is that uncommon?" Charlotte asked.

Preston shrugged. "It's not uncommon. Terry... He's late a lot. Doesn't seem to take the job seriously."

"Explain that, please," Charlotte added.

"Well, he was hired because my dad needed some more muscle at the job sites. We take down some large trees sometimes and it requires a few guys. He didn't have any experience and when we tried training him—"

"We?" Mona asked.

Preston nodded. "I'm in charge of training all the new employees, along with my dad. But Terry always just seemed to want to do his own thing. He wasn't serious about the work."

"Why not fire him?" Charlotte asked.

"Dad needed the help. We've been short-staffed all summer, and not a lot of people want to go out and work in the heat, you know? Terry never seemed to mind that part, it was getting him to listen that was the problem."

"Do you have any idea where he could be?" Charlotte asked.

"I have his address on file somewhere," Preston replied, but Charlotte just shook her head.

"We've already been there. Anywhere else?"

The boy shrugged. "Sorry."

"What about his vehicle? Do you have his car on file?" Mona asked. Bowman was running the plates of the vehicles at the Brookmoor address, but there had only been two of them.

He nodded. "Yeah. We keep a record in case anyone has to use their personal vehicle for work. Sometimes we need to borrow a pickup or something with a hitch if the other vehicles are being used, you know." He typed something in his computer. "He drives a gray Ford F-150. License plate is 0GH-54BX."

Charlotte jotted it down. With Barker in the wind, they'd have to put out an APB. "Thanks for your help."

Preston nodded. "I don't know if it will do you any good, but the past couple of days, he's been bumming a ride to work."

"Why's that?" Charlotte asked.

"He said his car was in the shop. That he hit a deer or something." Charlotte and Mona exchanged a quick glance. "He did something, didn't he?"

"We just need to ask him some questions," Mona said, smiling.

But the question caused Charlotte to perk up. "Why do you ask?"

"Terry's been in a few... scuffles here," he said. "He's got a temper. I knew it would get him in trouble one day."

"What kind of temper?"

"He pushed one of the guys up against the cages in the back one time, held him there by his neck until my dad broke it up. He had to pay the guy a bonus not to sue us."

"And *that* wasn't enough to let him go?"

"Like I said, it's hard to find help this time of year. Pretty sure Dad is gonna let him go as soon as things calm down, though," he said. "I've never liked the guy."

Charlotte held up the notes with the plate number on it. "Thanks for this."

"Anytime."

"Good seeing you, Preston," Mona said. "Tell your dad I said hi."

The boy nodded. "Sure."

Back outside, Charlotte handed Mona the plate number, but she refused. "I remember it. I'll call in the APB."

"We need to find him right now. If he's not driving that car, he could be anywhere."

"We have a description from Kayleigh," Mona replied. "I'll make sure every cop in Oak Creek is on the lookout."

"Let's check with the parents too. Just in case."

"Mmm."

"Are you okay?" Charlotte asked as they got back in the car.

"Yes," Mona replied. "Fine." But Charlotte recognized that wall of hers going up again. She'd seen it too many times not to be able to tell what it was.

"Mona."

She took a deep breath. "Dr. Cross says if I'm ever going to get people to stop treating me like some kind of specimen, I need to keep trying to interact with them... to get to know them on a personal level."

"How's that going?" Charlotte asked.

Mona's shoulders slumped. "Not as well as I'd hoped. At my therapist's suggestion I signed up for a few of those online dating sites. Turns out it's hard to do in a small town where everyone knows you as the daughter of a serial killer."

"Don't beat yourself up too bad," she said. "Most people can't understand what we do. Which means they can't understand why we do it. Hell, my husband sure couldn't. But that wasn't entirely his fault. Still... I feel like he would have left eventually no matter what. The stress and pressure of this job... it's a lot for people."

"Except not us, right?" she asked, dialing the station on her phone.

"No, for us too," Charlotte replied. "We're not immune. Eventually, it wears you down, gets into your bones. But by then it's too late." She paused. "And then when someone tries to take it away, you find it's like someone reaching in and pulling out a vital organ."

Mona held her gaze a moment before finally turning away and calling in the APB.

Maybe Mona wasn't integrating into this new role as seamlessly as Charlotte had first suspected. Was that why she was here? Because Mona still didn't feel like she could handle this without some backup?

But now was not the time to analyze the situation. They had a suspect out there with a damaged car that could have very well have hit Mallory Wakefield. *And* he had a personal reason to attack Connor Peterson. They needed to find Terry as soon as possible.

Charlotte drove them to Terry's parents' house only to find the home empty. Apparently, both parents worked. It took them some time, but Charlotte and Mona managed to track down the father, who worked in an office in Crystal Lake. However, he admitted he hadn't seen his son in a few weeks, not since a family barbecue that had turned into another fight. His wife backed up the story when they spoke with her over the phone.

It seemed that no matter where Terry went, he got into a scuffle with someone, even family. And neither parent had any idea of where Terry might be.

Which meant they had to go back to basics.

"You gotta be kidding me," Logan said as Charlotte and Mona stepped into the interrogation room where he sat with Bowman and his lawyer.

"Please," Logan's lawyer said, standing as the two women entered. "Officers, take a seat. My client is cooperating fully."

Bowman snorted back a laugh. "Considering how many charges we're bringing against him he better be."

Charlotte had only taken a few minutes to look over the report as soon as they'd come back into the station. They'd found a felony-level number of pills in the home Logan, Donnie and Terry rented along with records for distribution. It was enough to charge the two they had in custody with possession with intent to distribute of a class-one narcotic. That was a twenty-year charge.

There had been evidence that more people than just Logan and Donnie had been staying at the house. Terry was probably only bumming a spot, and given the rental contract for the house was in Logan's name, it was impossible to tell how many people were actually staying there at any given time.

"We just thought we'd come down and pay Mr. Halter a visit," Charlotte said, rounding the table. Logan sneered back at her. "Just isn't your lucky day, is it, bucko?"

"Please, Detective. Direct all your questions to me," his lawyer said.

Charlotte appreciated the fact that Bowman didn't correct the lawyer and let him know that Charlotte was only here as an advisor. Still, she had the authority Earle had given her.

"How is your client feeling?" Charlotte asked. "Confident?"

"As I said. We're cooperating in every way possible," the lawyer replied.

Charlotte looked around the man at Logan again. "Pretty high-powered lawyer for a twenty-something. How'd you afford it? Oh, right, silly me." She grinned just as Logan continued to sneer harder.

She was pushing him and she knew it. But the kid was a shit and deserved it.

"Detectives, if there is nothing substantive here, we would like to get back—"

"We're here to offer Mr. Halter an opportunity," Charlotte said. She'd discussed the plan with both Mona and Sheriff Earle, and all of them had come to the same conclusion. It was worth it to find Terry Barker.

"A deal?" the lawyer asked.

"No, an *opportunity*," Charlotte replied. She turned to Mona.

"If you give up the location of Terry Barker, we'll reduce the charges to possession only."

"No," Logan said before his lawyer could interject. "I want the charges dropped. Completely." His lawyer sat and whispered in his ear, but Logan pulled away. "*No.* They want something, they gotta pay."

"Ah, a *negotiator*," Charlotte replied. "Look. This is the best deal you're gonna get. Otherwise we walk out that door and you stay in here for a very long time."

"You're not gonna just walk out of here," Logan replied. "Whatever Terry did must be real bad if you're willing to cut a deal just to find him."

Charlotte turned to Mona. "Told you this was a waste of time. He doesn't even know where he is."

"No, I know," Logan reiterated. "But it's gonna cost you."

"You can't bluff your way out of this one," Charlotte replied. "Give him up and we'll talk."

Logan just shook his head, despite his lawyer continuing to talk in his ear. That was the problem with entitled little brats. They didn't know a good thing when they were staring at it. Anyone with an ounce of sense would take this deal.

"Okay, fine," Charlotte said. "Deal's off the table. Thanks for your time." She and Mona turned, heading back out into the hallway.

"What now?" Mona asked. "It didn't work."

"Let's give him some time to stew on it," Charlotte replied. "Maybe once he sees he can't bravado his way out of it, he'll change his mind."

"And if he doesn't?"

Charlotte didn't have an answer for her. This job was occasionally a gamble. And sometimes it worked out.

Then again, sometimes it didn't.

FIFTEEN

Mona sat, typing idly at her computer as she waited to hear back from some of her contacts. It had been a few hours since they'd arrived back at the station and still Logan hadn't decided he was ready to help them find Terry. The APB hadn't done much good either; there had been no positive IDs despite every cop in the county looking for him.

His car had been found in a local repair garage, just as the kid from Advantage Tree and Lawn had told them, halfway torn apart to repair the damage from the collision. The mechanics said there hadn't been any blood on the vehicle when it arrived, otherwise they would have reported it, but when Mona asked if the damage could be consistent with a hit-and-run, they admitted it was possible.

The only problem was all the panels that had taken the damage had been hammered out and a lot of the body work had already been done, leaving little evidence for them to find. Still, Mona had impounded the car anyway. She'd also conferred with Bowman again about the results of the autopsy on the Peterson boy, which Whittle had finished up not too long ago. As expected, he'd died from asphyxiation, though his injuries were consistent with someone who had been struggling up there for a bit. Which meant just like Mallory, his death hadn't necessarily been quick.

Whoever was targeting these kids, whether it be Terry or someone else, wanted them to suffer. These were not easy deaths. But the question was why? What could they have done to deserve such horrible deaths? Other than a possible connection with Terry, they still hadn't found anything concrete connecting Mallory and Connor except they both happened to be twenty-four years old. But Mona was doing the background work regardless. She just wanted to get Barker into custody so they could at least take a breath. She'd forgotten how stressful it was to have a killer on the loose and no way to find them.

"Oh good, there you are," Charlotte said, coming around the corner. Her phone was turned up in her hand. "Hang on, I just found her."

Mona glanced over, pinching her features together. "What's going on?"

"I've got Roger on the phone," Charlotte said. "Roger, tell Mona what you just told me."

"Hi, Mona," Roger said down the line. "Charlotte sent me that second rune that was burned on the boy's skin. It took me a little longer than the first one, but I found it. It generally refers to *harvest* or *preparation*, usually in conjunction with the calendar. By that I mean the word generally shows up when referring to the fall more than any other season."

"Harvest?" Mona asked. "And the first one meant life-giver?"

"More or less."

"Okay, then—"

"Hang on," Charlotte said. "Roger, tell her the rest."

"After looking into it further, every single instance I've found of both this symbol and the first one paired together always come with three other symbols," he said. "They can be found on their own, but whenever they're found together, the three others always accompany them."

Mona's breath hitched. "Are you saying there are going to be three more victims?"

"I don't know," he replied. "But if the pattern holds, you can expect to find the other three."

"But... this is just... this is someone who might misunderstand, right?" Mona asked.

"I don't think we can take that chance," Charlotte replied. "Whoever is doing this is looking to send a message. And that message may include three more victims."

Mona took a breath. "Roger, what do all five symbols together mean?" she asked.

She could sense his hesitation on the other end. "I wouldn't take this to the grave, but it's something to the effect of *crops watered with blood bear fruit*. Like I said, it's not an exact translation, there is a lot of nuance surrounding these things, but I thought you should know."

Charlotte's face was like a stone rune itself, etched with concern and worry. "Was there anything else?"

"I'm still looking. If I find anything, I'll let you know."

"Thanks, Roger," Charlotte replied. "We'll be in touch."

"Anytime," he said. "Let me know if you find any more. Though I really hope you don't." He hung up.

"Five victims total," Mona said. "Do you think he's right?"

"I don't think we can just ignore the possibility," Charlotte replied. "Until we find the person doing this, we need to consider that our killer isn't done. Not by a long shot. We need to locate Terry and we need to do it now." Charlotte turned and headed back down the hallway as Mona fought to catch up.

"You were right, Roger is pretty smart. It's a good thing we have him."

A soft smile tugged at the corner of her mouth. "Yeah. We're lucky. He's always been studious. Kind of a nerd that way."

"You like him."

Charlotte turned to her, one eyebrow arched. "I suppose. He's helping with this case. I don't have any reason not to like him."

"No. I mean you *like* him," she replied.

"Don't be ridiculous," Charlotte snapped. "We're professional colleagues, that's it."

"Uh-huh. Except every time you talk to him, you can't quit grinning from ear to ear. It's cute."

As if to spite her, Charlotte frowned. "I'm not cute."

"You can be," Mona replied. "Sometimes. And you know what, I think he likes you too."

"This is irrelevant," Charlotte replied, though Mona caught a hint of red in her cheeks. There was no hiding human nature. "We have a case to work. Stop trying to distract me."

"Don't change the subject," Mona replied. "Aren't you always the one saying you should be true to your deepest self? Because your deepest self really likes Roger."

A hint of a smile appeared at the corner of Charlotte's mouth. "Okay. I'll admit he's handsome. And he can be charming when he wants to be. But it doesn't matter, it could never work out."

"Why not? You're divorced and I didn't see a wedding ring when we went to his shop."

"Remember that conversation about not everyone understanding what we do? If I were to... *pursue* anything with Roger, it'd end badly. He'd get hurt and so would I. At least this way we can remain friends."

"Why would he get hurt?"

Charlotte huffed. "Because I'm... me. And I'm a workaholic."

"But... you're retired."

The woman stopped, then glared at Mona. "Anyone ever tell you that you're too nosy for your own good?"

"All I'm saying is that I think you should ask him out. Or at least not dismiss the idea out of hand. You can't just shut everyone out all the time," Mona replied. "Trust me, I know. In fact, you were the one who encouraged me to push beyond my own personal boundaries and faults. And look at me now."

"Uh-huh. Thanks, Dr. LaSalle," Charlotte said, obviously not entertaining the idea any longer. "C'mon. Let's take another shot at Logan."

They headed back to the holding cells where Logan was waiting to be transferred to the local jail. The other boy, Donnie, had already been remanded back into the custody of his parents, given the lease of the home wasn't on his name and the DA didn't have as strong of a case against him. They would be pinning it all on Logan.

As soon as he saw Charlotte and Mona enter, he turned away, staring at the small window in the room.

"Feeling talkative yet?" Charlotte asked, but he didn't reply. Just kept looking defiantly in the other direction. "You know what is sad about all this? You know cooperating with us is the right move. And yet you're willing to spend more time in jail because of your pride."

"It's not pride," Logan finally said. "It's loyalty. Something you obviously know nothing about."

"Loyalty to your friends."

"That's right."

"You don't even know what we want with Terry. And yet here you are, willing to sacrifice your future for him." She tsked. "That's one hell of a friend. Wish I had friends that loyal."

Mona watched this whole conversation play out, carefully observing Logan to see if she could spot anything they might be able to use. Charlotte was right, he *was* sacrificing a lot for Terry. But why?

"What does he have on you?" Mona asked.

Logan finally turned to look at her. "What?"

"He's holding something over you," she said. "It's the only thing that makes sense. So what is it?"

Logan's eyes flashed for a brief moment before he turned to look out the window again. "You don't know what you're talking about."

"My partner is right," Charlotte replied. "You're not being loyal to him. You're protecting yourself. The question is, from what? What could be so bad that you'd be willing to spend an extra seven years in jail for?"

Something sparked in Mona's brain. "He's not in charge."

Charlotte turned to her, one eyebrow raised. But Mona was watching Logan. And she caught a nearly imperceptible jerk as she confronted him about it. "This is Terry's operation, isn't it? He pays you to use that house. To keep your name on it, so if things go south, he stays out of the light."

Logan didn't reply, but he readjusted himself several times, a classic sign that he was uncomfortable.

"Terry is the one running the show. Is that the kind of person he is? A planner? How much is he paying you to take the fall?" Mona asked. "Or maybe he isn't paying you at all. Maybe he's threatening you."

"Look, you don't know what you're talking about," Logan replied. "Just leave me alone."

"Can't do that, kid," Charlotte replied. "See, we need to find Terry and we need to find him yesterday. There's a good possibility he's connected to two local murders."

Sweat formed on Logan's brow. *There it was.* The telltale sign he wasn't loyal to Terry, he was *scared* of him. This only strengthened their case. If he had threatened Logan or someone he cared about and Logan believed without a doubt he would follow through with that threat, that might just encourage him to take the hit.

"Look," Logan said, his voice losing most of its power. "I can't say anything."

"Because he'll do something, won't he?" Charlotte asked, approaching the bars of the cell. "He'll hurt someone."

"You don't mess with Terry, okay?" Logan replied. "I'd rather do the time. It's safer."

"If you help us find him, we can get him off the streets," Mona replied. "We can hold him in custody."

Logan swallowed and finally looked at them again. "You'd arrest him?"

"If he did it, yes," Charlotte replied.

"But you don't know it's him," the boy replied. And he really *had* turned back into a boy. Gone was all the bravado and the attitude and in its place was a scared kid, terrified of what might happen if the man who threatened him found out he squealed.

"We don't know for sure, no," Charlotte admitted. "But we have good reason to believe it's him."

Logan shook his head, pinching his features together. "No. No deal."

"Detective?" Mona turned to see Officer Anderson in the doorway. She motioned with her head for them to join her out in the hallway.

"Looks like we might have gotten a hit on your suspect," she said as soon as they were out of earshot of Logan.

"Where?" Charlotte asked.

"Unit Sixty spotted someone matching his description getting into a black Jeep over on Blackridge Road, the service station. He pulled away, heading north. They're currently following at a safe distance."

"He hasn't spotted them?" Mona asked as she and Charlotte began heading for the exit.

"Not yet."

"Tell them to stay on him but not to engage until we get some backup out there. We have no idea what this kid could be carrying, he should be considered armed and extremely dangerous." Charlotte rushed forward, plowing through the doors back outside.

"Inform Earle that we're headed out there and to send two more backup units," Mona told Anderson. "We're not going to get another shot at this."

"You got it, Detective." She headed back in as Mona joined Charlotte at the car.

"Lucky break?" Mona asked.

"Maybe. But let's not count our chickens before they're hatched. We still don't know if he's our guy."

"But the evidence—"

"I know," Charlotte replied. "Still. Let's get him in custody first."

"What are we arresting him for?" Mona asked.

"The same thing we arrested Logan and Donnie for." Charlotte smiled. She looked like a woman who was about to enter the best race of her life. At least she was having a good time. Mona was glad one of them was.

"Okay," Mona said. "Lead the way."

SIXTEEN

Charlotte's leg bounced with a nervous energy as they sped down Route 34, the landscape blurring into a smear of greens and browns. The radio crackled with updates from the patrol units tracking Terry Barker's black Jeep heading north toward the county line.

"Unit Sixty reporting suspect vehicle has turned onto Westfield Road. Still maintaining visual contact."

"You know, I've been thinking," Mona said, leaning forward. "If Terry is branding these kids, he has to be using an iron brand, or some kind of metal, right?"

"Right," Charlotte replied, keeping her eyes on the road.

"So maybe we should be looking for a blacksmith," Mona replied. "Someone who knows metals and can create custom symbols."

"That's not a bad idea," Charlotte said, pushing the accelerator harder. "Let's just get this kid in custody first. But if he ends up not wanting to talk, that gives us another avenue to explore. And maybe we can save three more lives in the process."

Charlotte felt the engine respond beneath her lead foot. It had been years since she'd been involved in a pursuit, and the familiar rush of adrenaline coursed through her veins like an old friend returning. Yes. More of this.

"Dispatch, we're about three minutes out," Mona said into the radio, her voice steady and controlled. Charlotte glanced over, noting how Mona's posture had shifted—spine straight, shoulders squared, jaw set. She was preparing for battle, in more ways than one.

The rural road stretched before them, a narrow ribbon cutting through farmland. Charlotte took the next turn faster than she should have, the tires protesting with a brief squeal.

"Whoa," Mona said, gripping the door handle. "I don't think I've ever seen you drive pursuit before."

Charlotte nodded but didn't ease off the accelerator. "If this is our guy, I'm not letting him slip away. Not after what he did."

The radio crackled again. "This is Unit Sixty. Suspect appears to be increasing speed. He may have spotted us."

"Damn it," Charlotte muttered. They crested a small hill, and in the distance, she could see the flash of emergency lights. "There. I can see the patrol cars."

The black Jeep was visible now, weaving dangerously between lanes as it tried to outrun the pursuit. Charlotte's tactical mind clicked into gear, assessing angles and options.

"He's heading toward the rail crossing at Old Mill Road," Mona observed, studying the map on her phone. "If we cut through Easterly Lane, we might be able to intercept."

Charlotte didn't hesitate, taking the next turn sharply onto a narrow farm access road. The car bounced violently as they hit an unexpected pothole, and Charlotte felt a sharp pain shoot through her wrist as she fought to maintain control of the wheel.

"You okay?" Mona asked, noticing her wince.

"Yep," Charlotte replied through gritted teeth, ignoring the throbbing. The dull ache was nothing compared to the determination burning in her chest. She hadn't felt this way since retirement, and a deep part of her didn't want it to be cut short, especially not by a little twinge of the wrist.

The shortcut wound through a stand of trees before depositing them onto Old Mill Road. Charlotte could see the railroad crossing ahead, its warning lights just beginning to flash as a train approached in the distance.

"He's going to try to beat the train," Charlotte said, accelerating toward the crossing. Through the windshield, they could see the black Jeep speeding toward the same point from the perpendicular road.

"Charlotte, wait—" Mona started, but Charlotte had already committed, timing their approach to cut off the Jeep before it could cross the tracks.

The timing was perfect—or would have been, if Terry hadn't slammed on his brakes at the last second. The Jeep skidded wildly, spinning almost 180 degrees before coming to a stop mere feet from the tracks as the crossing gates descended.

Charlotte braked hard, positioning their vehicle to block any escape route. The patrol cars that had been in pursuit arrived seconds later, boxing in the Jeep from behind.

"He's running!" Mona shouted as a figure bolted from the driver's side door, vaulting over a nearby fence and sprinting across a fallow field.

They were out of the car in seconds. Charlotte's body moved on autopilot, muscle memory from decades of pursuits taking over as she followed Mona over the fence. Her landing was less graceful than intended; her right ankle rolled on the uneven ground, sending a spike of pain up her leg that she stubbornly ignored.

The train's horn blared as it approached the crossing, the ground vibrating beneath their feet. Terry was twenty yards ahead, running toward a dense thicket of trees at the field's edge.

"Split up!" Charlotte called to Mona, who nodded and veered left while Charlotte continued straight. The younger woman moved with remarkable speed, her training evident in her efficient stride. In fact, it was almost scary how quickly she could move. And for a brief second, Charlotte saw that strangeness about Mona that she knew everyone else saw. In some ways, the woman was uncanny.

But it was gone a second later.

Charlotte pushed herself harder, ignoring the protests from her ankle and wrist. Age was just a number, she told herself, even as her lungs burned from the exertion. The gap was closing—fifteen yards, then ten.

Terry glanced back, his face twisted with panic when he saw how close they were. He changed direction abruptly, heading for a shallow drainage ditch that cut across the field.

"Cut him off at the ditch!" Charlotte shouted, altering her own trajectory to maintain pursuit.

The suspect stumbled as he descended into the ditch, giving Charlotte the opening she needed. She launched herself forward in a diving tackle that connected solidly with his midsection, sending them both tumbling into the muddy bottom of the drainage channel.

The impact drove the air from her lungs and sent a fresh wave of pain through her already injured wrist. Terry thrashed beneath her, an elbow connecting with her ribs as he fought to escape.

"Stop resisting!" she gasped, struggling to pin his arms. Despite being retired, despite the pain radiating through her body, Charlotte found herself automatically reciting the words she'd said countless times throughout her career.

Mona appeared at the edge of the ditch, dropping down beside them with her weapon drawn. "Terry Barker, you're under arrest! Stop moving or I will restrain you by force!"

Something in her tone—a steel-edged authority that brooked no argument—caused Terry to cease his struggling. Charlotte rolled off him, breathing heavily as Mona secured his wrists with zip ties.

"Are you okay?" Mona asked, her eyes quickly scanning Charlotte for injuries.

"Never better," Charlotte replied, wincing as she pushed herself up to sitting. It was a lie, and they both knew it. Her wrist was swollen, her ankle throbbed, and she could feel a warm trickle of blood from a cut on her forearm she hadn't even noticed receiving.

The train thundered past on the nearby tracks, its rhythmic clacking providing a soundtrack to their labored breathing. Charlotte watched as Mona hauled Terry to his feet, reciting his rights with practiced efficiency.

"Need a hand?" Mona asked, extending her own after passing Terry off to the officers who had caught up to them.

Charlotte hesitated only briefly before accepting, allowing Mona to pull her to her feet. Her body screamed in protest as she put weight on her injured ankle. That, and the deep ache that came from her ribs.

"You should get checked out when we get back," Mona said, her warmth having returned as if it had never left.

"It's nothing," Charlotte insisted, limping alongside Mona as they made their way back toward the vehicles. "Just getting reacquainted with fieldwork."

Mona's expression said she wasn't convinced, but she didn't press the issue. "You know, most consultants don't tackle suspects into drainage ditches."

"Never have been very good at staying behind a desk," Charlotte replied with a grimace that was half smile, half pain.

As they approached the patrol cars where Terry was being secured in the back seat, Charlotte caught sight of her reflection in a side mirror—mud-streaked, disheveled, with a fire in her eyes she hadn't seen in months. Despite the pain, despite knowing she'd pushed too hard and would pay for it later, she couldn't deny the truth.

This was what she was meant to do. And she'd been a fool to think otherwise.

"Terry Barker," Charlotte said, sitting down across the metal table. She'd wrapped her ankle but could tell it was already going to swell and she'd be limping for a few days, not to mention the pain that radiated through her wrist and ribs from her encounter with Terry out in the field. He had barely said a word since they brought him in; instead, he just looked defiant the entire time, even as Mona had read him his rights.

He was a big kid, that much was for sure. At least two hundred and twenty pounds, his mugshot put him at a solid six-three with the square jawline to match. And while he was the size of a linebacker, he moved with the simple grace of someone who was completely aware of themselves at all times. For a few moments, Charlotte could see what Kayleigh saw in the boy—he was damn handsome. Something he no doubt used to his advantage whenever possible.

Barker didn't look up as Charlotte took a seat while Mona stood in the back of the room. They had agreed since Charlotte was the one who'd taken him down, she got first dibs on interrogating him.

"Need anything? A glass of water before we begin?" Charlotte asked.

"No," Barker replied, his stoic demeanor something Charlotte didn't see very often in someone so young. Usually, that kind of response was reserved for someone who'd had a lot of experience in the system, but from what they could tell, Terry only had a minor list of priors. A couple of possession charges that had amounted to nothing, a couple of misdemeanors and that's about it. Not much for someone who was an active participant in a drug den.

"First things first, you need to know why you're here," Charlotte replied. "We arrested you based on suspicion of possession and distribution of opioids, understand?"

Terry only stared back at her.

"But I want to talk to you about something else. Kayleigh Goole." His eyebrow arched. "Specifically, your relationship."

"We don't have a relationship," he replied.

"Not according to her," Charlotte said. "She told us you two have been seeing each other recently."

"Is that a crime?"

"No, but I'm curious why you're still seeing her when you know she's in another relationship with Connor Peterson." So far they'd managed to keep a lid on the Peterson story, limiting the media to reporting that an unidentified man had been found dead in his home until they could get Barker off the streets. Thankfully, the local news had been cooperative so far. But that would only last so long—eventually they'd release the details of the story no matter what. Probably on the eleven o'clock news tonight.

"That's her business," Barker finally replied. "I don't care who she sees."

"So it doesn't bother you that she's in a relationship with someone else at the same time she's seeing you?" Charlotte asked.

He shrugged. "Peterson's a pushover. Everyone knows it. They don't have sex. Why do you think she comes to me?"

Interesting. From the way Kayleigh had spoken it sounded like the two of them had been intimate. "How do you know?"

"She tells me," he replied. "She's only with him because of their parents."

"What does that mean?" Charlotte asked.

"Their parents wanted them to get together," he said. "When they were little kids. Kinda sick, if you ask me. An arranged marriage at that age? Kayleigh doesn't want him, though. She has particular needs." He cocked his head. "So I satisfy her."

"Uh-huh," Charlotte said, taking this in. Kayleigh hadn't mentioned any of this in their interview. Then again it could all be a smokescreen on Barker's part to shift the spotlight away from him. "How well do you know Connor Peterson?"

"Never met the guy. Don't want to," Barker replied. "What does any of this have to do with anything?"

"Are you a big history buff, Terry?" Charlotte asked, trying a different avenue.

"No," he scoffed. "Why?"

"What about family history? Ever do one of those genealogy tests?"

He looked at her like she was crazy.

"Or maybe you were just doing an internet search one day and happened upon something that looked cool." She pulled up a picture of the rune from Peterson's body and showed it to Terry. The boy barely flinched, but it was there.

"Yeah," Charlotte said. "It was burned into him. Seen it before?"

"No," he replied a little too forcefully.

"You sure? Haven't been looking up symbols on the internet?"

"No," he said again. "Why would I waste my time with that?"

Charlotte ignored him. "Can you tell me where you were on Monday evening, between the hours of six in the evening to eight the following morning?"

He huffed. "Yeah, me and my uncles drove down to Indianapolis to deliver some furniture. I just got back a few hours ago."

"I thought you worked for Advantage Tree and Lawn," Charlotte said, looking through the file she'd brought with her. There was no reference in his work history that said anything about a delivery service.

"It was a personal favor," Barker replied. "He sold some stuff online but had to transport it. We loaded it up in the back of his pickup because mine was in the shop. Drove down last night and came back this morning."

"Where?" Charlotte asked.

"I dunno. Some shitty motel. Super 8 or something."

If that was true, it meant Terry couldn't be their killer. Whittle had put Connor's death between the hours of midnight and six am Tuesday morning, but if Terry was in a completely different state, then it would be a little difficult to pin him to the crime. Not to mention he didn't seem to know anything about the runes.

She glanced to the camera in the corner where she knew Bowman and the others were watching. They'd be scrambling to check traffic cameras and hotel records.

"We're going to need your uncle's information," Charlotte said.

"Why? I thought this was about Logan's house." He eyed her carefully.

"One last question, Terry. Why is your car in the shop?"

Terry shook his head like he couldn't believe he was being subjected to these questions. "I clipped a deer the other day and needed to get the dents out. What does that have to do with anything?"

Charlotte glanced to Mona, her lips pressed in a line. The odds of Terry being their killer were dropping by the second. The deer story was easy enough to fabricate, but they both knew they didn't have any usable evidence off his car that connected him to Mallory's death. Their big play had been Connor. Rolling Mallory into the mix would have been the icing on the cake.

"Terry, I'm going to level with you," Charlotte finally said. "You're not here because of some bullshit possession charge. Connor Peterson was found dead in his house yesterday morning. And there were signs of foul play."

"Wait a second," Terry said, scooting back from the table, clearly alarmed. "Was that *Connor's* body you showed me? I didn't have anything to do with that. Like I said, I didn't even know the guy. I don't even know what he looks like."

Charlotte found that hard to believe in this day and age. It wouldn't have been hard for Terry to find an image of Connor and Kayleigh together. The question now was if he wasn't here, could he have convinced someone else to do it for him?

"Let's talk about your roommates," Charlotte replied. "Logan and Donnie. How long have you known them?"

"Since high school," he replied. "Why?"

"Logan seems to be particularly scared of you." Charlotte leaned forward. "Why is that?"

"Because he's a pussy?" Terry replied, but it was in the form of a question. As if he didn't know himself.

"You don't know why he was willing to take the rap for you?" Charlotte asked.

"Rap for what?"

"Everything we found in his house."

"Hey, that's all his stuff. Not mine."

"Right. You had nothing to do with it."

He nodded. "Exactly."

Charlotte sat back. Pinning the drug charges to Terry would be difficult as well. He was smart—had built in multiple layers of protection to keep himself insulated. But there was a big leap for willing to a little time for someone versus killing another human for them. She took a deep breath, finding it hard to fully fill her lungs without stabs of pain in her abdomen. But she didn't have time to deal with that now. She had to find some way to nail this kid.

"We know Connor didn't kill himself, that much is clear, despite the killer wanting us to think that," Charlotte said, watching him carefully. "And we know that you're still seeing his girlfriend on the side. So you tell me, what do you think happened?"

"How the hell should I know?" he protested. "Like I said, I was out of town."

"But you see how it looks, right? You said yourself you didn't understand why they were together... that you thought it was *weird*. Maybe you got tired of playing second fiddle. Maybe you told one of your boys to take care of business for you while you were out of town. Maybe you even helped them set it up. And maybe you wanted to throw us off the scent with some strange symbols you found in the deep corners of the internet."

Terry held up his hands. "Wait a second here. Just wait, okay? Logan is a little bitch, Donnie too. I can barely get them to leave the house. I didn't tell anyone to kill anybody."

"But again... you see how it looks."

Terry bit his lip, looking around the room, at Charlotte, then at Mona and finally at the camera. "Look, if you want someone to blame, why don't you check into Connor's family? Those people are crazy. Kayleigh's too. That whole clan. They do that ritual shit. Ask them."

"What whole clan?" Charlotte asked.

"I don't know all the details. I just know her dad is head of some church out on the edge of town. She used to tell me about all the crazy stuff they did. Bonfires in the middle of the night, secret meetings. Connor's parents too. They're all in on it."

"You think Connor's parents killed their own son?" Charlotte gave him a skeptical look.

"I'm not the cop here, okay?" Terry shouted. "I don't know what happened. All I know is I had nothing to do with it. Check with my uncle. We. Were. In. Indianapolis." He said each word with extra punctuation as if to drive home his point.

She wasn't getting anywhere with him and they were starting to go in circles. Not to mention they didn't have any physical evidence attaching Terry to the murder scene. She had hoped shaking him down would give them something tangible, but the kid was either too smart or too stupid for that.

She couldn't decide which.

"Terry Barker, you're being charged on third-degree possession of a class-one narcotic. As well as distribution of more than one ounce of Fentanyl, which is a felony. You'll be remanded in custody until the time when a trial date can be set." She stood and joined Mona at the door, heading back out into the hallway.

"That didn't go very well," Mona said.

"No, it didn't," she admitted.

"So now what?"

"We check his alibi. If it checks out... then we'll explore your blacksmith angle. He didn't exhibit any traits of lying in there. Either he knows nothing about any of this or he's a master manipulator. And given what we know about him, I'm inclined to believe the former."

"Do you think he's telling the truth about Kayleigh's family?" Mona asked.

"I don't know. And I don't want to cause *another* incident with the people of this town without cause. We need to do some research."

"Great."

Charlotte could tell from the disappointment in her voice that Mona wasn't optimistic. In one fell swoop they'd lost their only lead and suspect all in one.

She just hoped they could find another before it was too late.

SEVENTEEN

It turned out Terry Barker had been telling the truth about being in Indianapolis the night of Connor Peterson's murder. Traffic cameras and tolls caught him heading through Chicago on his way to Indianapolis, and they even managed to find the motel where he and his uncle stayed the night. Mona and Bowman tracked down the uncle and interviewed him, and he backed up the alibi, despite not knowing Terry had been arrested.

It was all a lot of legwork to confirm what they already knew: Terry wasn't their guy. At least not directly. And they couldn't find any evidence he'd somehow orchestrated the killings.

Mona had volunteered to track down the information while Charlotte went to the local urgent care to get her ankle and ribs checked out. Mona had noticed how much she had been holding herself during Terry's interrogation and thought perhaps she'd hurt herself more than she'd wanted to admit. It had taken Mona demanding she get checked out for Charlotte to finally agree. By the time she returned to the station, it was close to ten in the evening and Mona was about to drop dead from exhaustion.

They'd given Charlotte a good round of painkillers, which meant she couldn't drive herself. Mona took her back to her hotel room with a promise that she'd be there first thing to pick her up again in the morning before heading home herself. She barely pulled into the driveway of her place before falling asleep at the wheel. The past few days had been a full whirlwind and Mona was feeling every inch of it.

As soon as she opened the door, Perigee was there to welcome her, rubbing up against her leg. "Oh," Mona said, having temporarily forgotten she now owned a cat. "Hello there." She picked up the purring animal who allowed itself to be cradled in her arms. Mona headed to the kitchen, checking to find Perigee's bowl was empty. "Poor thing. You're probably starving."

She put the cat down and retrieved a can of wet cat food from her pantry—a new addition—before opening it and mixing it as Perigee stared up at her, licking her lips. As soon as Mona set the food down, the cat went to work, chomping away.

Mona headed back to her bedroom and peeled off her clothes that felt like another layer of sweaty skin at this point. Once she was in a pair of oversized sweats, she returned to the living room to find Perigee stretched out on the couch, a satisfied look on her face.

That reminded her; she'd forgotten to eat something herself. But one look in the fridge confirmed what she already knew: she had nothing worth eating. She'd pick something up in the morning on the way to get Charlotte. Remembering to eat was important— she couldn't keep forgetting.

Ever since she'd "come out of her shell," she'd found the world a lot more complicated to deal with. She had to weigh her impact on others and vice versa, as well as navigate all the complex social situations that came with her job. She had to remember to be subdued when the situation called for it, or exuberant and excited when they had a breakthrough. Because if she didn't actively think about it, it was too easy to back into old habits. What she had unaffectionately started to think of as her "dad's persona" as a way to keep herself from doing it too often.

Still, it was difficult. And her sessions with Dr. Cross had revealed just how far she had to go. She'd made massive breakthroughs in a short time, and Dr. Cross said those didn't come without repercussions. Errant thoughts, attempts to self-correct or falling back into old patterns. She had to constantly monitor herself and it was exhausting.

And the worst part of all was she missed her old self. Not all of it of course, but there had been a simplicity to how she'd been before. It had made navigating everyday life easier. But now, with all she had to keep track of, things like eating easily fell off the to-do list. Dr. Cross had suggested building an easy-to-follow schedule, but how was she supposed to do that when her days changed from one to another? Five days ago she couldn't have predicted Charlotte would be here, helping her track down a killer who was leaving strange symbols on the bodies of his victims.

Frustrated she didn't have anything she could eat; Mona found an errant can of soup in the back of her pantry and took five minutes to heat it up. But by the time it was ready, she'd already lost the taste for it. Instead, she poured it back into a container and threw it in the fridge before heading to her bedroom. She needed a reset. They'd run themselves ragged today with little to show for it.

But tomorrow would be better. It had to be.

As she pulled the covers up and switched off the light, Perigee hopped up on the bed, startling her before curling into a little ball against her legs.

That's what you used to do with Mallory, wasn't it? Mona thought. Thankfully, the cat seemed to be adjusting to its new surroundings without too much trouble. But as Mona lay there, wishing for the exhaustion she felt to send her into a dreamless sleep, she couldn't help but think about all the things she'd forgotten to do in addition to eating. She'd forgotten again to get Perigee some cat toys so she didn't tear up the house, though there was no evidence of her destroying anything yet.

She also couldn't get Terry Barker out of her mind. He had seemed like the perfect suspect. And yet they had nothing connecting him to either murder. Which meant the killer was still out there, roaming around freely without a care in the world. She tried putting herself in his head, tried to figure out what could be driving him. Why these two victims? There was nothing solid connecting Mallory Wakefield and Connor Peterson. And were there really three more out there? Charlotte was right, they couldn't ignore the possibility.

What was it about these symbols?

Mona sat up. Between Charlotte heading to get herself checked out and she and Bowman doing the heavy lifting on Terry's uncle, she'd dropped the one thread that might give them a lead.

She grabbed her laptop from the nearby nightstand and opened it, her eyes taking a moment to adjust to the bright light. A quick search revealed only two possible blacksmiths in the general area with the ability to create the brands they'd seen on the victims. One was over in Fox Lake while the other was in Lawrence. It would mean a lot of driving tomorrow, but if they could find who made these brands, it might give them a clue to the identity of who ordered them.

Then again it was just as likely that the person who was using these things made them themselves, or sourced them from somewhere else.

At any rate, it was a long shot.

Mona closed the laptop and sighed. At her legs Perigee began to purr. Mona leaned over and ran her hand down the animal's soft fur. Why was she so conflicted lately? Hadn't she gotten everything she wanted? Sure, she'd only been on one date so far, but that was leagues better than where she'd started. And while most of the town still kept her at arm's length, she was beginning to chip away at that, little by little. So long as her dad remained locked up and she could disassociate herself from him completely. People would move on in time. And she'd made a lot of progress at work. People might still not know what to think about her, but at least they respected her.

And now she had a cat. Things were getting better. They just took time.

Maybe happiness wasn't a goal to be achieved, but more of a

state of mind. If that was the case, she still had a long way to go. Primarily because of where she had come from. Her father's shadow still loomed large over her life and that wasn't something she could just easily cut out.

Mona hesitated a second before flipping on the light in the room again and reaching over into her bedside drawer, removing a wrinkled piece of paper. She opened it, her eyes scanning the handwritten words a few times before she crumpled it back up and tossed it to the trash can in the corner, just as she had half a dozen times before.

In the morning she would flatten it back out, fold it carefully and place it back in her bedside table.

Just as she had also done half a dozen times before.

"Good morning," Mona said as Charlotte opened the door to her hotel room. Mona held a carrier with two coffees and a box of donut holes from Tim Hortons. She'd also grabbed a couple of egg sandwiches before coming over. Knowing Charlotte, she was as unlikely to have eaten as Mona.

The older detective looked a little worse for wear, a bruise having formed on her cheek. "Oh," she said, groggy. "Is it?"

"Seven thirty," Mona chirped. "I figured you'd want to be up early."

"I need to shower," Charlotte replied.

"That's okay, I can wait in the lobby," Mona said.

"Don't be ridiculous, come in," Charlotte said, moving to the side. "I'll just be a few minutes."

Mona stepped into the room, setting the food on the desk-slash-drawer-unit in the room under the TV mounted on the wall. A small duffel bag sat in the single chair while the bed itself was a mess of covers and pillows.

"Sleep okay?" Mona asked.

"Not really," Charlotte replied. "I may have overdone it yesterday. Couldn't get comfortable."

"Do you need to go back to urgent care?"

"Not as long as I have these," Charlotte said, picking up the bottle of painkillers she'd been prescribed. She popped a couple in her hand before tossing them back and drinking them down with the coffee. She winced, gritting her teeth. "Hot."

"Yeah," Mona said. "It's coffee."

"Okay, give me fifteen minutes," Charlotte said, heading for the bathroom. "I have to unwrap all these bandages."

"Need a hand?" Mona asked.

"I got it," she called from inside the room.

Mona took a deep breath and sat on the edge of the bed as she listened to the shower starting. A series of grunts and cusses emanated from behind the closed door of the bathroom and Mona thought about offering her assistance again, but if Charlotte wanted it, she'd ask.

"I think we should check out a couple of metalworkers I found last night," Mona called out.

"Metalworkers?" Charlotte asked.

"Yeah, you know. Blacksmiths. Anyone who could have created those brands. It's a long shot, but maybe he got them from somewhere local."

"Maybe," Charlotte replied. "It's just as possible that he made them himself."

"I thought that too," Mona said.

"I think we should go back to Kayleigh Goole," Charlotte replied. "Maybe we overshot our mark. Terry might have been just trying to shift blame yesterday, but I'd like to look into it, especially if their church has some ritual component. He might not have been the one who wanted Connor out of the way."

"You think she did it?"

"She's our next-most-likely suspect," she called back. "She may have had more motive than Terry." The water shut off, allowing Charlotte not to yell as loud. "I should have seen it before, but I got lazy... assumed Terry was our target."

"We *both* did," Mona replied.

Charlotte emerged from the bathroom with one towel wrapped around her head and another around her midsection. Mona couldn't help but notice the angry bruise on her ankle. Charlotte put pressure on it, but she could tell it was still tender. "I think the blacksmiths are a good idea, but we're limited on time. I have a bad feeling we haven't seen our last victim yet. Can you get Bowman on them while we speak with Kayleigh again today?"

Mona nodded. "I'm sure he doesn't mind making the drive." When Charlotte arched an eyebrow as she gathered clean clothes from her duffel bag, Mona explained both blacksmiths she'd found were outside of town.

It took Charlotte a fair bit more than fifteen minutes to finish getting ready. Apparently, she hadn't taken into account her injuries or how much they would slow her down. Mona even had to help her re-wrap her ankle before she got her boots on. In the meantime, she called Bowman and gave him the lowdown on the metalworkers. He agreed to take care of it and Mona again thought about how lucky she was to have such a good partner. Bowman had been surprisingly flexible about Charlotte coming in to assist. Something Ramsey never could accept.

Before they left, Charlotte grabbed the box from Tim Hortons. "Thanks for getting these. I keep forgetting to eat breakfast."

"Yeah," Mona replied. "I know the feeling."

EIGHTEEN

Charlotte winced as she eased herself into the passenger seat of Mona's car. The painkillers had taken the edge off, but every little movement still sent dull throbs of protest through her ankle and ribs. She tried not to let it show—the last thing she needed was for Mona to suggest she sit this one out. Thankfully, her wrist seemed to be the least of her injuries and didn't even hurt this morning.

But it wasn't her physical ailments that were giving her the most pause. It was the fact that there was now a very real chance Mona's case was connected to her original case from twenty-five years ago. Charlotte had continued to resist the idea until Roger had told them there were five runes in this sequence in total. Which meant it was possible they'd end up with five victims.

Just like her case.

She also had to consider the burns she'd found on her victims might have been someone's poor attempt at branding. The big difference was her victims were all found in one place, at the same time. Mona's victims so far had been spread apart. Still... she couldn't ignore the connection.

"You sure you're up for this?" Mona asked, catching Charlotte's grimace despite her best efforts to hide it.

"I'm fine, been through a lot worse," Charlotte replied,

adjusting her position to minimize the pressure on her ribs. "Nothing a little more field work won't cure."

Mona gave her a skeptical look but started the car without further comment. As they pulled away from the hotel, Charlotte found herself trying not to think about her injuries and failing: sprained ankle, bruised ribs, strained wrist, even though that had already begun to feel better. Not her worst day on the job by any means, but enough to make her feel every one of her years. Meanwhile, Mona had emerged from yesterday's pursuit without so much as a scratch.

Charlotte pushed the thought away. This wasn't a competition, and envy wouldn't help them catch a killer.

The drive to Kayleigh's apartment was mercifully short. When they arrived, Charlotte allowed Mona to take the lead, hanging back slightly as they approached the door.

Mona knocked on Kayleigh's door several times, each attempt met with silence. After the third try, they exchanged glances.

"Now what?" Mona said, her expression tight with concern.

The timing was too suspicious—especially after what they'd learned about Kayleigh's connection to both Connor and Terry.

Mona spoke briefly with the building manager, who confirmed he hadn't seen Kayleigh since yesterday morning. A quick check with neighbors yielded similar results—no one had seen or heard from her since the last time they'd been here.

Back in the car, Mona immediately called in an APB for Kayleigh while Charlotte reviewed what little they knew about the young woman. Her disappearance could mean several things: She might have fled out of fear, gone into hiding to avoid questioning, or—the possibility neither wanted to voice—become the killer's next target.

"What do we know about her parents?" Charlotte asked once Mona finished the call.

"Not much," Mona admitted, turning the car toward the station. "I've heard the name Goole around town, but I've never had any direct dealings with them. You still think Terry's accusations might have some teeth?"

"I think we're running out of time before another body turns up. Right now I'm willing to investigate any avenue."

Back at the station, they dug into the family's background. Joseph and Marie Goole owned a substantial parcel of land on the outskirts of town, where they operated a small church called the Circle of the Sacred Grove. Public records showed they'd established the church in the early 2000s after moving from Chicago, though information prior to their arrival in Oak Creek was surprisingly sparse.

"Got something," Charlotte said, pointing to the property records on Mona's computer screen. "Their residence is classified as an auxiliary building to the church. That's how they're avoiding property taxes on most of the land."

"Makes sense," Mona replied, scrolling through the documents. "Would have taken some savvy legal work to set that up."

After an hour of digging through public records, they'd built a basic profile: Joseph and Marie Goole, mid-sixties, no criminal records, minimal social media presence and seemingly respected in the community despite keeping a low profile. They were known for some philanthropy as well as some community outreach. But beyond that, details were frustratingly scarce.

"We're not getting anywhere with this," Charlotte said, leaning back in her chair with a grimace as her ribs protested the movement. "We need someone who actually knows them."

Mona was quiet for a moment, her face darkening. "I know who might be able to help But..."

"But what?" Charlotte asked.

"Well..." Mona said, her voice going up an octave. "Let's just say she's not the most *reliable* source."

"What does that mean?"

Mona huffed. "Do you know the Oak Creek Historical Society? Of course not, why would you? Anyway, Mrs. Carter runs it.

There's not a thing that happens in this town that she doesn't get wind of."

"Great," Charlotte replied. "What's the problem?"

"Oh, I mean she's perfectly nice. She's just... a busybody. The whole reason she runs the society is so she can have her fingers in everyone's business. The woman thrives on rumor and hearsay."

Charlotte sighed. "Any word from Bowman on those blacksmiths?"

Mona shook her head.

"Then I guess we don't have much of a choice."

Twenty minutes later, they pulled up to a quaint Victorian house that served as the town's historical society. The building was painted a cheerful yellow with white trim, looking more like someone's grandmother's house than a municipal building.

"Mrs. Carter is something of a local institution," Mona explained as they approached the front door. "She's been documenting Oak Creek's history and genealogy for over forty years. If anyone knows about the Gooles, it's her."

The door opened before they could knock, revealing a diminutive woman with silver hair pulled into a neat bun. Despite her age —Charlotte guessed mid-eighties, at least—her eyes were sharp and alert behind wire-rimmed glasses.

"Detective LaSalle," Mrs. Carter said, her voice surprisingly strong. "What a wonderful surprise." Her gaze shifted to Charlotte, assessing her with quick efficiency. "And you must be Detective Dawes from Chicago. I read about your work on that horrible business earlier in the year."

Charlotte exchanged a surprised glance with Mona. Mona hadn't been kidding.

The interior of the historical society was meticulously organized, with glass display cases showcasing artifacts from the town's past and walls lined with photographs documenting its evolution. Mrs. Carter led them to a small office in the back, gesturing for them to take seats while she settled behind a desk cluttered with papers and old ledgers.

"How can I help you, Detectives?" she asked, folding her hands on the desk. "As much as I'd like to believe otherwise, I know better than to assume this is a social call."

"I was told you're the authority on everything that goes on in this town," Charlotte said, giving the woman a quick smile that helped hide the pain she felt as she took a seat in one of the chairs opposite the desk.

"Oh, I wouldn't go that far," the woman replied. "I just like to keep records. I'm one of the oldest remaining residents of the town."

"That being the case, we hoped you could help fill in some blanks for us about the Goole family. Specifically, Joseph and Marie," Charlotte said.

"We're trying to locate Kayleigh Goole," Mona explained. "And we need to understand more about her family."

Mrs. Carter nodded thoughtfully. "The Gooles aren't originally from Oak Creek, you know. They came here in ninety-one or ninety-two, I believe. Joseph was quite charismatic—had a way of speaking that drew people in. They started their church in a small building downtown before acquiring that land on the outskirts."

"What kind of church is it exactly?" Charlotte asked.

"They call themselves non-denominational, but there's always been something... different about their practices." Mrs. Carter reached for a thick binder on a nearby shelf. "They keep to themselves mostly, though they're always polite when you encounter them in town. Their congregation isn't large—maybe thirty regular members, primarily families that came with them from Chicago."

She flipped through the binder until she found what she was looking for—a newspaper clipping from 2002 showing a younger Joseph and Marie Goole at a town festival.

"The interesting thing is how they've managed to maintain their privacy while still being part of the community," Mrs. Carter continued. "Joseph serves on the Chamber of Commerce, donates to local causes, but never allows outsiders to attend their services. Says they're 'intimate family gatherings,' not public worship."

Charlotte studied the photograph. Joseph Goole had been a handsome man with an intense gaze that seemed to pierce through the camera. Marie stood beside him, her expression serene but somehow distant. "I thought they did public outreach."

"They *used* to. But they haven't in a long time. It was only for a few years after they arrived. Since then they've more or less kept to themselves."

"Do you know the Petersons as well?" Mona asked.

"Oh yes," Mrs. Carter replied, flipping to another section of the binder. "Robert and Catherine Peterson were among those that arrived at the same time. The families have been close ever since. There was always talk that they'd arranged for Connor and Kayleigh to marry eventually—old-fashioned that way."

Charlotte felt that nagging sensation again, something just beyond her grasp. "What did Joseph do before founding the church? Do you know what brought them to Oak Creek from Chicago?"

Mrs. Carter closed the binder, her expression turning thoughtful. "He's never spoken much about their time in Chicago. I believe he worked in finance of some sort. As for why they left..." She paused, lowering her voice slightly. "There were rumors, of course. Nothing substantial, but whispers that they'd left under some kind of cloud."

"What kind of rumors?" Charlotte pressed.

"The kind people don't speak of directly," Mrs. Carter replied. "There was talk of some trouble with another religious group they'd been involved with. A split of some kind, possibly unpleasant. But Joseph and Marie were always so respectable here that most people dismissed the gossip."

She reached for another ledger, this one older and bound in worn leather. "What I can tell you is that their church practices some rather unusual traditions. Seasonal ceremonies, particularly around solstices and equinoxes. Nothing overtly concerning, but distinctive enough that it's kept them somewhat separate from the mainstream religious community."

Charlotte exchanged a glance with Mona. Solstices and equinoxes. Pagan elements incorporated into ostensibly Christian worship. It wasn't unheard-of, but combined with the symbols they'd found on the victims, it raised questions.

"Have you ever heard of ancient runes being used in their ceremonies?" Charlotte asked carefully.

Mrs. Carter looked up sharply. "What an interesting question. What sort of *runes* are you referring to?"

Charlotte pulled up the images from Mallory Wakefield and Connor Peterson, showing them both to Mrs. Carter.

"Fascinating," she whispered, leaning back in her chair. For an older woman, she seemed as spry as a teenager. "There was an incident, oh, must be fifteen years ago now. A teenage boy—not from their congregation—snuck onto the property during what he thought was a bonfire party. What he described seeing caused quite a stir, though most dismissed it as teenage exaggeration."

"What did he see?" Mona asked.

"Symbols drawn in the dirt around a fire. People wearing gray robes. Chanting." Mrs. Carter shrugged. "But no one could ever substantiate the rumors, nothing was ever found. And most people dismissed it. But then again, Oak Creek has had a long history of... let's say, *disturbing* incidents."

"What kind of incidents?" Mona asked.

Mrs. Carter smiled. "Nothing but hearsay, I'm afraid. But the town was founded by religious groups looking for... alternatives."

Charlotte's phone buzzed with an incoming message. She checked it quickly—a text from Roger asking how she was doing. She couldn't help but feel a quick shot of adrenaline, especially after what Mona had said. She dismissed it and shoved her phone back in her pocket. This was getting them nowhere. Mrs. Carter was obviously feeding on their curiosity. It struck Charlotte that the woman probably didn't receive many visitors.

"Do you know where we might find Kayleigh?" Mona asked. "Her apartment's empty, and we're concerned for her safety."

Mrs. Carter considered this for a moment. "If she's not at home and not with friends, she's likely at the church property. The Gooles are very protective of their own, especially in times of trouble. They might have brought her there for safety—or to keep her away from outsiders."

"Thank you," Charlotte said, standing again and suppressing a wince as she did. "You've been very helpful."

"Leaving already?" she asked. "I haven't even gotten to the most interesting part. Did you know the town's founders were considered heathens?"

"Another time, I'm afraid," Mona said, glancing at Charlotte. "We're on something of a time crunch."

The woman seemed to deflate in front of them. "Of course."

As they prepared to leave, the elderly woman placed a gentle hand on Charlotte's arm.

"Detective Dawes, be careful out there," she said quietly. "The Gooles have been part of this community for thirty years, but I've always sensed there are depths to them that we've never seen. And deep waters can be dangerous when stirred."

It seemed Mrs. Carter had a flair for the dramatic.

Back in the car, Charlotte scrolled through Roger's message while Mona called the station to update them on their plans to visit the Goole property.

"Who is that?" Mona asked, indicating Charlotte's phone as she waited on the other line.

"No one," she said, putting the phone away.

Mona shot her a suspicious look as someone picked up on the other end. She spoke for less than a minute before ending her call. "Bowman checked with those blacksmiths. Neither has made anything resembling our brands, but one mentioned that custom brands aren't difficult to make with basic blacksmithing equipment."

"Great. I guess that means we're going to church."

Mona nodded. "Guess so."

"How far is the Goole property?" she asked.

"About fifteen minutes from here," Mona replied. "It's relatively isolated—large parcel of land surrounded by woods on three sides."

"Great, doesn't sound creepy at all." Whatever was going on, she didn't like the implications. She wasn't sure if they could trust the information from Mrs. Carter, but it had been something, at least. Her thoughts kept returning to that case from all those years ago. Could they really be chasing the same killer? Could he have come back after all this time?

Mona's phone rang, breaking Charlotte's concentration. The caller ID on the car's screen identified the caller as Oak Creek PD.

"LaSalle," Mona said, tapping the answer button on her steering wheel. Charlotte still hadn't gotten used to people talking through their cars and she doubted she ever would.

"It's Earle," the gruff man said on the other end. "I need you out at Billy's Diner, on Highway Forty-Four. Bowman is already on his way."

"Don't tell me," Mona said, shooting Charlotte a look of concern.

"Afraid so. We got another one."

After pulling a harrowing U-turn in the middle of the road, the drive to Billy's Diner took only about ten minutes. But the entire way, Mona considered the implications of what another victim meant. One thing was for sure; Terry Barker was not their suspect. Not if the pattern held. Earle hadn't said anything about another symbol being found on the body, but she was sure they'd find one, regardless.

What was worse, he'd only told her that the victim was in her early twenties and blond. No other ID, leaving both Mona and Charlotte to wonder if their efforts to find Kayleigh Goole had been in vain.

Charlotte had cautioned against making too many assumptions before they arrived, but Mona couldn't help the wheels in her brain from turning. Roger's warning had made a bad situation worse. She had no reason to believe this wasn't part of the pattern. Which meant there were still two more victims out there. Had they already been targeted? How were they supposed to get ahead of this guy? This was Robin's case all over again. And this time, they didn't have Mona's father to blame.

If she could just get inside the killer's head—figure out what they were thinking. What was driving them...

No. She *wouldn't* do that. It was too dangerous. If she opened that part of herself back up, there was no telling what might come out. She was still her father's daughter. She could never let that part of herself out, no matter the circumstances. In fact, she had to keep fighting against it.

The restaurant sat on a corner lot with a large parking area behind it, now filled with patrol cars and an ambulance. Yellow crime scene tape cordoned off a section near the dumpsters, lit up by the lights of the nearby patrol cars.

Mona parked as close as she could and they made their way toward the scene. Charlotte's limp wasn't as pronounced as she kept pace with Mona, but she could tell Charlotte was doing everything she could not to draw attention to it.

Bowman met them at the tape, his face grim.

"Got an ID yet?" Mona asked, her heart practically thumping out of her chest.

"Justine Mercer. Twenty-three. Worked here as a server." Mona let out a breath as he lifted the tape for them to duck under. It wasn't Kayleigh. Still... another young woman dead.

"What happened?" Charlotte asked.

"Manager said she never clocked in for her shift. Another server found her when she went out for a smoke break after the evening rush."

The scene was brutal. The victim lay on her back near the dumpster, her throat cut so deeply it nearly separated her head from her body. Blood had pooled around her, darkening the asphalt. She wore the restaurant's uniform—black pants and a white button-up shirt, now soaked crimson.

"Jesus," Charlotte muttered, surveying the scene.

Whittle crouched beside the body, his usual professional detachment firmly in place. "Evening, Detectives."

"Poor girl," Mona said, pulling on gloves. "Have you been able to determine anything yet?"

"Female, early twenties. Cause of death is obvious—exsanguination from the laceration to the carotid artery and jugular vein." Whittle pointed to the wound. "Death would have been relatively quick, though not instantaneous."

"Time of death?" Charlotte asked.

"Based on liver temp and the blood coagulation, I'd estimate between six and eight this evening."

"What time was she found?"

"Call came in at nine thirty," Bowman replied, flipping through his notebook.

"Why did it take so long for someone to find her?" Mona asked.

"Manager said they were busy this evening, no one took a break until later. They were a person short, after all. She must have been the last one to come into work and was attacked before she could get to the back door."

"Any signs of struggle?" Mona asked, scanning the area around the body.

"None that I can see," Whittle replied. "No defensive wounds on her hands or arms. Whatever happened, she didn't fight back."

"Or she couldn't," Charlotte said, her eyes narrowed as she studied the scene. "It's possible she knew her attacker. Trusted them enough to turn her back."

Mona circled the body slowly, taking in every detail. "The positioning feels deliberate. Almost... displayed."

"Initial assessment suggests it's meant to look like a suicide," Whittle said. "There's a knife a few feet away that appears to match the wound. We're working on prints now."

Charlotte snorted. "Suicide? Who comes to work to kill themselves? And the angle's all wrong. If she cut her own throat, the blood spatter would be different."

"I agree," Whittle said. "Just telling you what it's staged to look like."

Mona continued her examination, methodically checking the victim's clothing, hands and exposed skin. When she reached the right arm, she carefully turned it, revealing what she was looking for—a burn mark just above the wrist.

"Charlotte," she called, pointing to the mark.

Charlotte leaned in, her expression darkening. "Same placement."

"Different symbol, though," Mona noted, pulling out her phone to photograph it. "Just like the others."

The mark was distinct—unlike either of the previous brands they'd found, but clearly created with the same method. This one resembled a box with a strike mark through it, and three small lines at the top.

"Can you send it to Roger?" Mona asked, straightening up.

Charlotte nodded, already typing on her phone. "Anything else distinct about the scene? Any witnesses?"

Bowman shook his head. "This part of the building isn't visible from the road or the neighboring buildings. All the kitchen staff servers were inside working. No one saw or heard anything."

"Security cameras?" Mona asked.

"One pointing at the back door, but it doesn't cover this area." Bowman gestured to where they stood. "Killer knew exactly where the blind spot was."

Mona felt a chill that had nothing to do with the morning air. "So our killer is either very lucky, or they scouted this location."

"I'd bet on the latter," Charlotte said, pocketing her phone. "They're getting more confident. The first two deaths could plausibly be written off as accidents or suicide if not investigated thoroughly. This one..." She gestured to the scene. "This is more brazen."

"They're escalating," Mona agreed, the knot in her stomach tightening further.

Charlotte turned to Whittle. "Any sign of sexual assault?"

"None that I can see, but I'll know more after the autopsy."

"What about personal effects?" Mona asked. "Phone? Wallet?"

"Wallet's in her back pocket, untouched," Bowman said. "No phone found yet."

"It's just like Mallory and Connor," Mona noted. "Killer takes the phone but leaves everything else." Was this another lure? As she stared at the scene, she couldn't help but build what had happened in her mind... how the killer must have made his attack. She could even picture it, coming out of the shadows, knife in hand and with one quick slice...

Stop it. Maintain your detachment. She squeezed her eyes together, pushing away the images and opened them again just to take in the details of the scene. Just the facts. No suppositions. No reliving the victim's last moments. That's something her father would want to do. Mona was better. *Had* to be better.

Charlotte stared at the victim's face, her expression unreadable. "Three victims. Three different methods. And three symbols in a deliberate pattern." Mona could tell she was turning it all over in her head, working it out. "I was hesitant before. But..."

"But what?" Mona asked.

"Ever since Roger mentioned there would be five victims, I keep going back to my original case. I don't think we can continue to ignore the possibility these two cases are connected. We know there will be at least two more victims. Maybe there's something in the old case files that could help."

Mona wasn't sure, but it looked like some of the color had drained from Charlotte's face. That might have been due to her injuries, but she didn't think so. "Are you okay?"

Charlotte swallowed hard. "Out of all the victims so far, this one is most like the ones back then. They were all sliced open... their blood... everywhere."

The parallel hung in the air between them. Mona had been reluctant to draw the connection after Charlotte's initial dismissal, but now it seemed impossible to ignore.

"The markings were different back then," Mona said. "If it's the same killer, why change the signature?"

"I don't know," Charlotte admitted. "But we need to find something that will lead us to whoever is doing this. And quickly."

Bowman cleared his throat. "I'll have CSI process everything, but honestly I'm not expecting much. Scene's too clean."

Mona shuddered, pushing away the thoughts darkening the corner of her mind again. "We still need to talk to the Gooles."

"More urgently now," Charlotte agreed. "If there's a connection between these victims and that church, we need to know what it is. Not to mention Kayleigh is not out of the woods."

Mona checked her phone for the time. It was closing in on eleven. "It's late."

"I know," Charlotte replied. "Let's swing by Kayleigh's place one more time then meet with the Gooles first thing in the morning. In the meantime, I'll contact my old partner. Maybe he can pull my old case files."

"I'll finish up here," Bowman said. "You two go ahead."

As they walked back to the car, Mona pushed away the dark thoughts threatening the edges of her consciousness. The town was becoming another bloodbath. They'd been able to reasonably contain the story before now. What would happen when word got out? Last time the FBI had gotten involved. And it had almost cost them everything. They couldn't afford to let this go on much longer.

"You really think your old case might be able to help?" Mona asked once they were back in the car.

Charlotte buckled her seat belt, wincing slightly as the movement pulled at her injured ribs. "I dismissed the idea too easily," she admitted. "I thought there was no way they could be intertwined when it was staring me in the face the entire time. I didn't *want* to think they could be. This case, I've never been able to get past it. I thought maybe I could just forget it. You don't know what it feels like to have the case of the century hanging over your head."

"But you got past it," Mona said.

"Only because I got lucky. I had a few other high-profile cases early in my career. And thankfully they overshadowed this one."

Mona might not know what it was like to be part of something so high-profile that had never been solved, but being the daughter of a serial killer had come with its own set of challenges. Challenges that she was sure would follow her through the rest of her life, no matter how many wins she had.

Charlotte paused, looking at her. "Are you okay?"

"Of course," Mona said too quickly. "I'm just... tired."

"Mona."

"Really," she lied. "I'm fine. I just... I can't let this happen again. Not after Robin."

Charlotte nodded. "I understand. Which is what makes this so strange. In Chicago, all five victims were killed at once, in the same location. Here, they're being picked off one by one. Different methods, different locations." She stared out the windshield. "And the burns don't match."

"Could it be a copycat?" Mona suggested. "Or someone inspired by the original killings?"

"Maybe. Or maybe it's the same killer, evolved. Twenty-five years is a long time to perfect your technique."

Mona started the car, her mind racing. "If they are connected, that at least gives us another lead."

"I'll talk to Dale about putting together a witness list from the original case," Charlotte said as her phone buzzed. She furrowed her brow as she checked the message. "It's Roger."

"Guess he's more than happy to help," Mona suggested, but either it went over Charlotte's head or she was intentionally ignoring Mona's prodding. "Well? What does he say?"

"Symbol is a match. He sent back the entire sequence. The one on Justine translates roughly to *sacrifice* or *offering* on its own." Charlotte looked up, her expression grim.

There was no longer any doubt. The killer was following the pattern exactly. But without the victims' cell phones, there was no way to track their digital footprints to find any commonalities.

Mona pulled away from the restaurant, the image of Justine Mercer's severed throat burned into her mind. Whatever they were dealing with, it went beyond simple murder. There was a specific purpose here.

And they were running out of time to decipher it.

TWENTY

Charlotte's ankle throbbed with each step as they approached the Goole property. She hadn't slept well, and the injuries had made her feel stiff and old. The painkillers had worn off faster than she'd anticipated, leaving her with a dull, persistent ache that traveled up her leg with every movement. She wouldn't admit it to Mona, but tackling Terry Barker had cost her more than she'd expected.

After discovering Justine, she and Mona had agreed to get some rest before starting again in the morning. They still had to investigate the Goole property based on Terry Barker's tip, but at the same time, Charlotte didn't want to waste any time on her original investigation. She had left a late-night message with Dale asking him to give her a call back as soon as possible. And because she hadn't slept well, Charlotte had already been awake and ready by the time Mona had shown up to drive them out to the Goole property.

Thankfully, Mona hadn't said anything else about Charlotte's injuries and she hoped to keep it that way. She didn't want to be the cause of yet *another* investigation not getting off the ground.

However, Mona had arrived with news that forensics had come back with the only prints on the knife that killed Justine being her own. Someone was going to a lot of trouble to stage these killings, but they were only doing a passable job at it. That told Charlotte whoever was doing this didn't have a lot of experience with this kind of thing. They were determined, effective, but not very knowledgeable. It wasn't much, but it was something to go on at least.

The Circle of the Sacred Grove sat at the end of a long gravel driveway, surrounded by towering oak trees. The church itself was a modest white clapboard building with a small steeple, the kind you might find in any rural American town. Behind it stood a larger two-story farmhouse, presumably the Gooles' residence.

What struck Charlotte immediately was how ordinary it all appeared. She'd half expected something more dramatic based on Mrs. Carter's descriptions—perhaps stone gargoyles or ominous fencing. Instead, it looked like a typical country church, complete with well-tended flower beds and a hand-painted sign welcoming visitors.

"Doesn't exactly scream 'cult headquarters,' does it?" Charlotte murmured.

Mona didn't respond immediately. Her attention seemed elsewhere, her eyes distant as they had been since they left the crime scene. Finally, she said, "The most dangerous places rarely advertise themselves as such."

As they approached the house, the front door opened before they could knock. A tall man with silver-streaked dark hair stood in the doorway, regarding them with calm interest. Despite being in his sixties, Joseph Goole carried himself with the straight-backed confidence of a much younger man. His eyes—a striking pale blue —assessed them quickly.

"Detectives," he said, his voice smooth and resonant. "I've been expecting you."

Charlotte exchanged a quick glance with Mona. They hadn't called ahead.

"Mr. Goole?" Charlotte asked, showing her consultant's badge. "I'm Charlotte Dawes, consulting with the Oak Creek Police Department. This is Detective Mona LaSalle."

"Please, call me Joseph." He stepped aside, gesturing for them to enter. "Everyone does."

The interior of the house was as unremarkable as its exterior—comfortable but not ostentatious, with traditional furniture and family photos lining the walls. Charlotte noted several pictures of Kayleigh at various ages, often posed with Connor Peterson.

"I assume you're here about Connor," Joseph said, leading them into a sitting room. "A terrible tragedy. Our community is devastated."

"Actually," Mona said, taking a seat on an offered sofa, "we're looking for your daughter, Kayleigh. She wasn't at her apartment and no one seems to be able to reach her."

Joseph settled into an armchair across from them, folding his hands in his lap. "Kayleigh is here, safe with us. After Connor's death, she was understandably distraught. My wife and I thought it best she come home for a while."

"We'd like to speak with her," Charlotte said.

"Of course." Joseph's smile didn't reach his eyes. "Though I should warn you, she's still quite fragile. We've been praying together for strength."

He rose and disappeared down a hallway, leaving Charlotte and Mona alone. Charlotte took the opportunity to scan the room more thoroughly. Nothing seemed out of place or suspicious—family photos, religious texts on bookshelves, a cross on the wall. Normal trappings of a religious household.

"Has she been here this entire time?" Mona whispered.

"Maybe. Kids tend to go home when they get scared," Charlotte said. Though that certainly wasn't the case with Haley.

"I don't know... Something feels... off about this place. I don't like it."

Charlotte turned to her. "Off how?"

Before she could respond, Joseph returned with Kayleigh. The young woman looked markedly different from when they'd interviewed her at her apartment. Her hair was pulled back in a severe ponytail, and she wore a simple gray dress that hung loosely on her frame. Her eyes were red-rimmed but dry.

"Hello, again," Charlotte said gently. "How are you holding up?"

Kayleigh glanced briefly at her father before answering. "I'm managing, with my family's support."

Joseph placed a hand on his daughter's shoulder. "Our daughter knows that she can always come home whenever she needs support. Our children are our most important treasure."

Charlotte noticed how Kayleigh stiffened slightly at her father's touch, though her expression remained neutral. "Kayleigh, we were concerned when we couldn't find you."

"I'm sorry about that," she replied, her voice barely above a whisper. "After what happened to Connor, I just... I couldn't stay there alone."

"Understandable," Mona said. "We have some additional questions about Connor, if you're up for it."

Kayleigh nodded, taking a seat beside her father.

"We spoke with Mr. Barker. He told us you and Connor weren't getting along?"

Kayleigh stiffened again, then glanced to her father before casting her eyes down. "No, that's not true at all. Everything was good between us."

"Barker?" Joseph asked. "Terrance Barker? Why would he know anything about Kayleigh?"

Charlotte didn't want to lie, but she had seen this kind of dynamic before. It was plainly obvious Joseph Goole was the head of the household and whatever he said, went. He also more than likely expected his daughter to be completely honest with him. And if Charlotte knew anything about religious households, finding out that his daughter had been having an affair with someone while practically engaged to the man her father had set her up with would *not* go over well.

"Mr. Barker is a witness for us. He had observed Connor and Kayleigh around town." She turned back to Kayleigh before Goole could interrupt. "Do you happen to know Justine Mercer?" Charlotte asked, watching her reaction carefully.

Confusion crossed Kayleigh's face. "Justine? Of course. Why?"

Joseph's expression remained impassive. "Justine works at Billy's Diner, doesn't she? Lovely girl."

"Worked," Mona corrected. "I'm sorry to inform you but she was found dead last night."

Kayleigh's hand flew to her mouth. "She's... dead? How?"

"Murdered," Charlotte said bluntly, still watching Kayleigh's face. The shock seemed genuine.

Joseph closed his eyes briefly. "Another tragedy. This town has seen far too much death recently."

"Did you know Justine well?" Charlotte asked Kayleigh.

"Not really. We went to school together as kids, but..." She trailed off, looking down at her hands.

"But?" Mona prompted.

"She hadn't attended our services for a while. She became involved in other... pursuits," Joseph finished for her. "Though of course, that doesn't make her death any less tragic. Have you spoken to her parents?"

"She was a member of your congregation?" Charlotte asked.

He nodded. "The entire family is. I've known them for decades. This will no doubt destroy them."

"Then... both Connor Peterson and Justine Mercer were members of the church," Mona said.

Charlotte shifted her full focus to Joseph. "Mr. Goole—Joseph—did you know Mallory Wakefield as well?"

Something flickered across his face—so brief Charlotte might have missed it if she hadn't been watching closely. "Yes, I did. Her parents were also members of our congregation for many years. Before their untimely deaths."

"Can you tell us about that?" Mona asked.

"They passed away in a car accident about five years ago. After that, Mallory distanced herself from us." A note of regret entered his voice. "I tried to reach out to her, offer support, but grief affects people differently. Some turn toward faith, others away from it. However, one would think that in a time of deep pain, the young girl would have reached out to her church family for help. My wife helped nurse her as a baby. She was like a second daughter to us."

Charlotte leaned forward, ignoring the twinge in her ribs. "Mr. Goole. Surely you see the pattern here. We've had three deaths in less than a week and it just so happens to turn out that all three victims were connected to your church. Do you have any reason to believe someone would target you?"

"No, we mostly keep to ourselves," he replied. "I can't imagine anyone would be upset enough with what little we do that they'd go to this extreme."

"What do you mean by 'what little you do'?"

"Exactly that," he replied. "We hold services. Encourage study. Don't pressure anyone or get into hateful or harmful rhetoric. We have a 'live and let live' policy that we abide by."

"So you don't think another religious organization would take offense to your practices."

He sat back, crossing one leg over the other. "Well, I can't say that for sure. Of course there will always be some unspoken tension between denominations. But what reason would anyone have to begin this now? We've been part of this community for the better part of two decades."

Charlotte studied him, trying to discern if he was being truthful. There was something practiced about his responses—too smooth, too ready. Like he'd anticipated their questions.

"Kayleigh," Charlotte said, turning her attention back to the young woman, "did Connor ever mention being worried about anything? Anyone who might have wanted to harm him?"

Kayleigh shook her head, but her eyes darted briefly toward her father. "No. Everyone loved Connor."

"And did you ever hear of anyone having a problem with Mallory Wakefield or Justine? Even if it was just in passing. This could be really important, so please think."

Joseph placed a hand on his daughter's arm. "Perhaps that's

enough for today. Kayleigh is still processing her grief. And you have just introduced yet another shock to her system." He physically ushered her off the couch and back through the adjacent doorway. "Why don't we pick this up in a few more days, once we've all had a little time to process?"

Mona stood to try and stop him. "Mr. Goole—"

"As I said, call me Joseph," he replied.

"Joseph," Mona corrected. "We really don't have time to waste here. Three of your own have been killed. I would think you'd want us doing everything in our power to stop what's happening."

"Oh, I do, Detective," he said, his eyes flashing. "But my daughter's health and happiness must come first. Right now she needs time to reflect and pray. Perhaps if you leave your card, we can get in contact when we're ready to speak again."

"Sir, I must insist—"

"Detective, I believe I've made my position on this clear," he replied, his voice sharper. "Now unless you have a warrant of some kind, I'll have to kindly ask you to leave."

Mona reluctantly pulled out a card, handing it to the man.

"We'll be praying for justice, Detectives. For Connor, Mallory, and now Justine."

As he walked them to the door, Charlotte decided on one last question. "Your church, Joseph—we've heard you hold special ceremonies during solstices and equinoxes?"

He smiled thinly. "I see Mrs. Carter has been working the rumor mill again. I wouldn't call them special ceremonies. Nothing more than an acknowledgement of the changing of the seasons. Many faith traditions do."

"These services—do they involve any particular symbols or rituals?"

"Symbols are powerful tools for faith, Ms. Dawes. They help us connect to something greater than ourselves." He gestured to the painting of a large and ancient tree hanging on the wall. "But I assure you, there's nothing sinister about our worship. In fact, the lives and continued safety of all our members is our top priority. I would do anything to keep our members safe. After all, isn't that what community is all about?"

Charlotte and Mona exchanged glances.

Goole's lips formed a line, obviously upset that his rhetoric wasn't getting him anywhere. "I would also like to take this chance to remind you that freedom of religion is a protected right."

Charlotte nodded, noting he hadn't really answered her question. "Thank you for your time. We'll be in touch soon."

"My door is always open to those seeking truth," Joseph replied, his pale eyes revealing nothing.

As they walked back to the car, Charlotte felt his gaze on their backs. She resisted the urge to turn around, instead focusing on controlling her limp. Her ankle felt like it was on fire.

"Let's take a look at that 'church' before we go," she said quietly to Mona once they were out of earshot.

Mona nodded, still seeming distracted. They circled around to the white clapboard building, which stood silent and empty. The front doors were locked, but they were able to peer through the windows. The interior was simple—wooden pews facing an altar, the same image of the ancient tree on the back wall. Nothing unusual.

"Around back," Charlotte suggested.

Behind the church, the property extended into a small cemetery enclosed by a low stone wall. Neat rows of headstones stretched across well-maintained grass. Charlotte pushed open the wrought iron gate, wincing as her weight shifted onto her injured ankle, traveling up through her abdomen to her ribs.

"You okay?" Mona asked, finally seeming to notice Charlotte's discomfort.

"Just peachy," Charlotte replied, moving carefully between the graves.

Most of the headstones were fairly standard—names, dates, perhaps a brief epitaph or religious verse. But as they moved deeper into the cemetery, Mona suddenly stopped.

"Charlotte," she said, pointing to a grave. "Look at this."

Charlotte peered at the headstone Mona indicated. "Dina and Casper Wakefield."

"Mallory's parents."

Charlotte supposed it would make sense they were buried here. After all, they had belonged to this congregation. "I guess Goole wasn't lying about that part." But as she began looking around, Charlotte realized most of the graves were much older than the ones before them. Older than when Goole had relocated here from Chicago.

They moved through the cemetery methodically, examining each stone. Many were eroded, the names and dates unreadable. But there were some that were legible. "Peterson," Charlotte read off one of them.

"Here's one that says Mercer," Mona said. "Ida Mercer. Died in nineteen thirty-seven."

"Something about all this is wrong," Charlotte said. "We need to figure out just how long this 'church' has been here."

"You think it could have something to do with the deaths?" Mona asked.

"I think Joseph and Marie Goole didn't just arrive here thirty years ago to establish this church. I think we're dealing with something much older."

"Some of these families obviously have roots here."

Charlotte nodded. "Let's see what we can find out. Because we're certainly not going to get a straight answer out of anyone living in that house." A sharp pain shot through her side and she just barely stopped from wincing.

"You okay?" Mona asked.

"Don't worry about me," she said, though she was having trouble catching her breath. She paused a moment, drew a deep breath in and back out again. The pain subsided.

Mona held her gaze for a second before thankfully letting it go and heading back to the car. As they reached it, Charlotte noticed Joseph Goole still standing on the porch of his house, watching them. "Seems we're still being monitored." When she turned to

Mona, she saw a troubled look on the young detective's face. "What's wrong?"

Mona hesitated. "Him. Reminds me of my father."

Charlotte didn't push for more. John McCormick's shadow still loomed large over Mona, and Charlotte knew better than to poke at that particular wound. Instead, she said, "Let's head back." Another stitch, this one worse than before, drove itself through her side like a spike. "Actually, can you drop me off at the hotel? I have a few things I need to take care of."

"You sure?" Mona asked.

"Yeah, just for a bit. You head back and get working on this church. I'll meet up with you later."

As they drove away, Charlotte glanced in the side mirror. Joseph Goole stood at the edge of his property, watching them leave. He raised one hand in what might have been a wave but looked more like a benediction.

Or a warning.

TWENTY-ONE

"Terry Barker posted bail."

Mona looked up as she headed into the station, Bowman's words catching her off-guard.

"What?"

Her partner nodded. "Yep. Turns out that lawyer is worth his salt. Got the judge to agree to allow both Logan and Terry to be released on their own recognizance if they could put up fifty grand."

Mona shook her head in disgust. Great. That meant Barker and the other kid would probably be out of town by this afternoon.

"That was a boneheaded move," she said, sitting down at her desk.

"The DA agrees," Bowman replied, glancing over, his eyes scanning behind Mona. "Where's Dawes?"

"I dropped her back off at her hotel," Mona said. "She said she had some things she needed to catch up on." She didn't mention how she'd noticed the pain on Charlotte's face with each pothole in the road. She'd really injured herself taking down Terry Barker, but Mona knew Charlotte well enough that if she continued asking her about it, Charlotte would shut down. Mona just hoped she was taking care of herself.

Bowman scoffed. "I like her. She's got a good head on her shoulders. Wouldn't expect anything else from a Chicago cop, though."

"Yeah," Mona replied, her mind drifting again. Ever since coming back from the Goole residence-slash-church she'd had trouble keeping her mind from wandering. The fact that Mallory's parents were buried in that cemetery didn't sit well with her. So far, that meant each of the victims was connected to the Gooles in some way. And had all been members of the church at one point. Not to mention the family lines went back further than they'd expected. How long had this church been a part of Oak Creek? They'd finally found the common thread they'd been looking for.

"Hey. What do you know about the Circle of the Sacred Grove?" she asked.

"I don't know," Bowman replied, taking a bite of a sandwich that sat perched precariously on the edge of his desk. "Never heard of it."

"It's a local group that operates just outside of town," Mona replied. "Small congregation. Keeps to themselves."

"That could describe any number of organizations around here," Bowman replied, his mouth full of sandwich. "Why?"

"Because everything about these murders seems to point to them." She explained how Mallory was connected, as well as Connor and now Justine.

"You think the church is responsible for their deaths?" Bowman asked.

"Not the church, but someone *in* the church," Mona replied. "We met with the leader, Joseph Goole. And something about him just struck me the wrong way."

"How so?"

She glanced up at Bowman but decided not to get into the particulars of her own traumas. How could she explain that the man not only reminded her of her father, but almost seemed to attract a dark part of her. Ever since this case had begun, Mona had been fighting against that part of her that she knew came from her father's side. The part of her that could be capable of terrible things. The part she'd do anything to bury and hide.

But coming face-to-face with Joseph Goole had in a way almost pulled that part back to the forefront, like a magnet.

"I don't know. It's just a feeling. Probably nothing."

"Why would anyone in the church want to hurt their own parishioners?" Bowman asked.

"It isn't really even about that," Mona said. "All the targets have been young people... children of the church. It's like someone is taking out their anger on them."

"Then we need to get a record of all the church members," Bowman replied.

Mona nodded. "Charlotte and I suspect there will be two more victims. We need to find out how many more members could be targets. And I want to start talking to some of the more established members. Maybe they know more than they think they do."

"Do you really think they'll break rank?" he asked. "Those communities are tight."

"That's the million-dollar question." When they'd confronted Goole about Justine, he hadn't even seemed fazed. And he'd seemed more concerned with Mallory leaving the church than her actual death. Mona could see a situation where perhaps someone wanted her to return and she refused and perhaps things got out of hand. But Connor and Justine were enigmas. As far as she could tell, Connor had attended regularly and was even planning on being engaged to Goole's daughter. Justine... Mona needed to do a deeper dive into her backstory.

"Earle's pissed," Bowman said, swallowing. "The media got wind of Justine's death this morning. We've got incoming. They're already calling Oak Creek the town where the streets run red with blood."

"Ugh," Mona said, leaning back in her chair. This was only going to make things more complicated. And the longer they didn't have any answers, the worse things would get.

"Do you have anything on Mercer yet?" Mona asked.

"Brought the parents in first thing this morning for an interview," Bowman replied. "They're divorced but are one of those weird couples that don't act like it. I remember when my parents got divorced, they couldn't even be in the same room with each other. But these two were still acting like they were married."

"Grief does strange things to people," Mona said, going into her computer to start looking into the Gooles' church.

"I guess. Still weird to see," Bowman replied, finishing off his sandwich. "Anyway, they didn't have any leads. Didn't know of anyone who would want to hurt Justine. She still lived with her mom and had left for work just like normal. As far as the mother knew, she hadn't received any strange calls or threats. But we're checking the girl's computer now. Still no phone. Earle sent a K-9 unit out there this morning too. Waiting to hear back."

"No other evidence on the scene?" Mona asked.

"Nothing concrete," Bowman replied. "A couple of partials on the door and the dumpsters, but the odds they belong to anyone significant are low."

Mona nodded. The area was high traffic. Lots of workers in and out every day. Unless the prints had specifically been pulled from the body then they were essentially useless.

Nothing they could use. And the only connection to the victims was this "church."

But after spending a solid hour researching anything on the Circle of the Sacred Grove, Mona came up almost completely empty-handed. They had no social media presence, no website, no contact information. A full list of members was out of the question. The only evidence she could find they existed at all was the tax exemption certificate they filed with the state each year for the Gooles' property, complete with the man's signature. A property that had been purchased in the early 2000s. Before that, it had belonged to a local farming couple as part of a larger parcel. But a series of motions and rezonings in the nineties had created the new parcel, which the Gooles now owned.

Mona sat back. Did that mean the cemetery had been there

when the property was part of the farm? It had to have been as there were no records of any graves being exhumed and moved anywhere in the area in the last thirty years.

Something about this didn't make sense. And it was starting to give Mona a headache. These people lived off the grid—literally. Which meant tracking their activities was proving to be difficult.

Finally, an email popped up from Michaels, the department's primary tech guy. Anytime they had a computer that needed cracking, Michaels was the one to do it. But as Mona read through the report contained in the email, her heart sank.

"You reading this?" Bowman asked.

"Yeah," she replied. There had been nothing useful found on Justine Mercer's computer. All her social media accounts had been dragged and nothing had come back with any flags. Mona used the information in the email to look at Justine Mercer's social media accounts herself, but they were all pictures of nature. Very rarely did she ever photograph herself or anyone else. And most of the time she just reposted things she liked—very little of it was her original content.

Mona sighed. This was going to be impossible. Was this why the killer was targeting these people? Because they had little connection outside of their church? In Mona's experience, it was always easier to target those who were already isolated. There were fewer ripple effects.

This was getting them nowhere. She needed help.

Mona did a quick search and pulled up Roger's information on her computer. So far he'd been the only one who had managed to decode these symbols, and she needed some clarification. She didn't think Charlotte would mind if she gave him a call without her knowledge.

Plus, there was something *else* she wanted to discuss.

"Hello?" his velvety voice answered as Mona called his business number.

"Roger? This is Mona LaSalle. Charlotte's friend."

"Mona, yes, how are you? How goes the investigation? I texted Charlotte last night—"

"Yes, thank you for that," Mona replied. "We're still trying to piece things together. So far we haven't made much progress."

"Oh," he replied. "I'm sorry to hear that."

"I wanted to ask you more about these symbols and where they originated," Mona said.

"Of course. All the literature dates them about a thousand years ago, deep in the Welsh countryside. That part of the world was in a bit of turmoil then, and we have lots of instances of smaller religious factions like this popping up and disappearing just as quickly."

A thousand years? "I'm trying to figure out how someone from today would have even found out about them," Mona said.

"Well, if I were to venture a guess, I'd have to say the knowledge was passed down through generations. That's usually how these things propagate."

She supposed she could understand that, but at the same time, she hadn't been able to find anything on these runes when she'd first started looking. And she considered herself a savvy searcher. "But how would an obscure medieval rune make its way to twenty-first-century Chicago?"

"There would have to be some strong beliefs," he added. "Something that could withstand the erosion of time. Secrecy also would play a large part. And in fact, the secrecy itself is what may have helped it survive. It's very possible people lived with this religion for centuries in Europe before bringing it to the new world."

Her headache was getting worse. "Other than what you showed us, there haven't been any other instances of runes like this being found *anywhere* in the world?"

"Well, I can't speak to that entirely," he replied. "As permanent as we like to think things like stone carvings are, they wear away with time like everything else. It's possible other evidence could have been lost to time. Or it could have been discovered and cataloged in some other obscure volume somewhere, no one having put the pieces together yet. In fact, the only reason I knew about it was because I *happened* to read that specific book during my graduate studies. Had I not, we may not know as much as we know now."

"Is there anything that you could see that would connect Oak Creek back to the old world?" Mona asked. There had to be a reason this was happening *here*, of all places.

"Well, give me a moment," he replied. In the background she heard the shuffling of papers and the clacking of keys as he typed. "You know, let me do a little research and get back to you on that. You want more information about the town history in particular?"

"Well, we have a town historian, but I'm looking for something a little less... *biased*."

"Understood," he said with a smile in his voice. "Let me see what I can find for you."

"I really appreciate that," Mona replied.

"Of course," he replied. "Is Charlotte okay?"

Mona smiled. "She's taking a quick break. She... overextended herself yesterday while chasing down a suspect."

"Yeah. She's tenacious like that."

"You really like her, don't you?" Mona asked.

"I mean, well..."

"It's okay," Mona said. "You guys have great chemistry. I'm sorry if I'm being blunt. I get accused of that sometimes. But she lights up every time she speaks to you."

"She does?"

Mona thought back to the young man she'd met for dinner a week ago. It seemed like a lifetime now. "I know how hard it is to put yourself out there. I've been doing it myself... to varying degrees of success. But if I'd found a connection like you found with Charlotte, I don't think I'd need to be looking anymore."

"We've always been colleagues," Roger replied. "I mean... it's a professional relationship."

"I think we both know there's more beneath the surface," Mona replied.

He was silent on the other side of the phone. Mona glanced up, seeing Bowman staring at her with a curious look on his face. "I should get to work on this for you," Roger finally said.

"Just something to think about," she replied. "In the meantime, I'm going to update her on what you've given me so far. Maybe it will help us find our killer before it's too late. Thanks for your help. Speak soon." She hung up.

"What the hell was that?" Bowman asked.

"What?" she asked.

"Were you... matchmaking?"

"Nope," Mona replied innocently. "Just doing a friend a favor."

TWENTY-TWO

There was definitely something wrong. As soon as Charlotte made it back to the hotel, she'd laid down, hoping she could get the pain to subside. But it had only intensified. Finally, she'd been forced to call the hospital, and while she'd wanted to drive herself, she knew it wasn't a good idea. Instead, she'd taken a ride share—which was a hell of a lot cheaper than an ambulance *and* didn't draw any attention. The last thing she wanted was Mona getting wind of this.

They'd taken her in immediately and, based on what she'd told them, done a series of X-rays. Thankfully, because they hadn't been busy, she hadn't had to wait. The benefits of small-town care. It would have taken a full day back in Chicago.

"Mrs. Dawes," the doctor said, coming into the examination room where Charlotte had been forced to change into a smock and was now sitting on the edge of the table, holding her sore side.

"Mm-hmm," Charlotte said, sucking in as the pain shot through her again.

"It's good you decided to come in. You have two broken ribs."

"*What?*"

The doctor nodded. "I checked your chart. You were in here yesterday for a sprained ankle and jarred wrist, is that correct?"

Charlotte nodded. "And yet you neglected to tell us about the pain in your abdomen."

"It wasn't a problem yesterday," Charlotte replied. "Just a little sore."

"Probably because you have a high pain tolerance," he said. "Have you done any strenuous activity over the past twenty-four hours?"

"Define strenuous," Charlotte replied, glaring at him.

"Anything that would cause you to build up a sweat."

She pursed her lips. They'd had to examine Justine's scene, interview Goole, tramped around the cemetery and half a dozen other things. So yeah, she'd built up a sweat.

"Okay," the doctor said without waiting for a verbal answer. "I'm putting you on full bedrest for the next five to seven days. If you're feeling better—"

"I can't go on bedrest for five to seven days," Charlotte argued. "I'm in the middle of a case."

"Mrs. Dawes, you need to limit your movements for the time being and give your body a chance to heal," the doctor said, more insistent. "We can move your ribs back into place and wrap them, but until they heal, you need to not move around as much as possible."

Charlotte couldn't believe this. All she'd done was tackle the kid and she'd broken *two* ribs? What was she, made of glass? And now she was supposed to just sit around and wait to get better while a killer was out there murdering at random?

"Can't you give me something to... I dunno, make it heal faster?"

He cocked his head at her with a rueful smile. "Unfortunately, the only treatment is time and rest. Those are the two best things you can do right now. Otherwise, you risk injuring yourself further. Those sharp pains you're feeling? That's the bone pressing into organs it shouldn't be."

That didn't sound good.

"What about painkillers?" Charlotte asked.

"We can up the dosage from what you're taking for the ankle," he said. "Which, I might add, looks more swollen than it did in your initial evaluation. You need to stay off it too. I see in your file it says you're retired, but you're working with the local police?"

She nodded. "Consulting on a case."

He closed the file. "Well, for the next few weeks, you'll need to do your consulting from the couch."

"I can't just quit," Charlotte shot back. "I'm not going to sit around—"

"Mrs. Dawes, if you do not take this seriously, there is a very high chance you will re-injure yourself. You could even puncture a vital organ, in which case you will bleed out within minutes. I don't think I need to reiterate how serious this is."

Charlotte huffed, glancing at the ceiling. "Fine. Do what you can."

He nodded. "We'll get you sorted as quickly as we can. And I'll go ahead and refill your prescription for the time being. Where are you staying?"

"At the Blue Bird Inn."

"You'd be best heading back home," he replied. "Where you can relax. Do you have someone who can assist you for the next few weeks? A family member?"

"I'll take care of it," Charlotte grumbled. "Just get me out of this place."

The doctor seemed to accept he'd pushed her as far as he dared. He nodded and excused himself with a promise they would wrap her up and have her out as soon as they could.

She couldn't believe this. Sidelined by her own failing body *again*. This was her hands all over again. She was in the middle of an investigation, and she was just supposed to quit? And what? Go back home and lay on the couch while Givens came over and fed her soup?

No way. Not happening.

She'd been in tougher scrapes before and had come out okay. But she'd been a younger woman then—someone who wasn't saddled with a broken old body that seemed to betray her at every turn.

Broken ribs or not, she wasn't going to let this stop her from working on this case. This was the first time she'd actually felt like herself in *months*. And if she had to endure a little pain to keep that feeling, then that's what she'd do.

Two hours and a careful wrap job later, Charlotte got back out of the ride share vehicle. While she'd told the doctor she was headed back to the hotel and would return home within the day, she instructed the ride share driver to take her to the only place that mattered right now: the Oak Creek Police Station.

"Oh, hey," Mona said, looking up as Charlotte entered. Thanks to the painkillers, the sharp pain in her side had subsided and she barely even felt the soreness in her ankle anymore. "Everything okay?"

Charlotte nodded. "Yep. Just had to take care of some business. Figured it was easier for me to come back over here to you than for you to come get me again." She nodded to Bowman who gave her a quick salute. "Made any progress?"

As Mona filled her in on what little she'd managed to find on Justine Mercer and the Circle of the Sacred Grove, Charlotte scrutinized how she was feeling. The pain wasn't too bad right now—she could manage this. Doctors. Always assuming the worst. He was probably just being paranoid because he didn't want to get sued. But the reality was she was more or less okay. She'd just be careful over the next week or so. No more chasing down suspects on foot.

"That's... not much," Charlotte said after Mona had finished.

"No, Justine looks like a dead end. But we did manage to make a little progress on Mallory Wakefield. It seems she left the church years ago, after her parents died in that accident. And it took some scouring, but there were some old social media posts from her about the 'evils' of the Sanctuary. Some of that could have been nothing but misplaced anger. But then again..."

"Can I see the posts?" Charlotte asked.

"Sure," Bowman said and pulled up the files on his computer. She and Mona went over to his desk, Charlotte monitoring her pain as they did.

"From what we've been able to gather, she used to run gaming livestreams as a means of income. Most have nothing to do with anything in her real life, but there were a few. This was the first," Bowman said. He pulled up a grainy video of a younger Mallory Wakefield, probably only seventeen or eighteen. Her eyes were streaked with mascara.

"Sorry, guys, I can't do a livestream tonight," she said, wiping her eyes. "*Apparently*, WoW is the land of the devil." She exhaled. "I'll never understand what my parents saw in that *cult*. It's just a bunch of bored, middle-aged people, reciting ancient languages out in the middle of the woods and pretending like it means something. They act like it's the end of the world if they don't *give thanks*. I was just coming back from the grocery store and I ran into my old pastor. And it was like nothing had even happened. He wanted to know when I was coming back to the church and it took everything I had not to spit in his face. I mean, my parents haven't been dead a month and he's already pretending like everything is normal. There's something wrong with those people."

"Huh," Charlotte said. It wasn't uncommon for children to rebel against religion, especially in times of trauma. Though she would have thought Goole would be more open and empathetic towards someone who'd just lost both her parents. "Give thanks."

"Yep," Bowman said. "And here's another one."

He clicked over to a second video, this one from a few years later where Mallory was closer in age to when she'd died. "Guys, I swear I need to get out of this town," she said. "I can't wait until I have enough money to get out on my own. The rest of them may be happy with how things are, but I'm tired of people looking over my shoulder all the time."

"That one obviously doesn't mention the church," Mona said, "but we think that's the implication. We also think people are encouraged not to talk about the Circle, which is why we can't find anything."

"It's more like a secret society than a true religion," Charlotte said. "You know, this is the second time someone has mentioned odd ceremonies."

"You're thinking back to Terry Barker."

Charlotte nodded. "And while he had a good motive to lie, I'm more inclined to believe Mallory."

"Unfortunately," Mona replied, "that's about all we have." Charlotte caught Bowman staring at her, but he averted his gaze as soon as she saw him. She furrowed his brow.

"There was one other thing, though," Mona said, drawing Charlotte's attention again. "I gave Roger a call."

A very strange sensation bloomed in Charlotte's chest, and for a hot second, she thought it was the pain from her ribs coming back. But then she realized it wasn't that at all. It was *jealousy*. "Oh?"

"I thought he might be able to help give us some context on why these symbols are showing up now... here. It feels deliberate to me. I hope you don't mind."

"Why would I mind?" Charlotte asked, hearing the distance in her own voice and hating it.

"Well, because he's your contact, not mine," Mona replied. "But I wasn't sure how long you'd be... occupied and it was—"

"No, it's fine," Charlotte clipped. "What did he say?"

"Just gave us some insight on how this belief system or religion or whatever it is may have made its way across the ocean a couple hundred years ago. I have him looking more in-depth into Oak Creek, to see if we can't draw any parallels."

"Didn't want to go back to Mrs. Carter, huh?"

Mona gave her a tense smile. "She's nice enough, but I think this is a better plan. In the meantime, we're trying to track down all the members of the Circle of the Sacred Grove. Partially because we believe the next two victims will come from there, and also because we're not entirely convinced someone *within* the church isn't doing this."

"Killing their own members?" Charlotte asked.

"You saw how cagey Goole was when we tried to speak to him," Mona countered. "He's hiding something. In fact, he's hiding everything. We haven't even figured out exactly *who* is a member of the church. Except for the families of the victims, of course."

Charlotte thought back through the pain to the Goole family. "Did you look into the Gooles any further?"

"After his performance? You bet we did. But the information on them is scarce. We got more from Mrs. Carter than I can find online. Which is intentional... I think. Little to no modern-day presence."

"And yet they're not the types to be put off by technology," Charlotte replied. "Goole himself was wearing a Movado. It's not a Rolex, but it's not a cheap watch either. What about Kayleigh? Anything on her social media?"

"We suspect she may have other accounts under different names," Mona replied. "Her 'official' account is similar to Connor's and Justine's. Landscapes, nature, very tame."

"Speaking of which, did you see how different she was in the presence of her parents?" Charlotte almost couldn't believe it had been the same girl. She'd been so subdued... almost subservient.

Mona nodded. "I'm sure that's the product of growing up in a strict religious home. Also probably why she sought out Terry Barker in favor of Connor Peterson."

Charlotte sat thinking for a moment. She'd been pondering this all day, even through the examinations. Everything pointed back to the Gooles and the church, but it still didn't make sense. What incentive would they have to kill anyone, especially members of their own congregation?

"What about your old case files?" Mona asked as the conversation between them had fallen into a lull. "Has there been any development?"

She hadn't heard from Dale yet, which meant he probably wasn't taking this as seriously as he should. She would need to reiterate to him how time-sensitive this was. "I'm working on it. But right now I think we should focus on Goole. He's the common point here."

"We already went to his house. I don't think he's going to give us much more," Mona replied, moving her seat back over to her desk. "Especially not a list of his members."

"Maybe not. But you know where we could find the list?" Charlotte asked. "*Inside* the church itself. There have to be records somewhere."

"Can't get a warrant," Mona said. "We don't have anything to base a search on. I doubt Goole will just let us stroll through the place."

"You're not wrong," Charlotte replied. "Goole is a bully. He may not look like one on the outside, but I can guarantee he's the kind of man who is used to getting what he wants and who will push others around to do so."

"Then what do we do?" Mona asked.

Charlotte pushed herself back up, ignoring the pain in her body as she did so. "Let's go out for a drive."

"To the church?" Mona asked.

Charlotte shrugged. "Who knows? Maybe they accidentally left a door unlocked. It would be irresponsible of us not to double-check and make sure their building is secure."

The hint of a smile appeared on Mona's face. "Is that legal?"

Charlotte shrugged. "I don't recall any *no trespassing* signs." She checked her watch. "Plus, it's getting dark. Less chance of being seen."

Bowman snorted a laugh but kept his head down.

"Okay," Mona replied. "I'm game if you are." She paused. "You're okay to..."

"Of course," Charlotte replied. "Completely fine." Even though the doctor's words echoed in her head, she pushed them away. He was just being overly cautious. Plus, what was strenuous about walking around an old building in the evening?

"I'll go get the car," Mona said, hopping up.

Charlotte moved to follow. "Dawes," Bowman said, causing her to pause.

She let out a breath. "If you're going to lecture me on the legality of searching a sealed property—"

"No," he replied. "In fact, I think it's a good idea."

"Then what?" she asked, looking after Mona who was already out the door.

"LaSalle is a sweet kid. And she looks up to you. You know she'd never do anything to undermine you."

Charlotte screwed up her features.

"That call? To your contact? She's trying to get you set up with him. She thinks you're too lonely."

"That's preposterous," Charlotte said too quickly. It was too defensive and she knew it.

Bowman smiled. "Yeah. Anyway. She's just trying to watch out for you. Don't hold it against her."

Charlotte nodded. "Message received. Thanks." She shouldn't have gone cold when Mona mentioned calling Roger. And if it had been anyone else, she probably wouldn't have. She might be forced to admit she felt more for the man than she purported. But things like that could wait until later.

Because right now all that mattered was finding this killer before they found another body.

TWENTY-THREE

A full moon had settled over the church property by the time they arrived, casting long shadows across the small cemetery they'd explored earlier. Mona parked a quarter mile down the road, tucking her car behind a stand of trees where it wouldn't be visible from the main driveway. The precaution felt excessive—there had been no vehicles at the Goole residence when they'd driven past—but instinct told her to be cautious.

Charlotte moved with careful deliberation as they made their way toward the white clapboard building, her gait betraying her injuries despite her obvious efforts to conceal them. Mona slowed her pace, pretending to scan their surroundings while giving Charlotte time to keep up. Internally, she was screaming that this was a bad idea. Charlotte was injured whether she wanted to admit it or not. Which meant if they got in a bind, they might not be able to get back out quickly. She just hoped Charlotte knew what she was doing.

"Stay low," Mona whispered as they approached the rear of the church. The building's silhouette was stark against the darkening sky, its steeple a sharp point piercing the gathering dusk. No lights shone from within, and the property appeared deserted.

The silence felt wrong somehow—too complete, as if the

normal sounds of evening had been deliberately muted. No crickets chirped, no nocturnal birds called. Even the wind seemed to hold its breath. Mona felt her pulse quicken, that familiar hyper-awareness setting in as her senses cataloged every detail of their surroundings.

She circled the building, testing each window and door. The front entrance was securely locked, but a side door near the rear yielded slightly when she applied pressure. The wood around the lock appeared weathered, weakened by years of exposure to the elements.

"This one," she murmured to Charlotte, who stood watch at the corner of the building.

Charlotte nodded, joining her at the door. "Not exactly a security-conscious congregation," she observed quietly.

Mona worked the edge of her ID card into the gap between door and frame, feeling for the latch. It took only moments before the lock surrendered with a soft click. She paused, listening for any response from within, but the church remained silent.

"After you," she whispered, holding the door open just enough for Charlotte to slip through. The older woman moved with surprising stealth despite her injuries, and Mona followed, easing the door closed behind them.

The interior was dim, illuminated only by what little moonlight filtered through the stained-glass windows. Mona clicked on her small flashlight, keeping the beam pointed downward to minimize the risk of it being seen from outside. The sanctuary stretched before them—rows of wooden pews facing a simple altar. A large wooden cross dominated the wall behind the pulpit.

Perfectly ordinary. Perfectly innocent.

Except it wasn't.

The air inside felt heavy, charged with something Mona couldn't quite name. The hair on her arms stood on end as they moved deeper into the sanctuary. She swept her light across the floor, noting the well-worn carpet runner down the center aisle, the hymnals neatly arranged in their holders.

Charlotte moved toward the altar, her fingers trailing lightly over the back of the last pew. "Let's check the offices," she suggested, voice barely audible. "That's the most likely location of the list."

They found a narrow hallway behind the pulpit that led to several small rooms. The first appeared to be a simple storage area, containing folding chairs and tables. The second was a small kitchen, its counters clean and bare. The third—locked.

Mona worked the lock again, this time with greater difficulty. When the door finally opened, she stepped into what was clearly Joseph Goole's office. A large desk dominated the space, its surface meticulously organized. Bookshelves lined the walls, filled with religious texts and reference materials.

Charlotte moved immediately to the desk, carefully opening drawers while Mona examined the bookshelves. Most contained expected titles—religious commentaries, theological works, church management guides. But on the bottom shelf, partially hidden behind a row of identical black binders, she found something unexpected.

A thin volume bound in worn leather, its spine unmarked. She pulled it free, opening it carefully.

The pages were covered with handwritten text in faded ink, interspersed with drawings—intricate symbols and diagrams. The text was in a language she didn't recognize and none of the symbols matched the ones they'd seen on the bodies, but they seemed to be of similar design. However, there was one symbol that was more familiar than the others. And it took Mona a few seconds to realize where she'd seen it before.

"Charlotte," she whispered, turning to show her the book.

"Find something?"

"Recognize this?" Mona asked, pointing at the small symbol amongst the others. "It's the same one that was on the necklace Mrs. Peterson wore."

Charlotte pulled out her phone, snapping a series of pictures. "I want Roger to take a look at these." She tried texting them, but found she was only at one bar, and the texts failed to go through. It seemed the rural wilds had both their benefits *and* drawbacks.

"None of these matches the ones on the bodies," Mona said. "They're all different."

"But they're close," Charlotte said. "That's what matters. It's obviously the same written language. Which means Goole or one of his followers has *something* to do with this. Any luck on finding a list of members?"

"Nothing yet," Mona said, working her way through the shelves. "Nothing in the desk?"

"Everything is locked," Charlotte replied.

Next to one of the half bookcases sat a stack of file folders. Mona started going through them one by one, but they were mostly financial statements or property records.

"Wait a second," Mona whispered as she pulled out a sheet from the list.

"What is it?" Charlotte asked.

"I think it's a dues list. See here: *Peterson, twenty-six hundred. Mercer, twenty-six hundred. Waterson, eleven hundred. Castillo, two twenty.* Etc."

"Dues?" Charlotte asked. "I thought the church operated on tithes."

"Most do," Mona replied. "But this looks more like what you'd find at a country club than a church.

"Is this... *monthly?*" Charlotte asked.

Mona checked the date at the top. "Looks like it." If she added up all the numbers, it meant the church was getting over thirty thousand dollars in "dues" per month.

"What are they doing with all that cash?" Charlotte asked. "Clearly they're not putting it back into the facilities." The building they were in wasn't rundown by any means, but it was clear it hadn't been updated in a while. And the Goole family lived in a modest house. This was mansion money.

"No, but look at this. *Nathaniel Bradshaw, negative twelve thousand.* Looks like he hasn't paid in over nine months."

"Difference of opinion on how things are being done maybe?"

"Or maybe he's trying to leave and isn't being allowed," Mona suggested. "What if he's being pressured... or even blackmailed?"

"Are you thinking it might speak to motive?" Charlotte asked. "It's a long way from blackmail to murder."

"Still... might be worth a look." Mona caught a flicker of movement through the window—headlights sweeping across the property as a vehicle approached.

"Someone's coming," she hissed, quickly returning everything back where they found it, save the dues document.

They doused their flashlights, plunging the office back into darkness as they listened to the sound of car doors slamming, followed by voices—men's voices, their tone urgent.

Mona peered through the blinds, her breath catching as she spotted two figures moving toward the church. Even in the dim light, the shotguns they carried were unmistakable. They must have tripped a silent alarm somewhere without realizing it.

"Armed company," she whispered, already calculating their options. "Back door."

They retraced their steps through the hallway, moving as quietly as possible. Charlotte winced as she bumped against a folding chair in the storage room, the metal legs scraping briefly against the floor.

The sound was barely audible, but in the silence of the church, it might as well have been a gunshot.

"Did you hear that?" a voice called from the front of the building. "Someone's inside!"

Mona grabbed Charlotte's arm, pulling her toward the rear exit they'd used to enter. They slipped outside just as the beam of a flashlight swept through the hallway behind them.

"This way," Mona urged, leading them toward the tree line beyond the cemetery. The woods would provide cover, assuming they could reach them before being spotted.

They moved as quickly as Charlotte's injuries would allow,

keeping low as they crossed the open ground. Behind them, the church door banged open.

"Hey! Stop right there!"

The command was punctuated by the distinctive sound of a shotgun being racked.

Mona glanced back, catching sight of two men silhouetted in the doorway. One raised his shotgun, pointing it in their direction.

"Go," she urged Charlotte, giving her a push toward the trees as she drew her service weapon. "I'll cover you."

Charlotte hesitated for only a moment before moving, her breathing labored as she pushed herself toward the safety of the woods. Mona followed, keeping herself between Charlotte and their pursuers.

The first shot came as they reached the tree line—a warning, fired high above their heads. The blast echoed across the property, scattering birds from nearby trees.

"Next one won't miss!" one of the men shouted.

Once inside the cover of the woods, Mona pulled Charlotte deeper into the underbrush, finding a hollow behind a fallen log where they could catch their breath. Charlotte slumped against the decaying wood, one hand pressed to her side, her face contorted with pain.

"You should have told me how badly you were injured," Mona whispered, the concern evident in her voice despite her efforts to remain calm.

"I'm fine," Charlotte insisted, though her pallor suggested otherwise. "Just need a minute."

Mona wasn't convinced, but the sound of the men crashing through the underbrush behind them demanded her attention. She peered over the log, tracking their pursuers by the beams of their flashlights.

"They're splitting up," she reported quietly. "Trying to flank us."

Charlotte straightened, her jaw set with determination despite the pain evident in her eyes. "We need to keep moving."

"Not yet," Mona cautioned, placing a restraining hand on Charlotte's arm. "Wait until they pass."

They huddled in silence as one of the men approached their position, his flashlight beam sweeping back and forth across the forest floor. Mona held her breath, her hand resting on her service weapon. She wouldn't fire unless absolutely necessary—the situation was complicated enough without adding a shooting to the mix —but she wouldn't hesitate to defend them if it came to that.

The man paused, his light illuminating a patch of ground just yards from their hiding place. For a moment, Mona thought they'd been spotted. But then the light moved on, and the man continued past their position.

"That was Peterson," Mona whispered once he was out of earshot. "Connor's father."

Charlotte's eyes widened slightly. "You're sure?"

Mona nodded. The brief glimpse she'd caught of his face had been enough to confirm it. She recognized him from the pictures that had decorated Connor's home. Connor's father, armed and hunting for intruders on church property late at night. The implications were troubling.

They waited until both men had moved deeper into the woods before cautiously emerging from their hiding place. Charlotte moved with visible difficulty, her breathing shallow and controlled.

"We need to circle back to the car," Mona said, orienting herself in the darkness. "Can you make it?"

Charlotte nodded, her face drawn in pain. "Of course I can. Lead the way."

Mona took the lead, heading deeper into the woods away from the men and in the general direction of their car. The brush wasn't thick, but they had to step carefully not to make any sounds. Every foot they put between themselves and those guns was a welcome reprieve.

Finally, Mona realized they were on an old trail that cut through the woods but wasn't often used based on how little the path had been worn. But if she squinted in the moonlight, it was easy to see how it cut straight through. And given Charlotte's condition, it was easier to stay on this than try to make their way through the underbrush.

As they continued on, the trail opened into a small clearing. And even though it had been dark in the woods, the clearing was fully illuminated by the moon, almost as if it were being bathed in daylight.

And there, in the middle of the clearing, was a large stone altar, ancient and weathered. Its surface was stained dark, the discoloration visible even in the limited light.

Mona approached cautiously, Charlotte following close behind. The altar stone was massive, at least four feet high and six feet long, carved from a single piece of granite. Its surface was worn smooth by time and use, with shallow channels carved into the stone that led to a collection basin at one end.

But it was what lay on the altar that made Mona's blood run cold. Fresh blood, still glistening wet in the moonlight, pooled in the central depression of the stone.

"That's recent," Charlotte whispered, leaning closer to examine the stain. "Very recent."

Mona scanned the clearing, taking in details with practiced efficiency. The ground around the altar had been cleared of vegetation, the earth packed smooth by frequent use. Melted wax from countless candles clung to the base of the stone. As Mona looked closer, she realized the stone held symbols carved deep into its side. The first was the same symbol that had been found on Mallory Wakefield's arm.

"Hey, look," Mona murmured.

Charlotte approached, her breathing heavy in the still air.

Mona nodded. "There are others." She recognized the symbol found on Justine Mercer. As well as the one found on Connor Peterson's arm. And strangely, another of the symbols matched the one his mother wore around her neck.

A twig snapped somewhere behind them, the sound unnaturally loud in the stillness of the clearing. Mona turned, weapon half-drawn, only to find the clearing empty save for themselves.

"We need to document this," Mona said, already reaching for her phone.

"Quickly," Charlotte agreed, her voice tight with pain. "I don't think our friends have given up the search."

Mona took several photos, making sure to capture the altar from multiple angles, the blood, and the carved symbols. As she worked, Charlotte moved around the perimeter of the clearing, examining the arrangement of candles and other items placed around the altar.

This was it. This was the evidence they'd been looking for. All five symbols Roger had provided to them had been carved into the altar, and not recently. This place... It was ancient. And given there was fresh blood on the scene—the implication was clear.

Mona finished taking pictures just as the sound of voices reached them—Peterson and his companion, returning from deeper in the woods.

"Time to go," she whispered, helping Charlotte to her feet.

They retreated from the clearing, moving as quietly as possible through the underbrush. Charlotte leaned heavily against Mona now, her earlier determination giving way to exhaustion and pain.

"Just a little further," Mona encouraged, supporting more of Charlotte's weight as they made their way back toward the road. "Car's not far now."

But as they navigated through the darkness, Mona couldn't shake the image of the bloodstained altar from her mind. Whatever was happening at the Circle of the Sacred Grove went far beyond unorthodox religious practices. They'd stumbled onto something ancient and bloody—a ritual that had already claimed three lives.

And as far as she was concerned, this was enough to nail Goole to the wall for good.

TWENTY-FOUR

By the time they made it back to the station, the pain in Charlotte's side had subsided. She was sure crouching and running through the woods hadn't been what the doctor meant when he'd told her to take it easy, and her slowness had nearly cost them their lives out there.

But none of that mattered now. Now they finally had the evidence they needed to get some real answers. Fresh blood on an altar that was either on or adjacent to Goole's property was damning. But it wasn't a slam dunk. But Charlotte could almost feel Mallory Wakefield reaching up from beyond the grave to guide them in the right direction. She'd been right about the ritual, now all they needed to do was figure out why.

Charlotte also had to consider that Goole himself might not be involved. They had the list of members now, which would require a deep dive to figure out who might have motive to start killing off members of their own congregation. But first they needed to start with Goole.

Despite multiple protests, Mona convinced Charlotte that she needed to head back for some rest. She said she and Bowman would take care of getting the warrants and convincing Earle that

Goole was at least a person of interest that should be brought in for questioning.

Charlotte had wanted to argue, but she knew she'd already pushed herself too far. She needed to at least get a good night's sleep before tackling what would be a difficult day ahead.

After Mona dropped her back off, Charlotte had taken a good ten minutes getting up to her room. Once she no longer needed to pretend, she found the pain was actually quite substantial. She wasn't sure how much longer she could keep this up, no matter how badly she wanted to.

In her room, she tossed back a couple more painkillers before limping her way to the bed and slowly lowering herself onto it. She pushed off one boot with her foot but the other was stuck and required more force for it to come off. As it did, she pulled back her sock to reveal her ankle had swollen yet again, the skin red and angry. Charlotte sighed and laid back on the bed, thankful not to be moving any longer. She knew she smelled of dirt and woods, but for the moment she couldn't move, much less take a shower.

She just needed to focus on her breathing.

Her eyes snapped open to find light streaming through her window.

"Christ," she said, rolling over to pick up her phone, but it was dead. She'd fallen asleep and had forgotten to charge it. Charlotte fumbled for the cord through gritted teeth, finally plugging it back up. The clock beside her bed showed 6:41 on the display.

She'd been asleep for nearly ten hours.

Pushing herself up, Charlotte held back a yelp from her body's protests. She was sore all over, mostly in her side which was practically throbbing. Her ankle actually looked slightly better, probably because she'd been off it for a considerable amount of time. It seemed like it was taking her phone forever to charge enough that she could open the damn thing. What if she'd missed a call from Mona? Did they already have Goole in custody?

Finally, the screen connected and the phone sprung to life.

Charlotte scanned through her emails finding nothing of note, then her messages and voicemails, but there was nothing from Mona.

She wouldn't leave Charlotte out of the operation... right?

Then she remembered what Bowman had said. Mona was looking out for Charlotte, and despite her best efforts, Charlotte had only been able to barely conceal her injuries. Mona wasn't stupid, and it had probably only been her respect for Charlotte that she hadn't asked about her injuries.

Still... Charlotte could see Mona thinking she couldn't handle a raid on the Goole house this morning. And there was part of Charlotte that didn't disagree with that assessment.

Carefully, she peeled off the clothes she'd accidentally slept in and headed for a shower. She unwrapped the bandages that held her ribs tight to find the area purple with bruises all over, signs of massive internal damage. But she was still breathing. And as far as Charlotte could tell, she hadn't critically injured herself yet. But she couldn't even touch the area without sending shockwaves of pain through the rest of her body.

Of everything, her wrist was the injury that hurt the least, thankfully. That meant she could still drive herself around, which would probably be necessary this morning. She didn't want to keep relying on ride shares or Mona's kindness to get her from place to place.

An excruciating and lengthy shower later, Charlotte took three times as long as usual to get dressed. She didn't bother drying her hair other than a towel dry as the jerky movements only made her ribs worse. She was doing well to get her clothes on, and despite the complaints from her ankle, she pulled her boots back on again. And thanks to how long it had taken her to shower, her phone was completely charged by the time she was done.

Even though it was still before eight, she called Mona anyway just to get an update to the situation.

"You've reached Detective Mona LaSalle with the Oak Creek—"

Charlotte hung up, shooting her a text instead. There was no way Mona was asleep. When she'd left her, she'd been heading back into the station to get the paperwork running on Goole and his property. They needed to get back out there before the blood on that altar "accidentally" got washed away. There was no telling who it could have belonged to: one of their existing victims? Justine Mercer seemed like the most likely, but it didn't make much sense. She had obviously been killed in the parking lot behind the restaurant. Someone would have had to collect her blood and transported it to the altar.

The other possibility was there was a fourth victim they hadn't found yet. Someone who had been killed on the altar itself. A blood and DNA analysis would answer that question relatively quickly.

Charlotte grabbed her bottle of painkillers and threw back three more, which was higher than the recommended dosage, but the recommended dosage assumed you'd be sitting on your ass all day, not out hunting a killer. Plus, the more she moved around, the better she felt. If she just stayed in bed all day, she'd be too sore to even stand.

Moving deliberately and carefully, Charlotte made her way back down to the lobby and grabbed something quick from the meager hotel breakfast before heading out to her car. Taking a deep breath, she slipped inside and sat down, holding herself tight against the pain. It was manageable... for now. She promised herself if it got worse, she'd pull back, do as the doctor suggested. But as long as she was able to move around without too much pain, she didn't see any reason why she couldn't still assist on this investigation.

As she drove, Charlotte found herself thinking of Roger. Not just because she wondered if he'd found anything in his research, but because she'd forgotten how much she enjoyed being around him. It hadn't really registered when she was younger, probably because she was so career focused that she hadn't paid much attention, but they had always gotten along. And she had to admit she'd really looked forward to introducing him to Mona. She hated to admit it, but Mona was right; Charlotte did have something of a crush on him. She always had, but because she'd been married to Ronson at the time she hadn't even entertained the possibility. Though... maybe once all this was over...

Charlotte arrived at the station to find Mona's vehicle missing. She debated going in and confronting Earle, but he'd only confirm what she already knew—that Mona and Bowman had gone after Goole first thing this morning. She backed out of the lot again and headed out toward Goole's place.

But before she even arrived, she saw the flashing lights surrounding the property. There were three patrol cars already on the scene, along with Whittle's vehicle and a CSI van. Mona's vehicle sat up in front of the church building, just adjacent to the Gooles' home.

The officer directing traffic around the property tried to stop Charlotte until he recognized her, then waved her through to the scene. She pulled up behind Mona's car and stepped out, just as Mona and Bowman emerged from the Goole home with Joseph Goole in custody.

"Do you understand these rights as we've read them to you?" Mona was asking the man as Charlotte made her way up to the house.

"Of course, Detective. I'm willing to cooperate completely. But I want to reiterate you are making a mistake."

"We'll make a note of that," Bowman said, directing Goole to a nearby patrol car where he helped him into the back, making sure he didn't hit his head.

"Oh," Mona said as soon as she saw Charlotte. She trotted over to meet her. "Good morning. You should have called me; I would have come and picked you up."

Charlotte waved her off, not bothering to tell her she tried calling already. "You're busy. I assume you had no problem with the warrant?"

"Judge signed it at six this morning. I called you, but it went straight to voicemail."

"Phone died," Charlotte replied. "Any trouble?"

"He's been perfectly cooperative," Mona said. "Says he knows nothing about blood on the altar in the woods. That it's just an old relic."

"The one that just happens to sit behind his church, *right*," Charlotte said.

"Are you... feeling okay this morning?" Mona asked.

"A little sore, but I'll be okay," Charlotte replied. "What's the situation? Need me to do anything?"

Mona shook her head. "Whittle and his team are over at the altar. I was just about to speak with Mrs. Goole and Kayleigh again. And we need to search the home."

"Great," Charlotte replied. "Let's get on it. Time's wasting." Mona nodded and they headed back to the front door. "Did you hear back from Roger?"

"I figured he'd call you before me," Mona replied. "We've been swamped with this. And I didn't... I didn't want to overstep again."

Charlotte stopped her with a hand on her shoulder. "You didn't overstep. Bowman told me what you did. I appreciate it. But I'm not ready to start dating yet. Not while I've got this going on."

"You might not be ready, but he is," Mona said. "And I wouldn't look a gift horse in the mouth if I were you." She grinned and headed inside.

"Wait a second, are you saying you don't think I can get a date?" Charlotte asked, following her in.

"Listen, I'm in the dating pool. It's a nightmare," Mona replied. "If I had someone as interested in me as Roger is in you, I'd jump on him in a second and never let go. You two have known each other a long time and there's obviously an attraction there. So why not go for it?"

Because, Charlotte's mind replied, *you haven't dated since your husband left.* There were a whole host of reasons Charlotte hadn't sought out companionship since Ronson, but the primary one was she wasn't sure she could take someone leaving her again. If she wasn't with someone, it was impossible for them to leave, right?

At least, that's what she'd justified to herself in all those years since. Plus, being partners with a detective was irritating at best, oppressive at worst. Ronson had made that abundantly clear. It was why work had become everything to Charlotte.

They entered the kitchen without Charlotte providing an answer for Mona. It was a conversation they could continue later, because right now, Mrs. Goole and her daughter sat at the four-person kitchen table, both of them staring off into space.

"Mrs. Goole, this is my associate Detective Dawes," Mona said. Neither woman really looked up, they just kind of sat there, blank looks in their eyes. "Is now a good time to talk?"

The woman didn't reply, just stared out the sliding glass door to the patio and backyard beyond.

"Sure." The response came from Kayleigh who peeled at one of her cuticles, though she looked up long enough to give Charlotte a terse smile.

"We know this is upsetting for you," Charlotte replied, taking a careful seat on the other side of Mrs. Goole while Mona sat opposite Kayleigh. "We'd just like to clear some things up, if that's okay."

The woman wasn't even blinking. In a way, it was creepy.

"Did either of you know about the altar that sits behind the church?" Mona asked.

Kayleigh shot a look at her mother before answering. "I knew it was there, but that's it," she said. "I used to play out there when I was a kid."

"Mrs. Goole?" Charlotte asked.

Finally, the woman met her gaze, but it was like she was looking through Charlotte, not at her. "I knew."

"Do you know what it's used for?"

Her voice was almost ethereal, spoken with a soft strength that commanded your attention. "It isn't used. It's just an old artifact."

"Someone used it," Mona replied. "Recently. There was fresh blood on the surface last night."

"I don't know anything about that," she replied. "But the land is easily accessible. Anyone could have been out there."

"When's the last time you went out there?" Charlotte asked.

"Years ago."

"Do you regularly attend your husband's services?" Charlotte asked.

"Yes."

Charlotte turned to Kayleigh. "Do you?"

"Not as much as she should," her mother answered for her, her tone harsher and more biting.

"Okay." Charlotte was beginning to think they weren't going to get any solid answers out of either of them. "In your experience, has Joseph or anyone else from the congregation ever used the altar for anything?"

"No," Mrs. Goole replied quickly.

Kayleigh shook her head.

"What about the symbols around the bottom," Mona asked. "Can you tell us about those?"

"I have no idea," Mrs. Goole replied without looking at either of them. "Like I said, it was there when we bought the property."

Out of the corner of her eye, she noticed Bowman stick his head in the doorway. "Detectives?"

"Excuse us for a moment," Mona said as both she and Charlotte got up, following Bowman deeper into the house.

"We found something," he said, leading them to the bedroom. "Chamber under the floorboard." As they entered into the large bedroom, the carpet had been pulled back, revealing a hatch in the old hardwoods beneath. It opened on a hinge and one of the other officers was pulling out items, setting them all on a nearby tarp that had been spread out.

Immediately, one of the items caught Charlotte's eye. It was a small piece of metal with a handle, and on the end was an engraved piece of iron or aluminum in the shape of the symbol found on Mallory Wakefield's body. Beside it were four more, all with identical handles and differing symbols, matching those of their victims.

"Damn," Mona said. "I think that's pretty conclusive."

Charlotte nodded. "We got the bastard."

TWENTY-FIVE

"I've been trying to tell you; I am a peaceful man."

Joseph Goole sat across from Mona and Charlotte at the very same table where they'd interrogated Terry Barker. Through the entire process he'd remained adamant that they had the wrong person, that he'd committed no crime. He'd even waived his right to a lawyer, saying it was unnecessary. But unlike when they'd had their discussion with Terry Barker, this time they had solid evidence against him.

"A peaceful man doesn't keep human branding irons in his floorboards," Mona said. Charlotte had been gracious enough to allow Mona to conduct most of the interview with Goole. Mona was afraid she'd upset her by not including her on the raid, but the truth was Mona had been worried. And she *had* tried to call Charlotte before they headed out, but she hadn't followed up or gotten in contact with the hotel to wake her up. She'd observed how much Charlotte had been struggling, and how hard she was pushing herself on this case. And given the night they'd had, she didn't need the woman to injure herself when all Mona and Bowman needed to do was pick up a suspect. It wasn't as if Mona had been expecting a shootout.

However, after Bowman had discovered the evidence at the

home, everyone agreed it was prudent to bring Mrs. Goole in for questioning as well. Kayleigh, for her part, had seemed more than shocked at what they'd found, asking her mother about it even as they'd led her out of the home. Mona was reasonably convinced Kayleigh didn't have anything to do with the murders, but she'd asked her to come down to the station regardless. If for no other reason than to see how her parents responded to her being there.

"Let's go back to the altar," Mona said. They'd already asked Goole over and over about the branding irons, but he *insisted* he knew nothing about them, that he didn't even know the house had a hatch underneath the floorboards. Mona suspected that was a lie, as the way they'd found it was Bowman had been walking around the bedroom and noticed his footsteps sounded different in one part versus the other, because one part of the floor echoed while the other didn't. Bowman was a big man, and it was probably easier to tell with him than of someone fifty pounds lighter, such as Goole. But still, she was willing to bet he knew. When the forensics came back, they'd have him dead to rights.

The other option was Goole was telling the truth, and Mrs. Goole was the culprit. They were currently checking the alibis of both suspects, though Mona bet when it came down to it, the husband was the more likely killer. He was the more controlling of the two of them—the leader of the congregation. He'd be more likely able to get his followers to do his bidding.

That was the other angle. It was possible Goole was the mastermind and pulling the strings behind the scenes. They currently had three other officers tracking down the whereabouts of every single person on the list Mona and Charlotte had obtained, with a particular interest in finding Nathaniel Bradshaw.

"Your wife told us the altar was on the property when you bought it—is that correct?" Mona asked.

"We certainly didn't put it there. It was a curiosity, nothing more," Goole replied. "My daughter used to play on it as a child."

"So she told us," Charlotte said.

"And you have no idea why it was covered in blood?" Mona asked.

"None."

Mona leaned forward. "When was the last time you visited the altar?"

"It's been a few years," he replied.

"We found candles that had been recently burned there," Mona said. "The ground around it trampled. *Someone* was using it. Who else knows about it?"

"I'm sure a few of my parishioners know," Goole replied. "But none of them would ever do anything like you're suggesting. We are not a violent people."

"What about Nathaniel Bradshaw?"

Goole paused for a brief second, either caught off guard that they knew who Bradshaw was or because he was trying to come up with a lie in real time. "Nathan is a good man. Strong. A family man. Why do you ask?"

Mona pulled out the paper from Goole's church. "Because it looks to me like he owes you a lot of money."

Goole's eyes hardened.

"Maybe he's upset that the church is pressuring him for money," Mona continued. "Maybe even upset enough to do something about it."

"You're suggesting one of my own congregants is behind these murders?" Goole said.

"Maybe you're in it together," Mona suggested. "And in lieu of payment, you're getting him to do your dirty work for you."

"That is as impossible as it is preposterous," Goole replied. "Nathaniel wouldn't harm a soul."

"So you keep saying. And yet we have three dead people in our morgue. People, I might add, that used to be part of your congregation. Someone is targeting your children and I want to know why."

"If I knew, I would be more than happy to tell you."

This was getting them nowhere. "Can you tell us more about the Circle of the Sacred Grove?" Charlotte asked.

The man pinched his features together. "I'd rather not. We like to keep our practices private. There tends to be a negative view of practices like ours which don't follow a more *mainstream* dogma. But we are honest, hardworking members of this community and have been for over twenty years."

"You moved here from Chicago, isn't that right?" Mona asked.

"Yes, my wife and I moved when we found out we were pregnant with Kayleigh," he replied.

"Did you operate the church while living in Chicago?"

"Less formally, yes," he replied. "But our meetings were in community centers, or sometimes private dining rooms. We made the decision to leave the city for our family's sake—to give our children a better life outside the pressures of somewhere such as Chicago."

Mona motioned to Charlotte. "You know, Detective Dawes is from Chicago. She's been a cop there for... how long?"

"Twenty-nine years," Charlotte replied, staring the man down. To his credit, he didn't shrink under her gaze like so many others. But he did avert his eyes.

"So you leave Chicago, move to Oak Creek. Buy a plot of land that happens to have an altar on it," Mona said. "An altar with symbols that match the ones we found on brands underneath your floorboards. See how that looks?"

"I don't know what to tell you, Detective," Goole replied, holding up his hands. "Whoever owned the property before us—"

"Was a ninety-two-year-old couple who had owned the farm their entire lives," Mona finished for him. "Which you already know because you're the one who negotiated with them to split off a portion of that land for you. And you built that house and that church on that land. So don't sit here and tell me it was *someone else* because there is no one else. Just you, Mr. Goole. And your wife."

"Marie has nothing to do with any of this," he said.

"One of you did," Charlotte replied. "And we're going to find out which one."

Mona checked the time. They'd been in with him for almost two hours, going in circles. "Sit tight, Mr. Goole. We'll be back in a few minutes." She stood while Charlotte followed, both of them heading back into the hallway.

Mona stopped at the water fountain and downed one cup followed by another. "I think you should take a crack at him when we go back in," she said between sips.

"Why? You're doing fine," Charlotte replied, getting her own cup of water.

"He's not saying anything, just pulling us around on a string," Mona protested.

"It doesn't matter. As soon as the forensics are back, we'll have everything we need. He's just stalling, hoping he can figure a way out of this."

They headed back to their desks where Bowman was already waiting for them. "Bad news. Both Marie and Joseph Goole were at a social function last Friday night when Mallory Wakefield was killed."

"Doesn't mean they couldn't have ordered Bradshaw or someone else to do it," Charlotte said. "Given them the brand."

"Their daughter also confirmed they were home when Justine Mercer's death took place," he replied. "If they are behind this, it's going to be damn hard to prove."

"We have the brands," Mona said. "How much more concrete can it get?"

"Detectives?" All three of them turned to Sheriff Earle who stood at the entrance to their section. "In my office. All of you."

Mona shot Charlotte a glance, but the woman only shrugged. Mona had noticed she was holding her side particularly close, which had been the same side she'd landed on when tackling Terry Barker. But her face hadn't betrayed any of that earlier pain. Maybe Mona had been overreacting after all.

They filed into Earle's office, with Charlotte closing the door behind them.

"I just heard from Whittle. No prints on the branding irons."

"That doesn't mean anything," Charlotte argued. "Goole's a smart man, he probably cleaned them after using them. Or just wore gloves. Or ordered one of his lackeys to wear gloves."

"And the brands don't match the wounds," Earle said.

"Of course they do," Mona said. "I saw them myself. Those marks. They are an exact match."

He shook his head, turning around his computer. On the screen was an image of the first brand found on Mallory Wakefield, and beside it, in another picture, the brand they'd obtained from Goole's home.

Mona squinted at the pair of images. Immediately, it was evident they weren't the same. They were close, but there were minor differences, just as the hook not being as pronounced or the Y-shape extending out longer. It was the same symbol but represented in two different ways. One was like a bad copy of the other. That... and the iron itself was twenty-five percent smaller than the actual burn on her arm.

"I don't understand," Mona said.

"Whittle compared all three burns to the brands you confiscated," Earle added. "All of them are like this. Small differences, different sizes. Whoever killed those people, they did not use *these* instruments on them."

"Great," Charlotte said, crossing her arms as she leaned against the door. "Any other good news?"

"The blood on the altar was found to be animal after all," Earle replied. "Specifically belonging to a deer or something with a hoof. I don't know, ask Whittle."

"How is that possible?" Mona asked. "The symbols match. The ones on the altar... they're the ones on the victims... There has to be—"

"I'm not saying it's not related," Earle replied, holding up his hand. "But this is far from a slam dunk. And if we don't have any other corroborating evidence, we can only keep the Gooles in custody for so long."

"Their alibis for two of the murders check out, chief," Bowman said. "Third is a wash. But one is from the daughter, so take that for what it is."

"He has to be coordinating this," Mona said. "With someone else. Bradshaw... or someone."

"Do you have any evidence to corroborate that?" Earle asked.

Mona went to answer, only to realize she didn't. There was nothing that physically connected the Gooles to anyone else who then connected to the deaths. It was all circumstantial. "We need to go after the individual members."

"They're a tight-knit group," Charlotte said. "They're not going to turn on each other. Peterson was out there hunting us with a shotgun."

"On Goole's order, no doubt."

"Look," Earle said. "We're not going to get into semantics here. Is it concerning there's paraphernalia in the Goole home that aligns with evidence from the crime scenes? Yes. Does it mean they're responsible? We don't know. All we know right now is we don't have enough to prove anything either way."

"We're just supposed to let them go?" Mona asked.

Earle grimaced. "We can hold them for twenty-four hours before we're required to release them. You have that long to figure out how they fit into this and why."

"This is ridiculous!" Mona stood, slamming her hands on Earle's desk. She hadn't even realized she'd done it until she was standing there, looking at Earle, her chest rising and falling. It was almost like she was watching from outside herself, like she had no control of what she was doing.

"Detective. Remove your hands from my desk," Earle growled.

Mona blinked, coming back into herself. "I'm sorry, sir. I don't know... I think I'm just tired. I... didn't get much sleep last night."

"We're all tired, LaSalle," he replied. "Go off on me again and you'll find yourself walking a patrol beat for the rest of your career."

"Yes, sir. Sorry, sir," Mona said again.

"That's it," he said. "Get on it. Time is wasting."

"Are you okay?" Charlotte asked as they headed back to their desks. Bowman seemed to walk around Mona, giving her a wide berth.

"I don't... I think this has been a little harder on me than I'd realized."

"Bad memories," Charlotte said.

"It's more than that." Mona clamped her mouth shut before she could say anything else. They didn't need to sit here discussing her mental state. Those conversations should be reserved for Dr. Cross. Which reminded her she'd missed her last appointment because she'd been working this case. She needed to make it up.

Charlotte leaned closer. "Do you want to talk about it?"

Mona glanced to Charlotte's ribs. "Do you want to talk about your thing?"

"Fair enough," Charlotte replied.

"So where do we go from here?"

"We work our angles. Track down Bradshaw and the other members of the church. Try to get a bead on anyone under the age of twenty-five. If the pattern holds, they are the next most likely victims. In the meantime, I need to go back to Chicago, pull the old case files myself."

"Wait, you're leaving?" Mona asked.

Charlotte nodded. "Apparently, my former partner doesn't understand the term *urgent*. It's only an hour there and an hour back. But we need to start going through those files again. There might be something in there that can help."

"Okay..." Mona said, unconvinced. It wasn't like she could keep Charlotte here. But it felt wrong that she was leaving. Maybe this was just an excuse and she realized this case would only turn out like her original case in Chicago.

No. That was the other talking. Charlotte hadn't given up on her yet and she wasn't about to do so now. Mona just wished there was some way she could stay close. Things felt... better when Charlotte was around.

"When will I hear from you again?"

"I'll be in touch soon, okay?" The woman smiled. "Trust me."

TWENTY-SIX

Charlotte winced as she drove along the highway, heading back to the city. The doctor had recommended she go home, but he hadn't said exactly *how* she was supposed to do that without causing further pain or injury. Sitting in the seat with the seat belt strapped over her was causing considerable pressure to her abdomen, which further caused her to hold herself tighter than normal. In addition, the foot she needed to use to operate the gas and brake pedals was the swollen one.

Still, Charlotte pushed through the pain. They were on a deadline here and she didn't want their one suspect to get away just because they didn't have enough evidence to convict him. She believed in Mona's ability to track down Bradshaw and the others while she was gone, because they needed those files. What was Dale's problem, anyway? She'd called and left three messages on his phone and hadn't heard back. How hard was it to get something from the archives?

Ever since finding that altar in the middle of the woods she was convinced more than ever the two cases were related. Five victims, each with burns on their arms. And while all the details didn't match up exactly, it was close enough.

There was also something about Goole himself that made her

want to nail him to the wall. He almost seemed familiar in a way; despite the fact Charlotte had never met the man in her life.

And yet...

She eased off the gas as she approached the next stoplight, and as the car rolled to a halt, she used the opportunity to take a deep breath. The pain was still there, hiding behind her injury and all the painkillers, but she could feel it. It was like a ticking time bomb and she wasn't sure how long she had left before it went off. She needed to make some progress before then.

Thirty minutes later, Charlotte pulled into the familiar parking garage in downtown. She pulled a ticket for the first time, having always used her badge in the past, and the gate raised, allowing her through. At least now she got to park in the visitors' parking, which were the first spots in the lot.

And she'd make sure they validated.

Taking longer than she'd like, she got out of the car and headed into the connected station, coming upon the security scanners just inside the door.

"Dawes!" Officer Rodrigo said, smiling. "Didn't think I'd see you again so soon. You that desperate for something to do you couldn't stay away?"

Charlotte smiled, putting her personal effects into the small bowl that ran through the scanner while she stepped under the open doorway. "You know me. Can't stop, won't stop."

"Retirement's that bad, huh?" he joked. "My wife says when I retire she's not going to let me out of her sight. Knows it's too tempting to come back."

"Guess I need to get me one of those, then," Charlotte said, taking her stuff back from the little tray.

"Have a good day, Detective," Rodrigo said as she headed down the hallway.

"You too." She'd expected this. She hadn't been back to the office since she'd had her formal retirement party three months ago. But this was a matter of some urgency, and she couldn't afford to wait.

As Charlotte entered the station's main lobby, the place was a buzz with activity. Officers coming and going, suspects lined up against one wall, some handcuffed, some just under supervision. Friends and family of victims or witnesses huddled in small groups in the expansive space. If there was one thing to say about her old precinct, it wasn't boring.

Charlotte approached the desk sergeant, a man she knew better than most, considering they used to be on a few task forces together. He was about five years younger than her and had developed a serious belly in the past few years, which is probably what prompted him to his most recent assignment.

"Dawes?" he said as she approached, setting aside his newspaper.

"Hey, Bolts," she said. Jim "Bolts" Bolton was a career cop, a man who had worked his way up from patrolman as a young kid all the way to lieutenant before getting busted back down for an infraction that had been sealed by the department. No one knew the full details, but Charlotte understood it had something to do with a couple of call girls and a very seedy club in the city. Beyond that, she only had her imagination.

"Jesus, you look like you just stepped off the ass-kicking line. What happened?"

"The risks of being retired," she said, giving him a quick smile. Bolts had always been observant, and he must have seen her limp and the way she was holding herself, despite her attempts to cover it up. That was the problem with working with cops. "Is Dale in?"

"Givens? Yeah, I think so. Want me to ring him for you?"

"Actually, I'll just go see him if that's okay," she said. "I don't want to pull him off of something if he's in the middle of it."

"Sure," Bolts said, buzzing her through the door just as a pair of officers began dragging a young man in by his arms. He was twisting back and forth, spewing obscenities all over the place. "I will *fuck your mothers*," the kid yelled as he tried to wrench himself out of their grasp. From a brief glance, Charlotte could tell he was on something, probably PCP. The two officers had to fight to keep him from completely breaking their grasp.

"Never a dull moment around here," Charlotte said, pushing through the entryway to the back.

"You know it," Bolts replied. "Good seeing you, Dawes."

"You too," she said and headed back further into the station. She weaved around the corridors, flashing quick smiles at the people she recognized. It was so strange—and yet so familiar—being back. Like she hadn't left at all, and also like she'd been gone a lifetime.

"Dale!" She found him at his desk, typing away at some report or another, his face glued to the screen.

"Char?" He blinked a couple of times like he couldn't believe it. "Wha—are you okay?" He'd noticed the same thing Bolts had, but Dale knew her well enough that it only took a glance, rather than a few seconds of careful observation.

"You can't call me back?"

"Call you back?" he asked. "About what?"

"About that case I asked you to pull. *Remember?*"

He blinked a few times. "Oh... right. Sorry, we've just been swamped here. The commissioner is on a mission to get this crime wave under control and it's taking everyone's full effort."

"Dale, I left you three messages," she said, more urgently.

"I'm sorry," he replied. "I figured it could wait. It's not like you're still on the clock." He furrowed his brow. "You're on the clock, aren't you?"

"Just help me get these things so I can get back to work," she said.

"You're supposed to be retired," he reiterated as she turned and headed for the archives.

He stood sind followed. "What happened to you?"

"It's nothing," she said, though she knew that wouldn't satisfy him. "Just an accident. That's all."

"Char, come on. It's me," he said.

She exhaled. "Fine. I've been up in Oak Creek. Mona—

LaSalle... from a few months ago? She called and asked for some help. So I've been helping."

"And you're limping."

"I don't need you to point out my failings," she snapped.

"I wasn't," he replied. "But is that a result of your... help?"

"Officially, it's a consult job, don't get your panties in a twist," she said, taking a nearby seat. It was exhausting just standing up for too long. Not a good sign.

"Doesn't look like just consulting," he said.

"Well, maybe if someone would have pulled the files like I asked, I wouldn't have had to come all the way back down here," she replied.

Givens sighed. He knew her well enough to know no matter what he said, she wouldn't give up this fight. Which is the whole reason she came to him. If she'd tried to request files through official channels, it would have taken *months*. Or even if she'd gone to Whiteside and tried to ask, she could have been turned down. But Givens, he knew how stubborn she could be. He also knew that whatever she was doing, it was important.

"Okay, message received," he finally said. "What case?"

"It's 44-GH26-95," she replied without even thinking.

He paused. "Wait. Is that the one I think it is?"

"Just tell me where the files are," she said.

"I'll need to go into the archives. Give me a few minutes."

"I'm coming with you," she replied, standing with some effort.

"Can you just let someone do something for you for once?" he asked, exasperated. She only glared at him. "Fine. Come on."

They made their way to the elevator, Charlotte doing her best not to look in the direction of her old boss's office. While they had left on good terms, they'd still been strained due to what happened in Oak Creek with Sheriff Franklin. Jeremy Whiteside had still been processing the loss of his friend, and in some ways, Charlotte suspected he blamed her for not finding John McCormick soon enough to save Franklin's life.

"I assume there's a reason you're going back to this one," Dale said as they got in the elevator. "Especially since you told me you never wanted to think about it again."

"New information has come to light," she said. "Something is going on in Oak Creek. And I think it might be related." That was the first time she'd verbalized it. Ever since Mona had asked her to assist on the case, the possibility had been there. But when the MOs began to differ and the symbols didn't match the burn marks on the arms, Charlotte had dismissed the possibility of the cases being connected too soon.

The elevator doors opened, revealing rows after rows of evidence, all held behind large, double-paned, bulletproof glass. The entire room was also fireproof, with its own fire suppression system. Everything held in the tightest security in the event of a disaster. There were a hundred years of evidence down here, from the beginning of Chicago's mob era. And no matter what, it couldn't be lost or destroyed.

"Morning, Irma," Dale said as they approached the middle-aged woman sitting behind the desk.

"Morning," she replied.

Dale signed in on the sheet and also provided his badge for logging. "One guest."

Irma glanced at Charlotte, and narrowed her eyes. "She'll have to stay out here."

"I'll bring it back out," Dale said as Charlotte moved to argue.

"But—"

"Hey," he said. "Don't get your panties in a twist." He winked as Irma buzzed him through, which opened the massive glass door and closed behind him. Dale looked at the number he'd written down and disappeared into the stacks.

"You used to work here," Irma said, eyeing Charlotte carefully.

"Recently retired," Charlotte said.

"Mmm. Looks like it didn't stick."

"Just taking care of some unfinished business."

Dale returned a few minutes later with two white banker's boxes. Irma buzzed him through again and he stopped again at her desk. "Checking these out for the day," he said, giving her the serial numbers on the side of the box.

"They're not to leave the building, and all items inside must be accounted for before being returned to storage," Irma said.

"I know the drill." Charlotte went to take one of the boxes, but Dale turned away. "No, ma'am. You get the door."

Back upstairs, they took one of the empty conference rooms and began unpacking the boxes.

"So what is it exactly you're looking for?" he asked as she gingerly removed evidence samples, reports and notes from the case.

Charlotte examined each carefully, a flood of memories coming back to her. Notes scribbled in Ortega's nearly indistinguishable scrawl, blood sample analyses, pieces of evidence from the scene and photographs, back before digital photos were the norm.

It was the latter that interested Charlotte the most. She pulled out the stack of photos, flipping through them one at a time. She'd gotten so used to digital photography she forgot what it was like back then. Overexposed images, dark backgrounds, never capturing all the detail you needed, even when a professional did it.

"I've never looked at this case before," Givens said, peering over her shoulder as she thumbed through the images of the victims, sprawled out on their tables, blood running everywhere. Mixed in with the pictures were close-up images of the burns on each of the victims' arms. Charlotte set those aside as she continued to look.

"It's not a pleasant one," she replied. Finally, she came to the photo she'd been looking for. She hadn't been sure it was in here, but thankfully, someone had done their due diligence.

The deaths had all been in a warehouse downtown—a structure that had long since been destroyed and replaced with a new high rise. But it had been a big building back then. She recalled a catwalk running above the murder scene. Thankfully, one of the

CSI photographers had climbed up there and snapped a few images from overhead.

And as Charlotte stared at the pictures, there was no doubt in her mind that her case was connected to the recent deaths in Oak Creek.

She just hadn't been able to see it before.

"I need copies of these," she said, laying each of the photographs out in a straight line. "Kill the lights for me, I don't want there to be a glare."

As soon as he did, Charlotte began snapping images of the photos with her phone until she had all of them, including the ones of the burns.

"I don't get it, what's going on?" he asked.

As soon as Charlotte finished with the pictures, she gathered them all back up and placed them in the box again. "Thanks, Dale, this has been a big help."

"Care to let me in on what you're doing?" he asked, growing impatient.

"Too much to explain right now, but I'll fill you in later. Over one of those dinners you won't stop annoying me about." She headed for the door. "See? Was that so hard?"

"You're welcome, I guess," he said, a confused look on his face.

Charlotte smiled. There had been more than she could have hoped for. Now she just had to make one more stop.

TWENTY-SEVEN

Mona's office looked like a war room. She'd commandeered the largest whiteboard in the station and covered it with photos, names, and timelines. Red string connected members of Goole's congregation to each other, to the victims and to key locations. Next to her desk, a separate board displayed photos of all three victims with their respective symbols beneath them.

After Charlotte had left, she and Bowman had done a deep dive into the list found at the church. They'd managed to identify forty-three active members, though they still hadn't managed to locate Nathaniel Bradshaw. There was a BOLO out on the man, but given they had literally nothing to charge him with, Mona was just hoping they'd get a hit so they could talk to him.

They'd also managed to identify four other possible victims: Micah Gibson, Annabelle Rountree, James Langford and, finally, Kayleigh Goole. They were the only four members of the congregation young enough to fit the pattern, and the department was having a hell of a time tracking them down.

Her phone buzzed. She checked it, hoping for word from Charlotte, but it was just a news alert about the latest death in Oak Creek. The media was having a field day.

Bowman appeared in the doorway with two cups of coffee. "Thought you could use this."

"Thanks." She accepted the cup gratefully, not mentioning she'd already had three. Sleep felt impossible with a killer still out there and their main suspect's detention clock ticking down.

"Any word from Dawes?"

Mona shook her head, trying not to let him see how much it bothered her that Charlotte had just... left. "Nothing. But she seems convinced there was something in those files that could help us."

"Any idea what?"

"None. And if she doesn't get back quick, Goole walks in eighteen hours."

They'd been interrogating various church members all morning, but each interview yielded the same result: blank stares, vague answers, and ironclad alibis. The church members protected each other, forming an impenetrable wall around whatever secrets they held.

Mona turned back to her timeline. "There has to be something we're missing."

She'd traced Joseph Goole's activities over the past month, looking for any pattern, any indication he was orchestrating these murders. But nothing concrete had emerged. Church meetings, community events, family dinners—all accounted for. Marie Goole's schedule was similarly innocuous.

"It's like they knew we'd be looking," Mona said, tapping her pen against the desk. "They've covered all their tracks."

"Maybe we're overthinking this," Bowman suggested, leaning against the doorframe. "What if it's not Joseph or the church at all? What if it's someone with a grudge against the church?"

Mona considered this. "The symbols point directly to their practices. And those brands were in their house."

"But they don't match exactly," Bowman reminded her. "You saw Whittle's report."

"Close enough to be connected," Mona insisted. "No way that's coincidence."

"I'm not saying they're not involved. I'm saying maybe Joseph isn't the mastermind we think he is."

Before Mona could respond, Sheriff Earle appeared in the doorway behind Bowman, his face grim. "We've got another one."

"Shit," Mona said. "Who?"

"The Gibson kid," Earle replied.

Dammit. They'd been too late again. "Same MO?"

"Reports of a symbol on the wrist," Earle said.

He didn't need to spell it out. With Goole sitting in police custody, proving he was behind the murders would be near impossible, even if he was somehow orchestrating them. Any lawyer worth their salt would be able to get him released in a second. They'd have to cut him loose, sooner than expected.

"Where?" she managed to ask, already reaching for her jacket.

"Island Palm Apartments. Unit three-seventeen." Earle handed her a slip of paper with the address. "First responders are securing the scene. Neighbor heard a gunshot, called it in."

"Gunshot?" Bowman asked. "That's different."

"Yeah, and unlike the others, it looks like the killer didn't have time to stage this one," Earle added. "Something must have spooked them."

Mona felt her chest tighten. Just like before. Escalating violence, escalating boldness. Which meant he was getting reckless, no longer caring about the consequences. Was he aware they were getting close?

"We'll head over now," she said, forcing her voice to remain steady. "We need to get those other three kids in protective custody."

"Just got a lock on Rountree. A unit is headed over to pick her up now."

One was better than none. But it still meant there was at least one more victim out there. Kayleigh Goole was safe at the station, and with Rountree accounted for, they just needed to find Langford. As she and Bowman hurried to her car, Mona tried to push away the memories that threatened to overwhelm her. She couldn't afford to be distracted, not now. There would be time for her to fall apart later.

"You okay?" Bowman asked as they pulled out of the station.

"Fine," she said automatically.

He didn't push, and she was grateful. Because right now she didn't have time to dissect what was happening inside her head. She needed to be focused on what was in front of her. The past would still be there tomorrow.

The scene at Island Palm Apartments was chaos. News vans lined the street, reporters jockeying for position behind the police tape. Uniformed officers struggled to keep curious onlookers at bay. Mona felt the weight of all those eyes on her as she and Bowman approached. This case had exploded into a circus.

"Detective LaSalle!" A reporter thrust a microphone toward her. "Is it true Oak Creek has another serial killer? Is this connected to John McCormick?"

Mona flinched at her father's name but kept walking.

"You have to make a statement!" another shouted. "People are scared!"

Bowman stepped between Mona and the press. "No comment at this time."

Inside the apartment building, the air felt thick and stale. They climbed to the third floor, where Officer Tao waited outside Unit 317.

"Single gunshot wound to the head, close range," Tao reported as they approached. "Neighbor in 319 heard the shot about forty minutes ago, came to check, found the door ajar and the victim on the floor."

"Witness see anyone?" Bowman asked.

Tao shook his head. "Says she heard footsteps running down the stairwell but didn't get a look."

Mona pulled on gloves before entering the apartment. Unlike the previous scenes, there was no attempt at staging here. The victim lay sprawled on his living room floor, a single bullet hole in his forehead. Blood pooled beneath his head, soaking into the carpet. His eyes were open, staring at nothing.

The stark violence of it—the brutality—sent a chill through Mona. This wasn't like the other deaths. This was rushed, panicked. The killer had been impatient to get this one over with. Could that mean they were getting close? Was he feeling the pressure of their investigation, or was he building to something more climactic?

"Poor kid," Bowman said, crouching beside the body.

Mona carefully turned the victim's arm. There, on his right wrist, was a fresh burn mark—the same location as the others, but a different symbol. This one was a circle with a straight line through it, and a small cross perched on top. It matched one of the symbols on the altar.

"Four for four," she murmured, photographing the mark with her phone.

Whittle arrived, pushing past them to examine the body. "Time of death is consistent with when the shot was reported. Ballistics will tell us more, but preliminary guess is a .38 or 9mm. Close range, probably pressed right against the skull."

Mona stood, scanning the apartment. It was sparse but neat. A small dining table with two chairs. A couch facing a modest television. A bookshelf with a few paperbacks and framed photos. And no phone in sight.

The photos caught her attention. She moved closer, examining each one. Micah at graduation. Micah at what appeared to be a family barbecue. And then—Mona felt her pulse quicken—Micah with his parents at what could only be a church gathering. Behind them stood Joseph Goole, his arm around Micah's mother.

"Bowman," she called, pointing to the photo. "Look."

Bowman joined her, squinting at the image. "Is that—"

Mona pointed to Micah's mother in the photo. Around her neck hung a pendant—a small metal charm on a chain. The symbol on it matched one of those they'd found carved into the altar. And the one Mrs. Peterson wore.

"Another connection," Bowman muttered.

Mona continued examining the photos, finding more evidence of Micah's connection to the church. In one, he stood with a group of young people around a bonfire, laughing as they cooked smores and hot dogs. Connor Peterson appeared in one of the photos. Justine Mercer in another.

"We need to find his parents," Mona said.

The Gibsons lived in a modest ranch-style home fifteen minutes from their son's apartment. When Mona and Bowman arrived, Mrs. Gibson was already being comforted by neighbors. News traveled fast in Oak Creek.

Mona swallowed hard as they approached the home, gently directing the onlookers away.

"Mrs. Gibson?" Mona said. "I'm Detective LaSalle, this is Detective Bowman. We're very sorry for your loss."

The woman looked up, her face ravaged by grief. "I don't understand. What is *happening*?"

"That's what we're trying to find out," Mona said, sitting beside her. "We understand your family is part of the Circle of the Sacred Grove?"

Mrs. Gibson nodded, clutching a tissue. "We've all been long-time members."

"And you know Joseph and Marie Goole?"

"Of course. Joseph has been our spiritual guide for decades."

Mona glanced at Bowman before continuing. "Mrs. Gibson, I noticed in photos that you wear a pendant with a symbol on it. May I ask about that?"

Mrs. Gibson's hand went to her throat, where the pendant rested. "This? It was a gift from Joseph, when I completed my spiritual journey twenty-five years ago. All female members receive one when they're ready."

"May I see it?"

Mrs. Gibson hesitated, then pulled the chain over her head and handed it to Mona. The symbol matched one of those carved into the altar stone—not one they'd found on any victim yet.

"What does it mean?" Mona asked.

"Protection," Mrs. Gibson said automatically. "It keeps us safe from harm."

"Not safe enough," Mr. Gibson muttered from the doorway. He'd been silent until now, watching them with red-rimmed eyes.

"Harold," his wife admonished.

"No. Enough secrets." He turned to Mona. "Joseph told us those symbols would protect our children. That as long as we followed his guidance, no harm would come to them."

"Harold, please—"

"Our son is dead, Katherine! Dead!" His voice broke. "And he's not the first. We all know what's happening. Connor. Mallory. Justine. All gone. It's all falling apart. That necklace might as well be made out of string and cardboard for all the protection it provides."

Mona's attention sharpened. "Are you saying there's some connection between the victims? Other than being part of the church?"

"Of course there is," Mr. Gibson replied bitterly. "They were the chosen ones."

"Chosen for what?" Bowman asked.

Mr. Gibson opened his mouth to answer, but his wife cut him off. "Remember your oath."

"What good is an oath when our son is dead?"

"*Harold.*" The word came out sharp and cold, like a knife.

The man deflated, suddenly looking years older. "Never mind. It's not important."

"What oath?" Mona asked. Neither person spoke. "If you know something about what's happening, you have a duty to tell us." But it was as if someone had clamped their mouths shut. They wouldn't even look at the two detectives.

"Fine, then I'll have you both arrested for obstructing an official investigation—is that what you want?"

"Do what you have to do," Harold replied, his eyes still downcast. "Doesn't matter now anyway."

Mona took a breath. Maybe a softer approach was necessary. "When was the last time you saw Joseph Goole?"

"Last Sunday for service," Mrs. Gibson answered. "I tried calling, but he's been... unavailable."

Because he was in custody. Mona exchanged a look with Bowman. If Joseph had been detained when Micah was killed, he couldn't have pulled the trigger. But that didn't mean he wasn't involved.

"Did Micah mention anyone threatening him? Acting strangely around him?"

Both parents shook their heads.

"Where were you both this morning?" Bowman asked.

"I was at work," Mr. Gibson said. "I manage the hardware store on Main."

"And I was at my sister's," Mrs. Gibson added. "We have coffee every Thursday."

Alibis they could verify. Mona handed Mrs. Gibson back her pendant. She wasn't about to arrest two people who had just lost their only child. But still, the fact they knew something would continue to gnaw at her. "Are you sure there's nothing else you can tell us?"

Both people just stared off into the distance.

Mona sighed. "Thank you for your time. Again, we're very sorry for your loss."

Outside, Mona and Bowman paused by their car.

"Chosen ones," Bowman repeated. "What the hell does that mean?"

"I don't know, but it connects all four victims." Mona rubbed her temples, fighting a growing headache. "They were all children of the congregation, all the same age, all marked with different symbols."

"With one more to go. But Goole physically couldn't have done it. And he hasn't made so much as a phone call since he was brought in. So he couldn't have coordinated it either."

"Which means either he's innocent, or—"

"—he preplanned all this," Bowman finished. "And someone like Bradshaw is carrying out these killings."

"But that still doesn't answer why. What's the motive?" Mona leaned against the car, feeling the weight of four deaths pressing down on her. "Why use different methods each time? Hit-and-run, hanging, throat cutting, gunshot—there's no consistency."

Mona's phone buzzed. She checked it, hoping for Charlotte, but it was Earle. "Sheriff wants us back at the station. Looks like after the news about Micah he finally decided to lawyer up. And the lawyer is demanding his release. Says we have no grounds to hold him with Micah's murder happening while he was in custody."

"He's right," Bowman said grimly. "We're going to have to cut him loose."

Mona stared out at the bustling suburban street, neighbors gawking at the house as a media van pulled up and parked in front of the home. She could feel that familiar sense of helplessness creeping in. Four young people dead. A killer still at large. And their prime suspect about to walk free.

She pulled out her phone and dialed Charlotte's number, but it went straight to voicemail. She sighed and left the woman a message anyway, telling her about Gibson. If she didn't get back here soon, there wouldn't be anyone left to save.

As they drove back to the station, Mona couldn't shake the feeling that they were missing something critical. Something hidden in plain sight. The connections were there—the church, the symbols, the victims' ages—but the pattern remained elusive.

What did "chosen ones" mean? Why these specific victims? And why now, after all these years?

Mona hoped Charlotte had found answers, because right now,

all she had were questions—and four bodies with no justice in sight.

TWENTY-EIGHT

Charlotte knocked on the door, despite the fact the sign on the front said, *Closed*. It was an hour past opening time, so where was he?

Finally, a head popped around the corner inside the store, an annoyed look on the man's face before seeing Charlotte and turning into a smile. He approached and opened the inside door, cocking his head and, in doing so, looking like a curious dog out on a walk.

"This is a welcome surprise," Roger said.

"You're supposed to be open," she said as he rolled up the gate to allow her in. He lowered it back down behind her.

"Ah. I like to take Friday mornings to myself. They're always slow anyway, so I come in just for some peace and quiet. I promise I'm not locking you in, but with my luck the one day I leave it open will be the day people begin flooding in. And I'm in the middle of some very important research." He closed the door, leading her inside. "Can I get you something? I have tea brewing in the back."

"No, thank you," she said, recalling what Mona had said. He probably thought this was a social visit. "I wish I could stay, but unfortunately I needed some help."

"Of course," he replied, setting aside some of the books stacked on the table in the next room over from the main bookshop. "Does this have to do with the case?"

"It does," she replied. "I know Mona asked you to look into Oak Creek, but this is a little more... intense," Charlotte said. "How squeamish are you?"

He leveled his gaze at her. "Please. I've cleaned up more vomit than any one man has a right to. It's amazing how many people like to use the library to get sick."

"Okay, you asked for it." She pulled out her phone and handed it over, open to the first picture she'd taken from the evidence box.

"Ah," he said, gritting his teeth. Suddenly, Charlotte thought she might have overstepped. "That's... graphic."

"It was."

"This isn't from the current case?" he asked.

"No, it's from a case twenty-five years ago. One of my first, actually," she said.

"Oh." He scrolled through the pictures. "That must have been difficult to manage."

She took a deep breath. "It taught me a lot. But that's neither here nor there. Can you take a look at that first picture, the one from above. And tell me if that reminds you of anything?"

He scrolled back to the picture of all the victims the photographer had taken from the catwalk above. At first, he winced, only for a realization to settle over his face. "No. Is this...?"

"You tell me."

He handed the phone back to her and went into the next room, returning momentarily with the same book he'd shown her and Mona when they'd last visited. He opened it, flipping through the pages until he came to the image of an old stone carving, with a symbol prominently displayed in the middle.

"I would say that's coincidence, but I don't think that's the case," Roger said. "Your victims, they're arranged to look like this symbol here."

Charlotte nodded. "That's what I thought too."

"But how did you know?" he asked.

"We found a stone altar, in Oak Creek," she said. "With six different runes carved into it. Five were the ones you sent us. But the sixth..." She pointed to the last image in the book. "I first saw one of the victims' mothers wearing it around her neck. Then, when we found it on the altar, I knew it couldn't be a coincidence. Mona insisted to me that these cases were related, and I didn't want to believe it at first. But now, there is no doubt in my mind. We didn't know it at the time, but the bodies were arranged in the shape of one of your runes."

"Wait, what altar?" he asked.

Charlotte scrolled back to the images, showing him.

"Charlotte, these are incredible," he said. "Do you know what this means? It's probably the most significant find of this language in modern history!"

He turned to a pile of books that were off to the side, along with large parcel maps. "I've been looking into that town of yours, and from what I can tell, it's no ordinary small town."

"What do you mean?"

"I found records that it was settled in the early seventeen hundreds by Welsh refugees who had fled England under religious persecution. This book," he held up the first one he'd pulled for Charlotte and Mona, "is the only written text on the religion I can find. They were known as *Cylch Coed Sanctaidd*, which roughly translates into 'Circle of the Sacred Grove.'"

"That's the name of their congregation. Which sounds harmless enough," Charlotte said.

"It does. But what little history I've managed to uncover has revealed some dark practices. Blood rite sacrifices, intended to 'purify' members or ensure the safety and longevity of those in the order. And as far as I can tell, these practices go back over a thousand years or more. Charlotte, the town was *founded* by the people who were part of this order. Almost three centuries ago."

"So you're saying these people brought their practices over with them and continued to operate in secret through the modern age?"

Roger tightened his features, some of the excitement leaving his face. "I wish I could. But like I said, any text on these practices is scarce at best. Your discovery of that altar is the first confirmed structure on this side of the Atlantic to bear any of these symbols. I've actually reached out to some of my colleagues across the pond to see if they can't help provide some more context."

"Okay," Charlotte said. "So how do Goole and his followers get mixed up in this? They were originally from Chicago. As best we could tell, none of them were born in Oak Creek. And the congregation is small. Certainly not the entire town."

"It was common for families to move away from small towns in the thirties and forties," Roger said. "Most of the jobs moved to the larger cities. Maybe they took their practices with them."

"You're suggesting they didn't leave Chicago looking for a new home, but instead an *old* one."

He nodded. "Makes sense to me. Especially if these practices had been passed down. They would have known about their ancestral history in Oak Creek."

As Charlotte pondered the idea, Roger cleared his throat. "You know, as someone who skews more scientific, I'm remiss to even mention this. But as I get older, I find I'm starting to believe things that seemed preposterous when I was young."

"What do you mean?"

He grabbed one of the books, opening it to show Charlotte a hand-drawn image of what looked to be a large tree with a circle around it. The image itself looked like it was in the style of the medieval ages. But at the base was a person who had been cut open, their insides spilling out. "I'm a practical person. But I also know that life generates energy, and that energy has to go somewhere. The areas of the Welsh countryside where these people operated remain mostly deserted to this day, and I think there's a good reason."

"Roger," Charlotte said, narrowing her gaze.

"I know," he replied. "It sounds crazy. But I don't think you can do these kinds of things without attracting something... unnatural.

This sixth image, the one you found on the pendant... it means *protection*."

"Protection from what?" she asked.

"That's the million-dollar question," he replied. "There are a few other interpretations, but I'd say it's more prevalent than the others. It also shows up in more places. Whatever these people are doing, they are trying to protect themselves from the consequences."

"You mean like killing five people and arranging them into one of the symbols," Charlotte said.

He nodded.

Something stuck in the back of Charlotte's mind. "This... dark energy they're protecting themselves from... could it attract something else?"

"What do you mean?"

She couldn't believe she was about to ask this. But in for a penny... "Could it attract someone who might have a propensity for killing?"

"I don't know," he replied. "Maybe."

Mona and her mother had escaped to Oak Creek, trying to outrun Mona's father. But he'd managed to find them anyway and Charlotte had never been able to square that. Out of all the towns in the entire country, he *happened* upon the right one. Was it because there was something about Oak Creek that had *pulled* him in?

"There's something else," Charlotte said, setting that aside for the moment. Right now she didn't have the time to chase fairy tales. There was a real-life killer out there. "It involves the burns."

"The brands?"

"Not exactly." She scrolled to the images of the burns on her victims from twenty-five years ago. The official autopsy photos were clearer than what Charlotte had seen in the dark warehouse that night. And while she'd likely glanced at them in the course of her investigation, she'd never really taken a good, hard look until now.

Maybe now it was because she knew exactly what she was looking for.

She showed Roger the first image, a dark burn that had left the skin peeling in places, almost black from where it had charred the skin. He pulled back from the phone, not really examining the photo.

"I'm sorry," Charlotte said, covering it back up. "Sometimes I forget how desensitized I am to this stuff."

"No, that's okay," Roger said and gently took her hand, moving it to the side. As he did she felt a jolt of electricity race up her arm, not unlike when she used to feel the pain in her hands from her injury. But this was completely different. This was a *good* feeling. The kind that made her want to shiver all over.

Roger pulled his hand back quickly, like he'd just realized what he'd done. He took a nearby napkin and dabbed his brow. "Um... right. So it's a burn mark. Quite bad, it appears."

Charlotte smiled, indulging the feeling for a brief second. Maybe Mona wasn't as far off the mark as she'd thought. She turned her attention back to the photo. "Look at the edges of the burn. See anything?"

He squinted. "Yes. Looks like markings beyond the burn radius. Wait a second." He flipped the book to another page. "Is that the *bottom* of this rune here?" He pointed to the rune that had appeared on Mallory Wakefield. The shepherd's hook with the Y shape bisecting it.

"I believe it is." She showed him the other pictures. Some were too burned to be able to tell, but in at least three, there were hints of what had been on the victims before the burns.

"You're saying that each of these victims was marked with the same runes you're investigating?" Roger asked.

Twenty-five years ago, Charlotte had assumed the burns had been some sort of signature of their own. Something the killer did to their victims as part of a ritual or a calling card of some kind. She hadn't considered the possibility that the burns had been to *cover up* other, more immediate evidence. Someone had tried burning those marks off the bodies... marks that could have been brands. And given the size of them, they were much more likely to match those that were confiscated from Joseph Goole's home.

"Back then we didn't know about the runes—the symbols," she said. "If we had, we might have been able to put it together. Someone covered it up so we wouldn't be able to investigate."

"And now they're back at it again," he said. "After all this time."

Charlotte nodded. "It certainly looks that way."

TWENTY-NINE

Mona watched Charlotte's car pull into the parking lot with a mixture of relief and apprehension. She'd been waiting outside the station for twenty minutes, too restless to stay indoors after everything that had happened. The weight of Micah Gibson's death hung heavily in the air around her, made worse by the knowledge that Joseph and Marie Goole had been released a few hours ago, along with their daughter. Mona had tried to argue that Kayleigh was safer at the station, that she should remain in police protection, but Goole hadn't wanted to hear a word of it. Apparently, they had burned any remaining goodwill with the family by bringing them in on murder charges. Goole had insisted that they could protect Kayleigh themselves.

Charlotte parked haphazardly across two spaces, something so unlike her that Mona's concern immediately deepened. As the older detective got out of the car, Mona could see she was moving with extreme caution, her face tight with pain she was trying desperately to conceal.

"You look terrible," Mona said bluntly as Charlotte approached.

"Good to see you too," Charlotte replied, her voice strained. "I have something."

"So do I. There's been another murder."

Charlotte stopped short. "Who?"

"Micah Gibson. Twenty-four years old. Single gunshot wound to the head. And the same placement of a symbol on his wrist."

"When?"

"This morning. While Joseph Goole was in custody."

Charlotte's expression shifted, calculation replacing the pain in her eyes for a brief moment. "Shit. That changes things."

"And not in our favor," Mona replied. "We had to release them both. Joseph's lawyer was adamant—we had nothing concrete to hold him on, especially with this latest killing happening while he was here. We managed to identify three other potential victims, and two are under guard at this moment. Bowman just tracked down Langford."

"And the third?"

"It's Kayleigh," Mona admitted. "And the Gooles weren't leaving her here."

Charlotte nodded slowly. "When did they leave?"

"About an hour ago." Mona hesitated, then added, "But that's not all. There's something else that connects the victims."

They moved to a bench near the entrance, away from prying ears. Charlotte lowered herself with obvious difficulty, and Mona pretended not to notice the way she had to brace herself against the armrest.

"Gibson's father called them 'the chosen ones,'" Mona explained. "All four victims grew up in the church together. They were all only children. They were all the *same age*. And get this—Mrs. Gibson was wearing the same pendant necklace with that symbol we found on the altar and around Mrs. Peterson's neck."

Charlotte's eyes widened. "Protection."

"What?"

"The symbol. The one on the pendants. It means 'protection.'" Charlotte pulled out her phone, showing Mona a page from what looked like an ancient text with a familiar symbol. "Roger confirmed it."

"That's exactly what Mrs. Gibson told us about her pendant," Mona said. "She said Joseph and Marie gave it to her when she 'completed her spiritual journey' twenty-five years ago."

"Twenty-five years." Charlotte's voice was hollow. "Right before the kids were born."

Mona nodded. "All of them were born within four months of each other. That can't be a coincidence. Did you find anything in the case files?"

"You were right from the beginning. The cases are connected." Charlotte swiped through several photos on her phone—crime scene photos from decades ago, showing five bodies arranged in very odd pattern, blood everywhere. "Look at the arrangement from above."

Mona studied the horrific image, then suddenly saw what Charlotte was pointing out. "It's the same symbol."

"Exactly. And there's more." Charlotte showed her close-ups of burn marks on the victims' wrists. "These burns were covering up something. Brands. The same kind of brands we found in Goole's house."

Mona felt a chill run through her that had nothing to do with the evening air. "So Joseph and Marie were involved with what happened in Chicago."

Charlotte nodded. "There's more." She filled Mona in about what Roger had found on the town, though she left out her inquiry into Mona's father. They had enough to deal with at the moment.

"I wonder if Mrs. Carter knows," Mona said. "She has the town's history. Do you think she might be involved with this..."

"*Cylch Coed Sanctaidd?*"

"There's no telling," Charlotte replied. "It seems a lot of people in this town know more than what they're willing to say."

"So what do we do?" Mona asked.

"Let's double the security on the potential victims. With Micah Gibson that makes four, giving our killer only one more target before they're done. Then I think we need to sit down with every single member of this group—whatever they want to call themselves—until we get some answers. Did you find Bradshaw yet?"

Mona shook her head. "And Bowman and I have gone through twenty interviews already. No one is talking. I thought we could get something out of the Gibsons, but even with their son dead, they weren't willing to reveal anything. They are definitely hiding something, though."

"Maybe they'll be more cooperative if I have a talk with them."

Mona had to admit, she looked stronger than she had over the past two days, but still, the injuries had to be taking a toll on her. Mona didn't want to be the one to suggest Charlotte sit this one out, but at the same time, could she live with herself if something happened?

"We go back to the source. I want to sit down with Mrs. Goole. The women in this group seem to know as much if not more than the men. I believe we were interviewing the wrong person."

"I know you don't want to—" Mona's phone rang, cutting her off. She frowned at the screen. "Unknown number."

She answered, putting it on speaker. "This is Detective LaSalle."

"Detective." The voice was female, barely audible. "I need your help."

Mona put the phone on speaker. "Mrs. Goole?"

"Please. She's gone. Kayleigh is gone." The woman's voice broke. "When we got home, she wasn't here. Her things are still here, but she's not."

"I thought she returned home *with* you," Mona said.

"She was only five or ten minutes ahead of us," Mrs. Goole replied. "I don't know what could have happened."

"Is her cell phone still there?" Mona asked.

The woman was breathless on the other end. "I think he's going to kill her. Like the others."

"Stay where you are," Mona said. "We're coming to you."

. . .

They arrived at the Goole residence within fifteen minutes. Marie Goole sat alone at the kitchen table, her face ashen, hands clutched around a mug of untouched tea. She didn't look up when they entered, didn't acknowledge their presence at all.

"Mrs. Goole?" Mona approached carefully. "Where's your husband?"

"Looking for her," Marie whispered. Her voice had the same distant quality it had held when they'd spoken with her earlier, but now there was a tremor underneath it. "He thinks she might have gotten scared and left on her own."

Mona pulled out a chair across from Marie while Charlotte stood back, observing. "Give us the entire sequence of events. Starting from when you left the station."

She nodded. "Joseph and I were speaking with the lawyer. Kayleigh said she would meet us back home. We told her we'd be right behind her." Marie's eyes remained fixed on her mug. "Her car is still here. Her phone. Everything."

"Did she leave a note? Any indication of where she might have gone?"

Marie shook her head slightly.

"Has she ever disappeared like this before?" Charlotte asked from her position by the doorway.

"No." Marie finally looked up, her pale eyes rimmed with red. "Never."

Mona studied the woman carefully. There was something off about her reactions—a detachment that went beyond shock or grief. It was almost like she'd been expecting this.

"Mrs. Goole," Mona said gently, "I couldn't help but notice the pendant you wear." She pointed to the silver charm hanging around Marie's neck. "Several other members of your congregation wear similar ones. Can you tell me more about them?"

Marie's hand went to her throat, clutching the pendant. "Protection," she murmured. "They're meant to ward off bad things."

"What kinds of bad things?"

"The past. But it doesn't work that way." Her gaze drifted back to her tea. "The past doesn't forgive. The past doesn't forget."

Charlotte moved closer, wincing slightly as she lowered herself into a chair. "We know you lived in Chicago before you moved here. Or should I say, moved *back* here. What happened that caused you to return?"

The woman didn't respond.

"Four children from your congregation are dead," Charlotte pressed. "All the same age. All marked with symbols like the ones on the altar behind your home."

"And now Kayleigh is missing," Mona added. "We want to help her, but we need to understand what's happening."

Marie's fingers tightened around her pendant. "They were chosen," she whispered. "One for each family. A gift."

"A gift to whom?" Charlotte asked.

"For protection. For all of us."

Mona felt a familiar prickle of dread crawl up her spine. "Are you saying that what happened to these victims—to Mallory, Connor, Justine, and Micah—was planned?"

Marie's eyes snapped to Mona's, suddenly lucid and intense. "No! That wasn't supposed to happen. They were supposed to be *safe*. They were our miracles."

"Tell us about the brands," Charlotte prompted. "The ones we found here in the house."

"Sacred symbols. Given at birth." Marie's breathing quickened. "*Trees watered with blood bear fruit.*"

Mona exchanged a quick glance with Charlotte. The five symbols, that was their rough translation.

"Five children... to continue... to make sure everything survives..."

"But you think someone is targeting them specifically," Mona said, trying to bring the woman back to them. "Someone who knows about the symbols, about your church."

"We're paying the price," Marie said, her voice rising. "All of us. For what we did. For what we agreed to."

"What did you agree to, Marie?" Charlotte asked quietly.

"The sacrifice." Marie's eyes welled with tears. "The exchange."

"Exchange of what?"

"Life for life." Marie's hand shook so badly that tea sloshed over the rim of her mug. "Five lives for our children. That was the bargain."

Mona exchanged a glance with Charlotte. This was starting to sound like a confession to the Chicago murders from twenty-five years ago.

"Are you talking about what happened in the warehouse in Chicago?" Mona asked. "The five people who were killed?"

Marie's face contorted. "We... we were different then. It was wrong... I *knew* it was wrong. But it was tradition. Joseph said... it was the only way. Anything else was blasphemy. I went along with it. We... didn't think we had a choice. All we wanted was a future." She suddenly grabbed Mona's wrist with surprising strength. "Can you understand that, Detective? Do you have any *idea* what we did for our children? What we *sacrificed*?" Her fingernails dug into Mona's arm, breaking the skin, and she tried to work to get out of the woman's grip.

"Mrs. Goole—" She struggled until another hand grabbed Marie's wrist and in one simple move applied enough pressure that the other woman cried out, crumpling under the grip. Charlotte released her as Mona grabbed a nearby napkin, applying pressure against the four puncture marks in her skin.

"Are you okay?" Charlotte asked.

Mona nodded, though the wounds burned.

"Mrs. Goole, I'm placing you back under arrest for assault on an officer of the law," Charlotte said, but Marie had retreated into herself, her eyes vacant again.

"The past doesn't forgive," she repeated. "The past doesn't forget. We're paying the price."

"It's okay," Mona said. "Leave her. I don't think it was intentional." She turned back to her attacker. "Mrs. Goole, does

Kayleigh have somewhere she likes to go when she's scared? Is there somewhere special to her? Somewhere she might feel safe?"

Marie didn't seem to hear the question. She began rocking slightly in her chair, her breathing becoming more erratic. "He's going to take her. Like the others. And there's nothing I can do. Nothing any of us can do."

"Who is going to take her?" Mona asked, trying to keep her voice calm despite the growing sense of urgency. "Who killed the others?"

"The past doesn't forgive," Marie said again, her voice rising to a near-shout. "The past doesn't forget!"

She kept repeating the phrase, her rocking becoming more violent, hands clutching at her pendant so tightly that the chain began to cut into her neck.

"I need to call for medical assistance," Mona said to Charlotte, already reaching for her phone.

Charlotte nodded, her face grim. "Do it."

While Mona made the call, Charlotte continued trying to break through to Marie, but the woman had descended into a state of near-catatonia, repeating her mantra over and over, occasionally punctuated by soft, keening wails.

The paramedics arrived within minutes, administering a mild sedative to calm Marie. They also wrapped Mona's arm as a precaution. As they prepared to transport her to the hospital for evaluation, Mona pulled Charlotte aside.

"What do you make of that?" she asked in a low voice.

Charlotte's face was drawn with pain and fatigue, but her eyes remained sharp. "The answers are locked inside there somewhere. She knows who's behind this. But I'm not sure she knows where Kayleigh is. Otherwise, why call us?"

"She clearly believes she's the next target."

"And if the pattern holds, Kayleigh will be the last." Charlotte leaned against the wall, a subtle gesture that Mona recognized as an attempt to take weight off her injured ankle. "But she gave us something to work with. She talked about a bargain, a sacrifice. Five lives in Chicago for their children's protection."

"And now someone's collecting on that debt?" Mona suggested.

"Maybe." Charlotte's gaze followed the paramedics as they guided Marie toward the ambulance. "Or maybe someone thinks the bargain was broken."

"The past doesn't forgive," Mona murmured. "The past doesn't forget."

"*Someone* sure hasn't." Charlotte pushed herself away from the wall with visible effort. "We need to figure out who else was involved in what happened in Chicago. Who knew about the bargain, about the sacrifice."

"And we need to find Kayleigh before she becomes victim number five," Mona added grimly.

Charlotte nodded, then suddenly grimaced, her hand flying to her side.

"Hey," Mona said, stepping closer. "You need to get checked out. Those ribs—"

"I'm fine," Charlotte insisted, but her ashen complexion said otherwise.

"No, you're not. You can barely stand." Mona kept her voice firm but gentle. "Look, I know this case matters to you. It matters to me too. But you pushing yourself until you collapse isn't going to help us solve it any faster."

Charlotte met Mona's gaze, and for a moment, Mona saw the struggle playing out behind her eyes—the battle between pride and practicality, between determination and physical limitation.

"I need to see this through," Charlotte said quietly.

"And you will," Mona assured her. "But you need to be smart about it. Let me take the lead on the legwork. You focus on connecting the dots, on figuring out who from your original case might still be in play."

"We don't have time for that," she said. "I'm not failing these people again."

Mona let out a long sigh. This was not an argument she would win. She had been the one to bring Charlotte in on this case, and now the woman was determined to see it through, no matter the consequences. "Okay. Then what do we do?"

"Where would Kayleigh go? What would she do if she were scared?"

"She knows the other victims were being tracked using their phones," Mona replied. "Which would explain why she left hers behind. But that makes her nearly impossible to find. She could be half a state away by now."

"I don't think so. She's still a kid. She's scared. Where would you go when you're scared?"

Mona looked up. "To the one person you thought could protect you."

Charlotte nodded. "Exactly. We need to find Terry Barker."

As they quickly made their way back to their vehicle, Mona couldn't help but feel a familiar unease rising within her—not just concern for Charlotte's condition or for Kayleigh's safety, but a deeper fear about what they might discover when they finally unraveled this mystery.

She thought of her father, of the methodical way he'd arranged his kills, of the symbols and rituals that had given meaning to his madness. Was she looking at something similar here? A carefully orchestrated series of deaths designed to fulfill some twisted purpose?

And if so, how would she react when she came face-to-face with the person responsible? Would she see something of herself in them, some shadow of the darkness she'd inherited?

Mona pushed the thought away. She couldn't afford those kinds of doubts, not now. A young woman's life hung in the balance, and the clock was ticking.

"Start with Logan's place," Charlotte said. "And we'll work from there."

"You really think he went back there after getting out on bail?" Mona asked.

"Only if we're lucky."

Mona couldn't shake the feeling that they were running out of time—not just for Kayleigh, but for all of them. Whatever bargain had been struck in blood twenty-five years ago was coming due, and someone was determined to collect, no matter the cost.

Mona only hoped they could change the ending before history repeated itself one final time.

THIRTY

Charlotte had to suppress a grunt of pain as the car hit the next pothole. She was pushing it and knew it, but she couldn't give up now. She'd rest as soon as they found Kayleigh Goole and made sure she was safe. Until then, she just had to bear it.

To her credit, Mona had picked up on just how injured Charlotte was. But thankfully she hadn't removed her from the case. Charlotte doubted the thought even entered Mona's mind, despite the fact she was well within her authority to do it. But Mona was just as concerned with finding Kayleigh as Charlotte was, and they both knew they were on a ticking clock.

As they pulled up to the same beaten-down and battered home, Charlotte steeled herself. She couldn't afford to look weak or injured in front of Logan—assuming he was even home. A lone vehicle sat in the driveway littered with weeds. The sun was threatening to set, and Charlotte suspected that if they didn't find her, Kayleigh may not survive the night.

She hung back while Mona headed up to the front door, knocking vociferously. A few moments later the door opened to reveal Logan, only for him to realize who was on the other side before trying to slam the door in their faces. Fortunately, Mona had been ready for it and had stuck her foot between the door and jamb, keeping it from closing entirely.

"Logan," she said. "We're looking for Terry. Is he here?"

"Get the hell off my property," he spat.

"You're renting, it's not your property," Mona replied.

"I don't have to talk to you," he said. "My lawyer is gonna—"

"Your lawyer isn't here right now," Charlotte said, coming up to the kid and pushing the door open. "Where's Terry?"

"Fuck you," he replied, backing up a few steps.

"Do you even understand what's happening out there?" Charlotte asked, bearing down on the boy, despite the pain it caused her. "Have you been watching the news at all?"

This seemed to catch him off guard as he continued backing up, his bravado once again falling away quickly to reveal the scared kid underneath. "No. I'm not ninety like you."

"Four people, Logan. Four people have been murdered in the past week. All people your age. The last one was killed with a gunshot to the head."

"S-so?" he asked.

"So the killer is still out there. Targeting people. And he's looking for Kayleigh. Maybe Terry too. Maybe he's even looking for you. He doesn't seem to discriminate who he goes after. Just as long as they're young adults. I'd say that puts you firmly in his crosshairs."

"This is bullshit," he said. "You're just trying to scare me."

"Why do you think we brought you into the station? Because of some bullshit drug charge? I don't care about that." Charlotte took a few steps closer. "I care about people getting mercilessly murdered for no apparent reason. And this guy is a ghost. We still don't have any witnesses."

"I—I don't believe you," he said, though she could tell he was beginning to crack.

"If you're not going to help us, at least help yourself," Charlotte added. "The sooner we find this guy, the sooner everyone can go back to life as normal. *Or*, after we leave, you can keep looking over your shoulder."

"Why would he come after me?" Logan stumbled back and ended up sitting on his ratty couch.

"No reason. It's been completely random so far. But you're an easy target. And this house isn't very secure. I'd be willing to bet I could find a couple of windows that could be opened with just a little work. Did I mention Justine Mercer? Her throat was sliced from ear to ear. She never even saw it coming."

"Okay, *fine*," he said. "Jeez, get off my back."

"Terry. Now."

Logan huffed. "His dad has an old hunting cabin out on Chambers Highway. He sometimes takes girls out there when he wants to be alone."

"Why doesn't he live out there?" Mona asked. "If it belongs to his family?"

"It's small. Barely a bedroom," Logan replied. "Plus, it's a long way from town."

Charlotte leaned forward. "Do you have an address?"

Logan dug his phone out of his pocket and tapped away for a few moments. Finally, he turned it around to show Charlotte the map. "There."

"Sixty-two Chambers Highway," Charlotte said. "Have you had any contact with Terry today?"

"No, he was gone by the time I got up."

"Call him." He looked at her incredulously. "He won't pick up if we call. Call him. Now." Logan tapped Terry's name on his phone and it began ringing. "Put it on speaker." The call rang four times before going to Terry's voicemail.

"Terry B." Then there was a beep. Logan hung up.

"Try again," Charlotte said. "He may be screening."

She had him call Terry four times, but after the fifth, it was unlikely he would pick up.

"Service can be spotty out there too," Logan said. "He might get them all at once."

Mona handed over her business card. "If he calls you back, let us know immediately." Logan hesitated taking the card. "Unless you want their blood on your hands."

He huffed again, taking the card from her.

"C'mon," Charlotte said. "We need to get out there and check it." She pointed at Logan. "You understand how serious this is."

"Yeah, yeah, I got it," he replied, waving the card back at her. "I'll call."

They headed back out to the car and Charlotte finally released how hard she'd been holding herself in there. Ribbons of pain shot through her side, causing her to grimace. She put a hand to her abdomen, as if she were trying to hold the pain in and keep it from leeching out.

"Are you—"

"I'm fine," Charlotte replied. "Let's just get out there. Quickly."

Thankfully, Mona didn't argue. But she could tell the younger detective wanted to. They were so close now. All they needed to do was find Kayleigh and get her to safety. *Then* Charlotte could take a break.

The drive out to the cabin was long—longer than she'd expected. Logan hadn't been kidding when he said it wasn't close to anything. It sat in a remote part of the county surrounded not by farmland, but by woods and old-growth trees. By the time they arrived, the sun had fully disappeared, leaving the entire area in complete darkness.

The road up to the cabin wasn't paved, and Charlotte felt each and every bump as they traversed the gravel road. Each jolt sent another shot of pain through her and she expected the next one would be the one that dislodged her rib and punctured a vital organ.

Finally, they pulled up to the cabin itself. Charlotte wiped the sweat from her brow, taking in the scene. "Barker's car is here."

The cabin itself was small, as Logan had described. But from what they could tell there were no lights on inside. At least none on this end of the building, where there was only one small window.

"Think they're alone in there?" Mona asked.

"I sure hope so," Charlotte replied. She winced getting out of the car and had to hold on to the hood for a second until the pain subsided.

"Charlotte," Mona said in a low voice. "Just stay here. I'll take care of this."

"No, I—"

"You're not doing me any good by going up there and getting in the way," Mona shot back. "Right now you're a liability. Stay with the car."

The words hit Charlotte like cold water. Mona had never spoken to her like that before, and in a brief instant she saw the same Mona she'd seen in that basement when she thought she'd been under the spell of her father. A momentary viciousness that was so unlike her, and yet fit Mona like a glove.

"Can't let you go alone," Charlotte finally said.

"You're not going up there," Mona replied, pulling out her weapon. Charlotte knew she didn't mean to use it on her; she probably hadn't even thought about it. But still, the visual of Mona with the gun caused Charlotte to back down. She was in no condition to put up a fight. Mona was right. She *was* a liability right now. And she needed to stay back.

"If you think that's best."

"I'll be back in a minute," Mona said, her old self returning. "Just try not to die on me while I'm gone."

Charlotte nodded, opening the side door and slumping back in as Mona headed up the path to the cabin. Confronting Logan had taken almost all the rest of her strength. She should have let Mona and her partner handle this, instead of insisting she be a part of it. Her damn pride was going to get her killed if she wasn't careful.

She just hoped Mona could handle herself up there.

THIRTY-ONE

Mona crept quietly towards the house. She wasn't trying to completely obscure her presence, but she also didn't want to announce herself. It was possible Terry and Kayleigh were otherwise pre-occupied with each other and hadn't seen the headlights bearing down on the cabin from the road. Though, given she knew her life could be in danger, that wasn't very likely.

As she approached the rickety front porch, which looked like it had been the meal of a hundred different termite families, she carefully stepped up to the door, listening first for any movement on the other side. But it was completely silent.

She pushed gently on the door, which had no real latch, only a bar that acted as a handle. It opened freely, the door creaking on its old, rusty hinges as it opened into the space. Using what little light that filtered down in from the moon, Mona scanned the inside of the cabin, finding it to be empty. As Logan had described, it was a one-room place with little more than a fireplace for a kitchen and an old couch that could be pulled out into a bed. A small wooden table sat under the single window on the far side, with three chairs around it. It seemed like there was space for a fourth chair, but it was missing. There was also a back door that was partially ajar.

Mona scanned the space, finding Terry's personal effects

discarded on the nearby table. His wallet, and the keys to his car lay on the surface beside an old camping lamp. Mona placed her hand on the base, finding the lamp was still slightly warm.

They had been here not long ago. But where would they go without his car? And in the middle of the night?

Mona headed to the back door, opening it carefully. Out beyond the house lay a path that led to a large pond behind the property, surrounded by woods. And in the moonlight she could see figures standing out on a dock that led out into the pond, their silhouettes dark against the calm water.

For a second she thought it might be Terry and Kayleigh, out enjoying the scenery, but as she looked closer she realized something was very wrong. One of the figures was sitting in a chair and the other looked like they were tying ropes around the person, affixing them to the chair.

Mona rushed forward along the path, nearly tripping when her foot hit a large root.

But when she looked down, she realized it wasn't a root at all. The dead eyes of Terry Barker stared back at her. The middle of his white shirt was dark with crimson blood and it had pooled all around his body. She didn't need to check his pulse to know that he was gone. There was no life left in him at all. Someone had stuck him like a pig and left him to die there.

Mona pulled out her phone as she continued running towards the dock. She tried dialing Charlotte, but the phone wouldn't connect, even though they couldn't be more than a hundred yards from each other. She didn't want to yell out either, for fear of spooking whoever was on the dock into early action. Her best bet was to try and interrupt whatever they were doing before being spotted.

Mona shoved her phone back in her pocket and kept low, making her way forward as the two figures became clearer. Even from here, she recognized Kayleigh as the person in the chair. As far as she could tell, she was still alive, as she was jerking back and forth as her captor continued working on the lashings to bind her.

Her legs and arms had already been tied, and he was currently tying a series of ropes around her midsection, as well as her neck to make sure she wouldn't be able to get free. The chair itself was perched on the edge of the dock and Mona could already see what was about to happen. He meant to drown her in that pond, weighing her down so she couldn't float back up to the surface.

The figure doing the lashing was turned away from Mona, mostly obscured by the chair itself, which allowed her to get close. However, Kayleigh was facing her and saw Mona before she wanted her to. She began thrashing harder, an adrenaline-fueled panic brought on by Mona's mere presence.

"Quit wiggling, girl, you're only making this worse," the voice behind Kayleigh said.

Mona emerged onto the dock and raised her weapon, pointing it straight at the man behind her. Mona noticed that Kayleigh's arm already bore the brand burned into her skin: the final symbol from the altar. The iron brand sat nearby on the dock itself, next to a small travel furnace.

"Stop right there," Mona said, her weapon trained dead on the man.

He froze, not coming out from behind Kayleigh.

"Come out slowly, with your hands in the air and where I can see them," Mona ordered.

He wore dark chinos and a pullover, but she still couldn't see his face. "You're early," he said.

"I think I'm right on time," Mona replied. "Come out. Now."

"I'm sorry about Mr. Barker," the man said. "He got in the way. He wasn't supposed to be part of this."

"Just come out and we can talk." Mona tried to get a good bead on him, but he was using Kayleigh as a makeshift shield, making it difficult for her to get a clean shot.

"If I come out, you'll kill me," he said.

"No. I don't want to kill you," Mona replied. "But I do want you to let Kayleigh go."

"Can't do that," he said. "She's the last one. After her, it's all done." Kayleigh tried crying out in response, but only a muffled scream emanated from behind the tape on her mouth.

"The last one of what?" Mona asked.

"The crop," the man replied. "The *miracles*."

Mona couldn't be sure, but the man didn't seem to be that old from the sound of his voice. Maybe only in his early forties? She'd expected someone older. Someone who would have been there twenty-five years ago, in Chicago.

"Nathaniel Bradshaw?" she asked.

"Swing and a miss," he replied. He was almost playful, jubilant.

"What's your name?"

"That's not important," he replied. "Just let me finish my work. Then you can do whatever you want with me."

"I'm sorry, but I can't do that. You're about to kill an innocent girl."

"Innocence is granted upon those who come into this world without sin," he replied. "This one was born of it. As they all were."

Mona furrowed her brow. "I don't understand."

"You don't need to," he said, pulling Kayleigh's chair back closer to the edge of the water. Kayleigh screamed out again.

"*Stop!*" Mona yelled.

"Oh, how I wish I could," he replied. "But this is my life's purpose. I have been waiting for this moment for a quarter of a century. I won't be stopped now."

"Then you *were* there, in Chicago," Mona said. "You killed those other kids."

"*No!*" he yelled, the intensity of his voice surprising her. "I was not responsible. *He* was."

"Who?"

"Father Joseph Goole. The *faith* leader."

"Are you saying Goole killed those five victims?" Mona asked. "But why?"

Tears streamed down Kayleigh's face. The man put his lips to her ear while still watching Mona. "That's right. Your father is a cold-blooded killer. He sealed your fate before you were born. How does that feel?"

Kayleigh cried out.

"The cycle of death ends tonight," the man said. "The ritual has to die."

Behind them, at the edge of the pond, Mona caught the slightest movement. She had to squint, but there was another figure on the far bank of the pond. And from the way she was holding herself, Mona had no trouble discerning it was Charlotte.

Mona froze. What was she doing? Whatever it was, Mona needed to stall. To keep the man talking... at least until she could figure out what to do.

"The ritual? *Cylch Coed Sanctaidd*?"

The man paused. "You've done your homework. I'm impressed," he said, inching Kayleigh's chair back closer to the water. "But it was just superstition. What those people did—what they committed for their children... It was the greatest sin of all. And those born into sin must suffer it."

"These children," Mona said, watching Charlotte ease herself into the pond as quietly and carefully as she could. "They had no choice in the matter. They were born without a say. You've been killing them for something they couldn't control. For something they didn't decide."

"I've been doing them a favor," the man replied. "A darkness surrounds these people, Detective. Can't you feel it? They need to be free of this mortal coil. Otherwise, the cycle never ends."

"And their parents are the ones to suffer, is that right?"

He paused. "It's their time. They took, and now they bear the consequences."

"In fact, that's what all this is about, isn't it? Making the parents of these children suffer by taking away what they love the most."

He'd gone quiet. "You speak as someone with experience."

"You're right, I do have experience," Mona said. "I have seen the darkness personally. I've fought it. You could even say I was born into it."

"You?" he asked.

"My father... is a serial killer," Mona replied. It wasn't something she'd admitted aloud before. "He killed my best friend. He almost killed me."

Mona could barely see the ripple in the pond behind them, Charlotte making her way across like a silent alligator.

"What stopped him?" the man asked.

"I did. He thought I was like him. And maybe for a few short minutes I thought I was. But then I realized I could *decide* not to be. I didn't have to give into fate or destiny or anything else. I *decided* to be better. To make up for all the evil he had done. Doesn't Kayleigh deserve the same chance?"

The man had gone still, and Mona caught the first glimpse of his face. He wore glasses, one eye poking up over the shoulder of Kayleigh. His brown hair tousled and haphazard. But cleanly cut nonetheless. "I've never known anyone to escape the darkness."

"Now you do," Mona said. "Because I've done it."

His full attention was on her. And he didn't see the ripple getting closer and closer to him from behind.

"Come out," Mona said. "Give Kayleigh a chance to make up for her father's misdeeds."

He seemed to consider it for a brief moment. "No action can make up for what I've lost," he said. "I'm sorry."

He moved to tip Kayleigh into the water and three things happened at once. Kayleigh screamed as she felt the chair tilt back, and Mona rushed forward in a vain attempt to stop the man. But another scream pierced the air at the same time as Kayleigh's, coming from the man himself. Charlotte had reached the dock and grabbed the still hot branding iron, plunging it into the man's midsection and searing his pullover right onto his skin.

He fell back, writhing and screaming on the dock, letting go of the chair, which rocked back into a stable sitting position. Mona grabbed the man by the arms, pulling them back and handcuffing them behind him.

"No!" he yelled. "I have to finish! I owe her!"

"Shut up for one minute," Charlotte said, hanging onto the edge of the dock with one hand. The other still held the brand, which she tossed onto the dock itself.

"Need a hand?" Mona asked, stowing her weapon.

"Just help me get around to the shore," Charlotte said. "I don't think I can pull myself up." Mona helped her around until she was able to get her feet under her, and even then, Mona had to help Charlotte up onto the bank of the pond. She was holding her side and breathing heavily.

"Charlotte?" Mona asked, but the woman was going in and out of consciousness.

"Let me finish!" the man screamed.

But Mona wasn't worried about him. He wasn't going anywhere. Her primary concern was her partner.

She pulled out her phone and dialed emergency services, praying it would connect this time.

THIRTY-TWO

Charlotte blinked herself awake. For a second she didn't know where she was. But it came back to her the moment she recognized the harsh florescent lights above her as typical for a hospital. She was dressed in another one of those damn robes, lying on an adjustable bed with little more than a thin blanket covering her for warmth.

She lifted up one side of the blanket, noticing her wrist had been bandaged and sighed as she saw the near-complete encasement of her ribs in new wrappings. She also pulled off the cover to reveal her ankle had been treated again as well. With all these bandages, she felt like a mummy.

The TV in the room was on, but there was no sound. Nearby, her clothes and other personal effects sat on a nearby chair, folded neatly. She couldn't reach her phone; it was too far away. Outside the sun was shining, indicating it was at least midday. How long had she been out?

She grabbed the nearby controller for the bed and TV, nearly getting the cord tangled with the IV that ran into a needle that had been taped to her hand. She pressed the call button on the device and a little red light went on above her.

Charlotte tried taking a deep breath only to realize she

couldn't, that a heavy stitch prevented her from breathing deeply. Probably courtesy of her ribs.

"Ah," the nurse said, coming into the room. "Hang on, I'll get the doctor, Ms. Dawes. Are you in severe pain in any way?"

"No," Charlotte grunted. "Just the dull kind."

The nurse nodded and headed back out quickly.

Charlotte tried to recall what had happened. She'd grown worried when she hadn't heard from Mona in the cabin and, despite her better judgement, had followed her out there. Only by the time she'd gotten there, Mona had been on the dock in a standoff with their suspect.

Charlotte could have joined her on the dock, but considering she didn't have a weapon, all she would have done was make the situation worse. But he was close to the edge of the water. So she figured if she could get into the pond unseen, she could sneak up behind him, and maybe give Mona the edge.

She'd gotten in the water easily enough, and for the first time in days, the buoyancy had given her some temporary relief to her injuries, allowing her to float silently towards the dock. It had been then when she spotted the still red-hot brand on the dock beside the man. She'd made it her life's mission to get to that brand and shove it into his balls. In the end she'd only managed his midsection. But it had been enough for Mona to get the jump on him.

After that... she didn't recall much. All that had taken what little strength she had left. She'd needed help getting out of the water... but how had that happened? Had she accidentally gone under? She couldn't recall.

"Ms. Dawes," a woman's voice said, entering the room. She was dressed in a smart pantsuit and wore a white coat. The tag on her left pocket identified her as Dr. Bellen. "How are we feeling?"

"Four out of ten," Charlotte replied.

Dr. Bellen pulled out a pen light, shining it in each of Charlotte's eyes quickly before clicking it off again. "Given what you've put your body through, that's pretty good."

"How bad?" Charlotte asked.

"You had some internal hemorrhaging, which we managed to get under control, thankfully. But you were lucky. Most patients who experience that kind of injury don't get a second chance. I reviewed Dr. Anson's notes. You were supposed to be on bedrest after your last visit."

"Couldn't," Charlotte said. "I need to speak with Mona LaSalle."

"Detective LaSalle has already been here three times," Bellen replied. "And I believe she's coming back this afternoon. The question is, am I going to have to tell her to restrain you to this bed or are you going to cooperate?"

Charlotte gave her a rueful smile. "No. I'll cooperate."

"Good. And when I tell you that you need six weeks of recovery, I mean it. You are not to do anything but lay on your couch and let someone else do whatever you need. Understand?"

"Sorry, I'm not very good at sitting around," Charlotte said.

"Well, get good at it. Because if you don't let your injuries heal, you could very well kill yourself. You already almost succeeded once."

Charlotte swallowed hard. She hadn't meant to push herself so hard and so far. Ten, even five years ago, she could have handled injuries like this without much fuss. It was like her body was betraying her at a time when she needed it the most. "Six weeks. Understood."

"Good," Dr. Bellen replied. "I know it's probably hard, given your previous profession. But we make adjustments depending on where we are in life. We adapt. I read your medical file. You're no stranger to hardship."

Charlotte thought back to her hands. To the life she never got to lead. "No, I guess not."

"This is just a different kind of challenge," Bellen replied. "You can either embrace it or fight it. But it's happening regardless. It's up to you to decide what you want the rest of your life to look like."

"Which means give up," Charlotte said.

"No," Bellen replied. "It means you grow."

. . .

"I feel like an idiot."

"This was the only way," Mona said, pushing Charlotte in the wheelchair up the ramp to the station's entrance. "Either this or we do it through video chat."

"This," Charlotte replied quickly. "I'll stick with this."

It had been three days since her stint in the hospital, and five days since she and Mona had saved Kayleigh Goole from a watery grave. The entire town had been up in arms since then, after the media got hold of the fact that each of the victims was a member of the same religious group.

Their suspect—a middle-aged man by the name of Colt Hardin—had been held in custody without bail while he waited for a hearing date. Mona and Bowman had tried interviewing him multiple times, but he'd been reluctant to talk, his anger at Mona from keeping him from killing Kayleigh palpable.

Charlotte had been prepared to go home as the doctor ordered, *until* Mona had asked for one final favor. Hardin had waived the right to a lawyer, but he also hadn't confessed, and it was Mona's hope that Charlotte might be able to get something out of since he was obviously connected to Charlotte's case from twenty-five years ago.

She'd had a lot of time to think about what Dr. Bellen had said, and eventually Charlotte had decided she was right. Fighting her aging body was only going to make things worse. She needed to adapt and modify. Not give up—it didn't mean she could sit around eating chips and drinking beer all day. But it did mean to work within her limitations. And maybe sometimes push against them. A little.

But that didn't make this moment any less humiliating. Being wheeled into the precinct like someone in their nineties.

"Look out, coming through," Mona called, and Charlotte could tell she was enjoying this way too much.

"I've got an idea, why don't we switch places and I push you?" she suggested.

"Because Dr. Bellen would kill me if she knew I let you out of this chair," Mona replied. "Now get ready. They've already got him in interview room one."

"You really think he'll talk to me," Charlotte said.

"He refuses to talk to me," Mona replied. "Or anyone else for that matter. Even snubbed Earle when he tried to speak with him."

"I'm the one who burned him, remember?"

"You're also the one who investigated the case in Chicago. Whatever all this is about, it began there."

Charlotte took a deep breath as Mona wheeled her into the interview room where Colt Hardin sat, chained to the other side of the table. He scowled as soon as he saw Mona, but she just parked Charlotte on the near side of the table and left the room without a word.

Charlotte, for her part, wasn't used to not being physically in control of the situation. But she had to remember: Adapt. Don't force it.

"Morning, Mr. Hardin," Charlotte said. "I'm former detective Dawes."

"Former?" he asked, eyeing her carefully.

"I retired earlier this year," she replied. "Twenty-nine years on the Chicago police force."

"Congratulations," he said, deadpan. He was handsome, she had to give it to him. He wore clear-rimmed, prison-issue glasses in place of the ones he'd had on the other night. But his hair was thick and dark, showing no signs of the gray that would eventually make its mark. And he had a strong chin to boot; the kind she was sure made women swoon.

"In fact, it's my former career that brings me here to speak with you," she continued when he didn't respond. "One of my first cases as a detective was a multiple homicide. Perhaps you're aware of it. August twenty-ninth, 1999. The block district."

He stiffened.

She nodded. "We found five bodies that night. Each of which had their wrists and necks cut, allowing them to bleed out. And they all had these peculiar burns on their arms, right about here." She pointed to the middle of her forearm, causing Colt to look away. "I'll be honest, Mr. Hardin. We didn't know what to make of it. It's remained an unsolved case ever since. But I think you know what happened that night."

He continued looking away.

"I'm aware you already know the charges against you. You're looking at five counts of murder and an additional count of attempted murder. In addition to a slew of lesser charges. As you know this state no longer has the death penalty. But you would be looking at five life sentences at the bare minimum. And I've already spoken with the DA. He's looking to make those to be served in sequence.

"In other words, you are never seeing the light of day again. You understand that, don't you?"

He didn't respond.

"And the worst part of it was you never got your revenge. You never completed the work you started back in ninety-nine."

He turned to her, fury on his face. "The work *I* started? I didn't start anything. I was only fifteen back then."

"So I read," Charlotte replied, keeping her cool. "Impressive for a fifteen-year-old. My question is, how did you do it? How did you get them to kill themselves?"

He slammed a fist down on the table. "That wasn't me!"

"Then why start now, all these years later?" Charlotte asked. "Using the same brands?"

He perked up, his anger ebbing and flowing. "What?"

"You're using the same brands we found on the bodies back then," Charlotte replied.

He narrowed his eyes. "You found markings?"

She smiled. "I'll admit, I was a junior detective back then and really had no idea what I was looking at. I was more concerned with keeping my lunch down. But I recently went back to take a look. I found patterns beneath the initial burns that seem to match the five symbols we found on your victims. Symbols that someone tried to erase... to cover up, by burning the flesh away."

"You don't understand," he said. "You can't. No one can understand what I went through."

"Then tell me," Charlotte replied. "Maybe I can find a way to help. It's either that, or you spend the rest of your life asking, 'what if?'"

Hardin took a deep breath as if he were considering it. "If I tell you, will you make him pay?"

"Who?"

"Goole." The word came out like a curse.

"Depends. Let's start at the beginning."

"My real name isn't Hardin," he said. "It's Hocker. Colt Hocker."

Suddenly, everything made sense. It was like he'd removed a wall obscuring her vision. *Melissa* Hocker had been one of her victims twenty-five years ago. A recent college grad of Northwestern. Hers was the third body they finally identified when her parents began putting up missing posters around town.

"Your sister was one of the five," Charlotte said softly. He nodded. "I spoke with your parents back then. They told me they had a son in high school..."

"Yeah," he replied. "I dropped out."

Charlotte was sure Mona and Bowman were scrambling behind the scenes, trying to get as much information on Colt Hocker as they could. But she didn't need any of it. She remembered the file vividly.

"Your sister worked for a biochemical company, researching cancer, didn't she?"

He nodded.

"And your parents never had any idea about how she could have become involved in a cult killing like that. But you know... don't you?"

"A couple of months before, I overheard her talking to one of her friends on the phone," he said. "Talking about all kinds of weird stuff, rituals, ceremonies. I thought she was talking about a movie or something. When I asked about it, she pretended like it was nothing.

"So I did what any little brother would do. I started going through her personal things. I found her diary with all sorts of information about the Circle of the Sacred Grove. They'd approached her at work, asking if she would be interested in helping people, to be part of something bigger than herself. My sister was always very level-headed about things like science and technology. But there was another part of her that yearned for the fantastic. And I think the idea appealed to her.

"She started going to meetings. She began making friends. And over the course of six months, became indoctrinated to the church. And to one man in particular: Joseph Goole."

Charlotte didn't dare interrupt. She could see Hocker reliving the events as if they'd happened yesterday.

"Back then, Goole was young, charismatic, handsome and powerful. And he drew young men and women to him like moths to a flame. He brought my sister into the group. But there is something you have to understand about the church. It is made up of two types of people: those in a couple and those not. My sister, obviously unattached at the time, was in the second group. The entire philosophy of the church is to propagate by bearing strong, resilient children, and it's all based on an ancient Welsh religion. I didn't realize it at the time, but the entire point of bringing in single people to the church was so they could... *support*... the couples. To help them have those strong children."

Charlotte could imagine Roger having a field day with this information. "You said you didn't realize it at the time. When did you discover this information?"

"The night of the twenty-ninth," he said. "It was a date she'd circled in her calendar. Listed in there as an Ascension Day. By then I was beginning to get worried. I'd followed her to a few meetings before but never gone inside. And this time... I did." He locked eyes with Charlotte. "I don't know why. Maybe I wanted to see this ascension ceremony. Maybe I was just stupid. But I'd heard Melissa say that some of the ceremonies were... erotic in nature. And as a fifteen-year-old boy, that's like telling him there's money in the street for taking."

Charlotte leaned forward. "Colt. What did you see?"

"My sister and four other people were all on these tables, and they each had these gray robes on. I was watching from a corner on the catwalk. I'd made my way in through one of the open windows on the second floor. My mom used to call me a spider monkey, because I was great a climbing into places I shouldn't have been. I remember... I remember my heart was pumping so hard I thought someone would hear it from down below."

"And then Goole showed up. He and his wife, both of them wearing black robes. He instructed each of the people on the tables, my sister included to strip. At first I was disgusted. Who wants to see their sister like that? So I looked at the others."

"Did you know them?"

He shook his head. "But they all seemed about Melissa's age. That was when I noticed that they'd each had a mark on their arms. A symbol."

"The brands."

He nodded. "They must have done it when they first arrived. It had taken me a little time to get into my spot so I didn't see it happen. But then Goole told them..." He paused, swallowing. "He told them it was time to ascend. He held this long knife. And they each put their arms out, face up. And..."

Colt stopped, caught in the memory. Reliving the moment his sister had died.

"I saw the aftermath," Charlotte said gently. "So it was Goole who did it."

He nodded. "But that wasn't the worst part. I was terrified. I'd never seen so much blood in my life. And it just poured out of them, onto the floor. I wanted to scream, to run to Melissa and get her to the hospital. But I couldn't. I was just... frozen. I couldn't even blink."

"You were fifteen," Charlotte said. "No one could have expected you to do anything else."

He swallowed, coming back into himself some more. "I watched then, in horror, as Goole and that wife of his removed their own robes. They were... naked. They laid down in the blood, both of them, and proceeded to fuck each other right there on the floor." His hands had balled into fists again, his face darkening. "And once they were done, the next couple came over and took their turn. And so on. Until all five couples were done."

Charlotte didn't know what to say.

"I remember sitting up there, staring at them. All of them, covered in my sister's blood. Smiles on their faces, supporting each other. Wishing each other good luck with the pregnancies. I remember all I wanted was to make them hurt in that moment like they had hurt me."

He sat back, breathing heavily. "But it's like you said, I was a kid. What could I do?"

"What happened next?" Charlotte asked.

"They just... left them there," he replied. "They didn't even bother to try to clean it up. To give my sister and the others the respect of a burial. They had *used* them and just discarded them like trash. I sat up there for what felt like days... until I was sure they weren't coming back. It was only then that I finally came down. And as I looked into the dead eyes of my sister, I made her a promise that I would make them all suffer a hundred times what they inflicted upon her."

"You tried to destroy the marks on their arms," Charlotte said.

He nodded. "I used my dad's blowtorch from home. But I made sure I copied down the symbols first. I knew I would need them. I wanted to kill Joseph and the others, but I knew that would be going too easy on them. They deserved worse. They deserved to live with the pain I felt and that I have felt every moment since that day."

"Why wait?" Charlotte asked. "Why now?"

"My sister was twenty-four when she died. As were the others. According to the tradition, the sacrifices must be in their 'prime' and be no more than a quarter century of age. I waited until their children were the same age of my sister. All five of them."

"But Mallory Wakefield's parents aren't even alive anymore," Charlotte said. "She had left the church."

"It didn't matter. She was still a product of that unholy union. I wanted Goole to know I was coming for him. I wanted him scared. His child had to be the last."

Charlotte sat back. It was a lot to take in. But she couldn't help but think with this new testimony they might actually have enough to bring charges against the Gooles. They had the original brands that would no doubt match up with Melissa and the other four victims. Given what Hocker had said, the entire case would need to be reopened. And five bodies would need to be exhumed.

"Colt," Charlotte said gently. "I can't imagine what that's been like for you all these years. I can't promise anything, but if you would be willing to testify against Goole, I will speak to the DA about your situation. Five murders are five murders, there's no changing that. But there might be other concessions that can be made."

"It doesn't matter anymore," he said. "I always knew it would end up this way. The other detective, she was right. Those people didn't do anything wrong. But someone had to pay for my sister's death. And now Goole will have to live with the fact everything he worked for has crumbled down around him. Don't you see? The cycle is broken now. They won't be able to go on."

Charlotte took that to mean he'd be willing to testify if they could swing it. But this was a lot. She could practically feel the hate seething off him. Imagine waiting twenty-five years to enact revenge. To be living in that hate for all those years.

There needed to be a brand-new investigation. She needed to get Givens up here. She might even call Ortega, though last she heard he was living on some beach in Alabama somewhere. If he was even still alive.

"Will you excuse me for a moment? I'll be right back."

Hocker nodded, a strange sense of serenity coming over him. It was like relating the story had been cathartic in a way.

Charlotte struggled with the chair but finally managed to maneuver it to the door, where she kicked it to get someone to open it for her. As soon as she was back out in the hall, Mona ran up to meet her from the other side of the station.

"Charlotte!"

"I know," she said. "It's a lot."

"What do we do now? He's just blown your case wide open."

"Get Chicago on the phone," Charlotte said. "I need to speak with them."

THIRTY-THREE

Mona sat in Earle's office as he read her final report. Bowman sat beside them, chewing on a pack of sunflower seeds he'd picked up from the vending machine. It had been almost three full weeks since Colt Hocker's explosive revelations and things were finally beginning to calm down.

But for Mona, the biggest change, other than now owning a cat, had been in her own demeanor. Something about witnessing Hocker nearly kill Kayleigh and being willing to do anything to stop it had silenced the voice in her head telling her she was too much like her father—that his legacy was an escapable black hole from which she'd never escape. And things had begun looking brighter. She'd even been on another date with Caleb again, one they'd actually managed to finish this time. It hadn't been as terrifying as she'd first thought. She wasn't sure it would ever lead anywhere, but right now she was just feeling things out. Dr. Cross said it would take time before she began to feel like she was part of something again, whether that was an intimate relationship or just in the course of her regular job. She'd also told her how proud of her she was for fully adopting Perigee. That the companionship would do her good.

"This is good," Sheriff Earle said, his eyes scanning the report. "Really good. Chicago is happy?"

Mona nodded. Both she and Charlotte had been working in conjunction with the Chicago police—Charlotte's old precinct specifically—to reopen and re-examine the case from twenty-five years ago. Charlotte, acting as a go-between for the two cases, managed to pull together the evidence found at the Goole home and admit it to her case, along with expert testimony from Roger that connected the brands directly to the deaths twenty-five years ago. Another, more thorough search of the Goole home had revealed a ceremonial knife, which both Mona and Charlotte believed had been the original murder weapon back then.

Joseph Goole, for his part, had remained tight-lipped behind his lawyer's advice. Both he and Marie Goole were currently in custody based on Colt Hocker's sworn testimony. However, for the DA to accept that testimony, Mona had to sign off that Colt Hocker would *not* receive any special compensation or treatment under incarceration. He was looking at five life sentences, one each for the people he killed. But he'd pleaded guilty to all five, saving the trouble of a lengthy trial.

The other remaining families, the Mercers, Petersons and Gibsons, were all under investigation as well for their part and participation in what had been deemed a ritual murder. Each of them being charged as an accessory. However, without more direct evidence, the DA in Chicago wasn't confident the charges would stick. Not unless Goole turned on them all. They'd also finally tracked down Nathaniel Bradshaw, who had left the state, attempting to flee Goole's influence. It turned out Goole *had* been blackmailing him; forcing him to hold further rituals at the altar in the woods as soon as Goole realized someone was coming after the kids. Nathaniel was one of the other spiritual leaders in the group and had been responsible for continuing to "bless" the families of the victims, using animal blood on the altar. He was also set to testify against the Gooles, though it was unclear if he had any knowledge of the full ritual from Chicago.

It was a mess of a case, requiring a lot of legwork from both departments over the past weeks. Thankfully, the media circus in Oak Creek had died down in favor of focusing on the more head-line-grabbing quintuple murder a quarter of a century ago.

"This looks open-and-shut from our end," Earle said. "I would congratulate you on getting justice for the victims' families, but in this case I'm not sure it's warranted." While Mallory Wakefield's parents were dead, she still had relatives out of state. The other victims also had aunts, uncles, cousins and extended family that had been affected by the case. It seemed that twenty-five years ago, Joseph Goole had brought a lot of people under his spell, using his connection with an ancient and obscure religion to persuade them into strange ritualistic practices.

They'd managed to find his and some of the other families' bloodlines reached back to Oak Creek's founding, their ancestors having originally settled the area two hundred and fifty years ago. Ancestors who apparently practiced *Cylch Coed Sanctaidd*—the ritual sacrifice of one person to ensure the successful union of two others. According to the literature found with the knife, only the blood of innocents could protect newly born members of the congregation.

Joseph, ever the narcissist, had taken the ritual to heart, along with four of his closest friends, creating a pact to conceive their children out of blood in a belief it would protect them for the rest of their lives and allow the ritual to continue. There was currently an investigation looking back generations to determine if other unsolved cases from the past might be related, since it was a once-in-a-generation kind of ritual.

Mona had sat in on a couple more session with Marie Goole—who was the only one talking. She described it like being in a dream-state, where they had just relinquished control over to Goole, allowing him to lead, to make decisions and ultimately to kill for their desires.

Their desires for strong, healthy children. Though, apparently, it was only for one child per family, which explained why all the victims had been only children. Protection, but at a cost.

Mona couldn't imagine wanting something so badly that you'd be willing to go along with murder to get it. But then again these weren't regular people. All of them had come from trauma of some kind in their past, including Goole himself, who had been the subject of strict upbringing by his own parents, using the rituals as a basis for punishment. Similarly, Marie Goole had been the victim of abuse from older family members.

Each member of the Circle of the Sacred Grove had a similar situation. They had all come together searching for a better future than the one they came from—and they'd each had a connection back to Oak Creek in some way. It had been how Goole had "chosen" them to reignite the old ways again. In truth, all they had wanted was a life free of the kind of pain they had experienced as children. Joseph Goole saw that and exploited it.

And now he would pay for it for the rest of his life. His daughter may have been the only one who was spared, but he would never see the outside of a jail cell again.

That was the other side of the coin. Charlotte and Mona had met with Kayleigh on multiple occasions and had finally gotten her in with a therapist to help her process everything. She'd been unaware of the ceremony that had killed Hocker's sister and the others, though she admitted her father had become more insistent about teaching her the "old ways" as she got older. Mona believe he was waiting until after she and Connor had been married to fully indoctrinate them and encourage them to perform the ritual themselves.

Most of the time they spent together, Kayleigh was in a state of shock. In a few short days she'd lost Connor, Terry *and* her parents, and the whole world now knew about what they'd done. She'd have a tough couple of years ahead. Mona knew what that was like, and she was determined to make sure she didn't suffer alone.

"I have to admit," Earle added. "When I took this job, I wasn't expecting *this*."

"None of us were," Bowman said.

"Thankfully, we had someone here with the experience to get us through," Earle said, nodding at Mona. "Good work, Detective."

"Thank you, sir," Mona said.

"I want you taking the next few days off." He set the report on his desk. "The both of you. You've been working your asses off without a break and I don't want you burned out. This was a big one. Take a vacation."

A vacation? Mona hadn't ever considered the idea before. She'd never needed to. Where would she go? She supposed she could spend some more time with her mother... or Adam. Or even Kayleigh. There was no shortage of people who needed her help.

"Thank God," Bowman said, standing. "I'll be out on the lake fishing for the next week. If anyone needs me, don't call." He headed out of the office without another word.

The edge of Earle's lip curled into a half smile. "I can see that was warranted. What about you, LaSalle? Any idea of what you'll do with your time?"

"Actually..." Mona said, thinking. "Yeah. I think so."

"Okay, where does this box go?"

Charlotte maneuvered herself out from under the desk, screwdriver in hand. Roger stood in the doorway, with yet another brown box in his arms. "What is it?" she asked.

He looked at the top. "Says, *Supplies.* That's it."

"Oh, put it over there on the shelf, I'll get to it in a minute," she said, pointing with the screwdriver.

"Yes, ma'am," he replied. Charlotte smiled to herself as she worked her way back under the desk. Her ribs were still slightly sore from her encounter with Terry Barker, but at least it was manageable. The doctor had cleared her for "light" activity. Whether that meant crawling up underneath a desk to fix a faulty drawer was another matter entirely.

"Only twelve more to go," Roger singsonged as he headed for the doorway yet again.

"You really don't have to do this," Charlotte said, affixing the final screw and pulling herself out from under the desk again.

"I'd rather not do anything else." He paused as Charlotte shot him a look. "Was that a double negative? I can't ever tell."

She chuckled. "Neither can I."

Her experience in Oak Creek had made one thing very clear to Charlotte: She wasn't ready to give up detective work just yet. And after some long conversations with both Mona and Givens, she'd decided the best thing she could do was try to keep helping people by offering up her services... for a price.

"When does the nameplate arrive?" Roger asked, looking at the door to the office.

"Another week, I think, you know those custom jobs," Charlotte replied, opening one of the boxes he'd retrieved and beginning to unpack a lot of the stuff that had gone into storage when she'd retired.

"Why, Detective LaSalle, what a pleasure." Charlotte glanced up to see Mona standing in the doorway, her eyes traveling over the room.

"Roger. I think we're beyond that. You can just call me Mona," she said.

He gave her a warm smile. "Of course." Roger turned back to Charlotte, hooking his thumb over his shoulder. "I'm going to grab the next few. Then you want some lunch?"

"Please," Charlotte replied. "I'm starving."

"You're welcome to join us," he said to Mona.

"Oh, I wouldn't want to interrupt," she began.

"Wouldn't hear of it," he said. "The more the merrier. I know this great spot two blocks from here."

He chuckled and headed back down the hall and down the stairs.

"He's so outgoing," Mona said.

"I know. It's probably good for me. But I'll keep pretending like it isn't." Charlotte motioned to the room; even in its unfinished condition, what they'd managed to do in two weeks was impressive. What had been an empty shell now contained shelves, new flooring and trim and a brand-new air-conditioning system, courtesy of the building's super. "What do you think?"

"It's looking great," Mona replied. She walked up and picked up a box of business cards on the antique desk Charlotte had found at an estate sale. "Charlotte Dawes, Discreet Private Investigations." She held it up. "*Discreet?*"

"No one wants to know they've got an investigator on their ass. And I'm pretty good at shadowing."

"I think it's great," Mona said. "But what's even better is you've finally got some company. Sounds like things are going well between you two."

"Well, he did find me this great spot," she said. "And only a block from his bookstore. Which means it won't need to be a long-distance relationship."

Mona smiled. "Not so opposed to it anymore?"

Charlotte continued removing items from the box. "I spent a lot of time thinking about it. And you were right. It's worth the risk. Plus, with this new job I'll actually have something to do with my time now. The trick will be balancing the two and not falling back into old habits."

"As an expert in falling back into old habits, I think I can help you there," Mona replied.

"Everything good with the case?" Charlotte asked. "I haven't talked to Givens in a few days."

Mona nodded. "Goole goes before the grand jury next week. After that... we'll see. But the DA is confident."

"And Hocker?"

"Cooperative, but that's about it. The DA is throwing the book at him."

Charlotte shrugged. It was tragic, but he *had* killed five innocent people. There was no getting around any of it. "That's the best he can expect, honestly."

Mona nodded. "You good? Not ignoring your doctors anymore?"

"Only a little." Charlotte smiled. "I guess you could say I've learned my lesson."

"Almost dying in the middle of the woods will do that."

Charlotte regarded her friend. She seemed lighter, like she'd escaped some dark place. But she couldn't be a hundred percent sure. Of everyone, Charlotte was probably the only person who really understood how much Mona's father affected her. And for a short moment, she'd seen that come out in Mona, if only for a millisecond.

"Are *you* good?"

Mona smiled. The only problem was Charlotte wasn't sure if it was genuine or not. "Getting better."

"Right then," Roger said, excusing himself past Mona as he set down the next box. "Who's hungry?"

As Charlotte moved aside the empty box and joined the other two for a brief lunch, she couldn't help but feel like she'd finally gotten it right. Retirement had only been the first step. She took a longing glance at Roger as he was in the middle of an animated conversation with Mona.

Life didn't have to end with just one decision.

You just had to be brave enough to take the next step.

A LETTER FROM THE AUTHOR

If you've made it this far, thank you. Seriously. Thank you for spending your time with Charlotte and Mona, for following them through the darkest corners of Oak Creek, and for sticking with them as they unraveled a mystery that tested every part of who they are.

Writing *Never Strike Twice* meant living with these characters for a long time—sitting with their fears, their doubts, the weight of what they've seen and what they carry. Charlotte, trying to figure out if she still has what it takes. Mona, wrestling with whether she's destined to become the violence she's spent her life fighting. Their partnership, built on trust and understanding even when everything else felt uncertain. I hope their journey hooked you the way it hooked me.

If you want to hear about what comes next—new releases, bonus content, maybe some behind-the-scenes glimpses into how these stories come together—I'd love for you to join my newsletter. You can sign up here:

www.stormpublishing.co/alex-sigmore

And if you have a few moments, leaving a review would mean the world to me. It doesn't need to be long or polished. Even a short review helps other readers discover this book for the first time, and that matters more than I can say.

This story came from thinking about the things we inherit—not just from our families, but from our experiences, our trauma, the cases we can't let go of. I wanted to write about people who do the hard work of investigating darkness while trying not to let it consume them. People who support each other through the worst of it. People who keep going even when they're not sure they should.

Thanks again for being part of this journey. I have more stories waiting—more mysteries, more characters who won't let me rest until I tell their stories. I hope you'll stick around.

Alex

instagram.com/alexsigmore

facebook.com/AlexSigmoreBooks

bookbub.com/authors/alex-sigmore

amazon.com/Alex-Sigmore/e/B0B1YXMZ7N

ACKNOWLEDGMENTS

Writing a book is never a solitary act, no matter how many hours you spend alone with your characters and your doubts. This story exists because of the people who believed in it and who encouraged me to grow as a writer.

To Kate, my editor at Storm Publishing—thank you for seeing what this book could be and for pushing me to get it there. Your insight made Charlotte and Mona sharper, the mystery tighter, and the emotional beats land exactly where they needed to. This book is better because of you.

To everyone at Storm Publishing who put their hands on this story—the designers, the marketers, the production team, all the people working behind the scenes to turn a manuscript into something readers can hold—thank you. You took what I created and made it real. That's no small thing.

My author community—you know who you are. Thank you for the late-night discussions, the encouragement when the words wouldn't come, the understanding when I needed to vent about plot holes or self-doubt. You remind me every day that I'm not alone in this, and that matters more than I can say.

To my family and friends, who've supported me through every draft and who understand when I needed to disappear to meet a deadline. Especially to my mother, who gave me the gift of story from the time I was young enough to sit in her lap and listen. You taught me that stories matter, that they shape us, and that I could create them if I was willing to work for it. You told me I could do anything I put my mind to, and I believed you. I still do.

But most importantly—to you, the reader. Without you, I'm

just someone typing words into the void. You're the reason any of this matters. You're the reason I get to call myself a writer. Every time you pick up one of my books, every time you lose yourself in the story, every time you care about what happens to these characters—you give meaning to all the hours I spent creating them. This doesn't work without you. None of it does. Thank you for choosing to spend your time with my stories. That gift is not lost on me.

And to my wife—thank you for everything. For believing in me in those moments when I quit believing in myself. For giving me the space to disappear into fictional worlds while still keeping me grounded in the real one. For your unconditional love and support through all of it. I couldn't do this without you. I wouldn't want to.